The
Lady, the
& Chef,
the
Courtesan

An Imprint of HarperCollins*Publishers*

The
Lady, *the*
& *Chef*,
the
Courtesan

a novel

MARISOL

HarperCollins books may be purchased for educational, business, or sales promotional use. For information, please write: Special Markets Department, HarperCollins Publishers Inc., 10 East 53rd Street, New York, NY 10022.

FIRST EDITION

Designed by Shubhani Sarkar

Library of Congress Cataloging-in-Publication Data

Marisol
   The lady, the chef, and the courtesan : a novel / by
   Marisol.—1st ed.
     p. cm.
   ISBN 0-06-053042-1 (acid-free paper)
   1. Women—South America—Fiction. 2. South
America—Fiction. I. Title.

PS3613.A753L33 2003
813'.6—dc21

                          2003046580

03 04 05 06 07 NMSG/QW 10 9 8 7 6 5 4 3 2 1

To kept promises

Contents

A woman must be

a lady in the living room,

a chef in the kitchen,

and a courtesan in the bedroom.

—SOUTH AMERICAN PROVERB

The
Lady, *the*
& **Chef,**
the
Courtesan

Magic first entered Pilar's life on the day of her grandmother's funeral.

"Ashes to ashes, dust to dust . . . for from dust you came, and to dust you shall return."

Pilar slowly crossed herself, powerless as she watched those last few seconds slip by irretrievably.

The archbishop made the blessing of the cross and scattered a handful of earth over the body of Gabriela Grenales, Pilar's beloved nana.

When the time came for the coffin to be nailed shut, the stupor induced by all funerals gave way, if only momentarily, to a fearful buzzing from the onlookers: a collective realization that under the rule of death, everything that had gone unsaid would now remain forever so.

As the coffin was slowly lowered into the grave, a few damp clods of soil broke free and fell, with thumps and echoes, onto the lid. The sound was haunting, unforgettable; the deafening sound of death.

Across from her, a man dressed in black emerged from the knot of mourners, grasped one of the gardenia wreaths in his large hands, and stepped to the edge of the grave, then leaned over it as if intending to speak to the deceased. Instead, he gently tossed the wreath and watched it fall onto the coffin. At a glance, the offering could have been taken for a mere gesture of respect, but there was something in the man's measured manner in which a careful observer could read Bible-long volumes of grief; that, unlike the grave beside which he stood, could never be contained. Pilar saw a flash as he unfolded the handkerchief he was clutching and plucked out a tiny object that caught a glimmer of sunlight. He flicked the charm into the grave, to be buried for all time in darkness.

As soon as he turned to walk away, Pilar heard her mother, Cristina, say to no one in particular, "Well, that has to be a first."

Pilar struggled back, if only momentarily, from the labyrinth of incoherent thoughts in which she had been lost.

"*What* has to be a first, Mamá?"

"Seeing a stranger at one's own mother's funeral."

All Pilar could manage in reply was a barely audible "I see." Her mother seemed not to have noticed the shiny milagro that now adorned Gabriela's grave. Pilar wondered who the man was, and she knew Cristina was wondering, too.

In the distance, on the other side of the city, as if echoing the last words of Archbishop Mariano Fermín del Toro—"*May her soul rest in peace*"—the bells of the Caracas Cathedral began ringing for High Mass. It was April 15, 2001, Easter Sunday.

Even from here Pilar could see, atop the balconies of the city's whitewashed houses, where terra-cotta *materos* hung brimming with red geraniums and emerald-green *helechos,* that perfect succession of scarlet-redbrick roof tiles, which gave Caracas both its picturesque colonial look and its quaint nickname, *La Ciudad de los Techos Rojos.* Distracted for a moment, she imagined some graceful señorita with lustrous black hair and vibrant red lips making her way slowly onto one of those balconies, where she would lean against a hand-carved column and gaze out at the sunset that bathed the valley in pink and red brushstrokes as the sun reluctantly commenced its daily descent behind Ávila Mountain.

This was where, twenty-six years before, Pilar Castillo had been born.

Her onyx eyes, a common trait in Venezuelan women—a legacy of the centuries-old thankless Spanish rule—were painted on her face at an angle, and had she chosen to veil her face that day as some of the other women mourners had done in honor of tradition, she might easily have passed for a snake charmer. When Pilar was flustered, which was not often, her tentative gaze was what gave her away.

As she and her mother were preparing to leave the graveside, Pilar saw a handsome young man walking toward them. With his usual grace and polish, Rafael Uslar Mancera greeted both women and then turned to the younger, whose eyes tried hard to avoid his. He kissed her gently on the cheek and whispered to her, "*Lo siento mucho cariño*—I know how much she meant to you."

When she heard his voice, Pilar thought of the saying *Donde hubo fuego cenizas quedan*—"For where once there was fire, embers continue to burn."

Holding back tears and too overcome to speak, Pilar simply nodded in reply. Rafael's words had brought back so many feelings, even as they reminded her that the only person in the world who could have helped her sort them out was really and truly gone. Pilar had never felt more vulnerable.

Although her love for the woman whose wisdom had so often guided her life reached deeper than the roots of a ceiba tree, Pilar was self-conscious and rarely given to outward displays of emotion. In the end, she bade her last farewell to her grandmother from behind a mask of false serenity. In the pit of her stomach there stirred a bilious brew of helplessness of having to give in, once again, to the intransigence of death.

As they left the cemetery, Pilar fought to stay on her feet in her uncomfortably high heels, which in spite of her careful steps kept getting caught in the cracks of the rough cobblestones. It was then that she realized what an otherworldly departure this Sunday was from her usual Sundays in Chicago, and immediately she began to miss the routine of her life in that city she'd never believed she would call home. Still, the image of the man with the shiny milagro stuck in her mind, as did the thought of the exhausting hours that lay ahead.

After the funeral, they went to Gabriela's house in the residential district of Los Rosales, which now seemed, like everything else Pilar had seen and felt over the past two days, to exist in another time. Upon entering the house, she was struck by an even stronger feeling, a sense that time never touched Venezuela at all, much less her family.

Hoping to avoid well-wishers, she crossed to the outside terrace, where she was met by an intoxicating mixture of scents: eucalyptus, orange blossoms, birds of paradise, and wine-red bougainvillea, denizens of the garden she had so often visited but so little appreciated when she was younger. Now, after her three years away amid the bustle of an American city, the sight and scent inspired in her an almost supernatural awe. Standing in the shadow of the mango tree, Pilar felt as if she were breathing in all the memories from her grandmother's past and thought that nothing smelled quite like nostalgia.

When she finally forced herself to go back inside, she felt a sliver of a smile unexpectedly play over her lips as she saw the black and white checkerboard floor on which, despite her nana's protestations, she had so loved to sit as a child. Such floors were a common feature in houses built in the early twentieth century by craftsmen who had left Spain for the New World; evocative of centuries-old homes in Barcelona and other Spanish cities, these expanses of marble were the only surfaces in the household not at the mercy of Venezuela's oftentimes infernal heat.

With her typical shyness—sometimes mistaken, unfairly, for aloofness—Pilar stood at the edge of the foyer by the main entrance and observed in silence as one person after another spoke to her mother, Cristina Knowles de Castillo. Cristina was Gabriela's only daughter, so everyone lined up to offer their condolences.

As visitors signed the guest book, Pilar considered for the first time how odd it was that her grandmother, who had always been at such pains to observe tradition, had never taken her husband's name. Rather than becoming Gabriela Grenales de Knowles, she had remained Gabriela Grenales. Pilar wondered how her grandfather Jonathan had felt about his wife's blatant and unusual refusal to assume his name and thus belong to him.

The deluge of callers persisted. There was the president of the art museum, whom Pilar overheard telling her mother that the museum's board could never hope to have another member so dedicated as Doña Gabriela. Then came the ladies from the school of fine arts, followed by a small, well-behaved group of children of various ages who had had piano lessons with Pilar's nana once a week. A distinguished-looking man and his wife identified themselves to Pilar's mother as Señor Marcos Santoro and Señora María Antonieta Colmenares de Santoro; Señor Santoro recalled how Doña Gabriela had once promised to do whatever she could to help with the restoration of the then dilapidated national theater of Caracas. Through her many connections and her boundless determination, Gabriela Grenales had coaxed and prodded potential benefactors until the refurbishment—a project that everyone had thought nearly impossible not so many years before—was complete and the restored theater spectacularly reopened. Pilar continued to eavesdrop as the effusive man recounted to the always aloof Cristina how Doña Gabriela, not content to stop there, had then worked with the Children's Foundation on a campaign to encourage theatergoers to donate a portion of their ticket price to sponsor free performances for poor youngsters. "Without her involvement, our Teatro Nacional would not be standing today—I can attest to that, Doña Cristina. We are going to miss her." These were Señor Santoro's final words before he moved on, ceding his place to the long line of guests who stood behind him, all equally anxious to tell similar stories.

In the midst of so many strangers, Pilar was grateful for the presence of Ana Carla. Her older sister was charming and confident and, unlike Pilar, utterly extroverted. Having received inordinate amounts of attention from the day she was born, the young Ana Carla, like most children over whom everyone makes a fuss, was extraordinarily adept at performing before an audience. The result was a lifelong, almost preconditioned need to please others at all costs. Today, wearing a smile that lay somewhere between invitation and resignation, Ana Carla seemed to be the only one of them able to manage both the right manner and the right tone, speaking the precise words that would most touch each guest and make him or her feel as if it were his or her family, not Ana Carla's, that had suffered such a great loss.

Acknowledging her younger sister's presence near the door, Ana Carla lifted her head and smiled warmly in Pilar's direction. Hugging guest after guest, she looked like a dancer performing movements that had been tirelessly rehearsed. Pilar returned the smile and once more admired the choreographed fluidity with which Ana Carla seemed always to move through the world around her.

From this vantage point, everything in her nana's house was just as she remembered it, except that the very high ceilings now appeared even higher—almost infinite—in comparison with those in her apartment back in Chicago. Pilar thought about the apartment and wondered if her grandmother would have liked it. Her mother certainly did not approve.

When most of the visitors had left, Pilar at last entered the house, where the traditional ritual resumed with the beginning of the novena, nine straight days of solemn prayer aimed at ensuring that the soul of the deceased would enter Heaven in God's good graces.

The living room and dining room were separated by an enormous arch that made both seem more grandiose than they really were. Each room was illuminated by an imposing teardrop crystal chandelier, the cleaning of which had been Nana's only self-assigned house chore: if anyone was to break these precious crystals, she used to say, she wanted it to be her. Before she commenced the meticulous cleaning of each and every teardrop, she would have Pilar obediently count, on her instructions, as she poured three drops of white vinegar into a small bowl of water.

Every month, Pilar would look forward to this little ritual, not for what it *was*—the mere cleaning, after all, of two ceiling lamps—but for what it *meant:* to her, handling those small crystals was like being allowed to play with the queen's jewels. Of course, that wasn't how her nana saw it. Over the years, Pilar had learned to appreciate her grandmother's trust in her. Whereas Gabriela delegated all the rest of the chores to her housemaids, her younger granddaughter was the only other person permitted to touch the delicate crystals whose reflection made her living and dining rooms shine like a palace. Remembering that now, staring at the chandeliers, Pilar smiled.

Shaking herself free of the memory, she continued on to her favorite room. No room in the house exuded greater propriety and respectability than the library. It was isolated from the rest of the house by a pair of elaborate frosted-glass doors with brass handles. The formality of the library was, like Pilar's grandfather, undeniably English. With its built-in mahogany shelves holding hundreds of carefully arranged volumes, it had been Grandpa Jonathan's sanctuary. Pilar noted the pendulum that still rested on the desk and fondly recalled the monotonous *tick-tack* that its polished lead marbles made from the moment they were touched to the instant the hypnotizing swaying stopped. She kept walking, avoiding everyone around her.

Suddenly, as if some border had been crossed, on leaving the library, the elegant European decor gave way, at the back of the house, to an almost mystical melange of colonial furniture, handmade Moorish rugs, and native paintings. Two of the most intriguing works hanging here were copies of the celebrated Gauguin paintings *Nevermore* and *The Dream*, which Nana had brought home with her from the Gauguin Museum in Tahiti after she and Grandpa vacationed on that island. Pilar remembered that when Ana Carla turned seventeen, Nana, just back from her trip, decided to throw her a big birthday party. But the star of the evening turned out to be Nana herself, who spent most of the party talking to anyone who would listen about her new paintings and the wonders of French Polynesia. How typical of her grandmother to have to share her bursting joy with everyone!

Even though Pilar had listened to her stories, the fuss Nana made over the two unframed pictures from Tahiti meant nothing to her at the time. But now, as she studied them, it occurred to her that just like some Latin American folk art, the two Gauguin replicas made an irresistible symbolic reference to native superstition. The background of *Nevermore* seemed to portray the ominous thoughts of the girl on the couch, rendering the painting much more than a simple nude. Even to the untrained eye, the work conveyed a sense of barbarian luxury overlaid by haunting fantasies of acts that were commonly considered sins.

The other picture, labeled *Te Rerioa* on a tiny gold plaque affixed to its frame, was no less intriguing. Pilar recalled Nana's remarking how strange it seemed that Gauguin should have chosen that title to mean "The Dream," when in the native Polynesian a *rerioa* was really a nightmare. She felt certain, knowing how Nana had loved symbolism, that the names of these two paintings and their adjacent placement were no mere coincidence.

If all of the paintings in this part of the house departed from tradition, they nevertheless united a diverse array of elements that, when joined, created a uniquely graceful and dignified whole. This was also the impression given, at least to the casual observer, by Nana's two-houses-in-one. But the artworks' emphasis on color had more than a decorative effect. By and large, the paintings offered philosophical reflections on the mysteries of life and the untamed fervor of emotional expression.

And just as art always revealed something about the soul of the artist, thought Pilar, this part of Nana's house seemed to harbor some unspoken secret. Like the shimmering colors on the canvases, these rooms held the traces of a mysterious life lived here. She thought of something Nana had once told her: *"Mi amor,* people *say* a lot of things, but in the end, it is what they *do* that gives them away."

So it was, she suspected, with this house. While it was immediately apparent that the owner had had both good taste and a good sense for what things went well together, it was also obvious that stuffy English pieces and wild shrill-red paintings hanging above airy wicker chairs could never, no matter how skilled the hand of the decorator, truly blend.

The jarring contrast explained, at least in part, the person that Pilar's mother had become. Pilar now felt sure—or as sure as one can ever be about a parent—that at some point during her childhood, unable to reconcile her mother's and father's two worlds, Cristina had decided that she must choose one over the other. Cristina, who always wore the same strand of pearls and always pinned her auburn hair tightly in a bun, who always selected her clothes according to both the weather and the occasion, did not resemble, in either manner or appearance, the rare mixture she might have been. Instead she had adopted her father's austerity, thus distinguishing herself from both her mother and her younger daughter.

Before returning to the front of the house, Pilar regarded, one last time, the painted world of *Nevermore,* with all its bright surface and its hidden depths, its metaphorical yet real connection to the grandmother she had loved so dearly and now missed so much.

Just beyond the library, Pilar was met by the spectacle of a live gallery of older women, rosaries in hand, who now sat inside Nana's great room, piously repeating unending scores of prayers: nine Misterios Dolorosos composed of ten Ave Marías and one Gloria each. The leader chanted, *"Dale Señor el descanso eterno,"* and the others replied in the same monotonous murmur, almost on cue: *"Y brille para ella la luz perpetua."* And perpetual light it would be, Pilar thought, for everyone who had ever met Gabriela Grenales knew that there was only one possible memory of her: life.

"Pilar, where have you been? Aren't you joining us for the novena?"

Startled by the prying voice seemingly coming out of nowhere, she turned to see her mother standing behind her, just outside the library door. Not wanting to call attention to herself, Pilar had avoided actually entering the great room.

"I'd rather watch from here, Mamá."

Every word spoken to her by her mother was like a spark charged with static, every conversation like a simmering pot of water that might come to a boil if not carefully watched.

After her father's unexpected death when Pilar was twelve, no one was left to temper her mother's scalding anger. Pilar recalled the last time she saw him: she was still half asleep, and he kissed and hugged her and whispered softly in her ear, "Hey, ladybug, don't forget how much I love you."

That night, he was taken to the hospital; she never saw him alive again. She had wept for days then, and now that she was again in the presence of death, her grief had been resurrected. She was surprised to find herself, after so long, once more mourning the absence of the man who had so brightened the early years of her life.

And here, still, was her mother. By her very presence, Pilar seemed always to be infringing on any number of her mother's countless personal rules, and to each trespass Cristina reacted as if it were the Original Sin.

With the wariness of one who has been scolded too often, Pilar crept past her mother's searing gaze and obediently joined the others in the great room.

But as she tried to negotiate her way through the group to join in the prayers, Pilar felt immediately and irreparably out of place. Even though she was dressed in a sober black pantsuit, she stood out in stark contrast to the women around her, all of whom were in full mourning. Some of them wore floor-length, wimple-style black dresses, their faces drawn with grief and covered by lace mantillas, the whisper-thin, ornate black veils that are traditionally worn as a sign of respect for the deceased.

The prayers did not end until late that night. Afterward, Pilar went back to her mother's house to sleep once more in her old room. It remained eerily unchanged, a reminder that she was expected in the near future to move back to Venezuela from Chicago.

She reached inside her suitcase and pulled out a cream-colored lace baby-doll nightgown she had bought in a lingerie store on Michigan Avenue. She smiled as she thought of Patrick making fun of her for wearing lace even in the middle of winter.

"I can't help myself," she'd told him.

"I guess I can't complain, and besides . . . it's gonna come off anyway," he'd replied, laughing.

"It's like . . . I see my mother watching me through the window to make sure I look feminine all the time."

Raising both his hands, Patrick had gazed up at the ceiling and ended the discussion with a mischievous, "It's all your fault, Mrs. Castillo. I can't help myself, either." More laughter had followed.

It was hot and humid in her bedroom, so Pilar took off her black pantsuit and underwear and went to throw open the double windows. Because few houses have air-conditioning in Venezuela, windows are generally closed during the day to keep the heat out, then opened in the evening to admit the cooler night air.

Freed from their silver latches, the colonial windows revealed the backyard. The scents of the pomarosa and guava trees, baked all day by the equatorial heat, began to waft slowly into Pilar's room, carried on the breeze.

Standing there, fully undressed, Pilar noticed her body for the first time in days. She thought about how Patrick would touch her if he were here. Before slipping her nightie over her head she traced, for a few seconds, ever so lightly, the contour of her breasts.

Finally she shook her long, thick black hair and tied it back in a ponytail. She didn't like putting her hair up, but she knew if she didn't she'd have to fight with it all night.

Still too restless to sleep, she sat on her bed and picked up the phone. She wanted to call Patrick. What's the code for the States again? she asked herself. She hadn't done this since she applied to graduate school at Northwestern and had to spend hours on the phone with the admissions counselor. She tried to remember: o for International; o1 for the U.S.; 312 for Chicago. . . . As she was about to dial, a thought broke in: Not from here. She put down the receiver and tried to put Patrick out of her mind.

Looking around this room she had grown up in, she was struck by the incongruity of the enormous hand-carved mahogany bed that she had slept in for years. The very week Pilar turned fifteen, her mother had bought the bed, complete with Spanish lace-trimmed white bed linens, and informed her young daughter that "this is where a señorita should sleep." Like most Latin mothers' decisions, the purchase of the bed on which Pilar was now preparing to sleep had been a unilateral action about which there could be no discussion. In the end, Pilar had had no choice but to learn to like it. But on moving to Chicago, she had chosen a completely different style for herself. The decor in her small apartment was as modern and simple as this room at home was colonial and elaborate. Shopping for her own things had felt like being let loose inside a pastry shop filled with sweet temptations.

During her visit to Chicago the year before, Cristina had remarked sarcastically on the sparsely arranged modular furniture that her daughter had selected: "*Hija*, is there anyplace I can sit, other than on this flat chair with no arms?" And her opinions didn't stop there: she was similarly unimpressed with Patrick.

Unlike most people, Patrick Russo was exactly wh... be. He was a naturally funny, attractive photographer who... a cheeseburger in two bites and then lick his fingers with plea... But he was not the kind of man Cristina wanted for her daughter, and she made that sufficiently clear to Pilar.

"Pilar, *por Dios,* can't you see there's nothing more to him?"

Even after her mother went back to Caracas, Pilar could still hear her saying, "Why can't you be more like your sister?"

Ana Carla was married and had two rambunctious boys, aged three and five. Their *tía* Pilar cared for them and spoiled them as if they were her own. Perhaps it was as close as she would ever get; sometimes, especially after visits such as this, she wondered if she would die a spinster. Would Patrick ask her to marry him someday? Or should she listen to her mother and come back to Rafael?

More confused than ever, Pilar decided to call Patrick after all. Just to hear his voice, she told herself.

She picked up the phone, dialed, and listened to it ring. No answer. He was probably in his darkroom, developing prints.

Then, finally, a click. Even though she knew it was just his voice mail, she got lost in his jovial greeting: "Patrick here—well, not really, but if you wanna talk, just leave a number, and I'll catch you later." Hearing Patrick's electronic self made Pilar realize how different he and Rafael were. Wouldn't it be great if I could blend the best of each of them into one perfect whole? she thought.

She didn't usually leave messages because she was too self-conscious about the sound of her own voice. This time, though, she opted for a brief "Hey, it's me—I miss you" before putting the receiver down. The instant she said the words, she felt insecure and began to wish she'd just hung up instead. Oh, well.

Alone in her bed, she imagined herself in Patrick's welcoming arms. She hugged her pillow and smiled. He always made her smile. She had never met anyone quite like him—so unconventional, so e so real. His charm, unlike Rafael's, was

re was nothing contrived about him. She

st the moment they met, he had started

nor of the delicate, nearly imperceptible lit-

e corners of her mouth whenever she smiled.

iad asked, feeling a bit embarrassed by his

ed him instantly. "Yeah! Dimples . . . to remind

he had told her, laughing that contagious laugh

oɪ ʰ̄.   ith a low peal in his throat and got louder and

louder until she ...d no choice but to laugh with him.

But still Pilar's mind would not rest. Thoughts of Rafael crept in, and she began to contemplate what life might be like with him. She remembered the long conversations they used to have, that feeling that she could talk to him forever. Then, too, Rafael was a promising young lawyer, and had always been her mother's choice. Without a doubt, life with Rafael would be very comfortable. *But was that love?* She wondered if she would ever be able to sort all this out. It seemed to her that the questions that most worried and confused her had grown even more complicated over the last couple of days.

She had already tried every trick she could think of to clear her doubt-ridden mind—tiresome unpacking, reading, saying her prayers— but nothing seemed to erase the incoherent, choppy notions that floated in and out of her head, jumbled fragments of thought that could not be strung into a sentence but that nevertheless made her feel as rest- less as if they had been fully formed. Then she felt a sudden, stabbing pain, and images of her grandmother's funeral started flashing in her mind.

Emotionally, mentally, and physically exhausted (she had, after all, flown overnight to make it to the ceremony), she decided to force herself to sleep. But just as she was about to turn off the lamp on her nightstand, there was a knock on her bedroom door. It was her mother.

"Pilar, before I forget, your nana wanted you to have this. I'm sorry I did not give it to you earlier."

Cristina presented her with a heavy, handmade white brocaded box.

"Do you know what's inside, Mamá?"

"I have no idea. You know how Nana loved secrets. God knows what it could be."

"*Gracias*, Mamá." Then, "*Buenas noches.*"

"*Buenas noches*, Pilar. Try to get some rest. I've never seen you looking so pale."

Pilar regarded the box for a few minutes before opening it. How like Nana it was to prepare surprise gifts for others, even after she was gone. But why her? she wondered. Had Ana Carla gotten a box as well?

When at last she lifted the lid, Pilar was nearly overcome by the scent of Nana's sweet perfume, bringing a rush of warm childhood memories. She brushed her forehead with her fingers and began carefully to untie the red silk ribbon that bound the box's contents: three books. With black leather covers and beveled spines gilt-stamped with Roman numerals and the initials GG, they seemed to her a treasure, relics in their own right.

Seeing her own name on an envelope at the bottom of the box made Pilar gasp and for a fleeting instant gave her the peculiar feeling that her grandmother was still alive. She ran her index finger across the writing and tried to imagine how and when her grandmother's graceful hand had held the calligraphy pen and formed the letters: *Pilar*. When she turned the envelope over, she saw that it had been sealed with red wax. The envelope, and the box itself, were meant for her and her alone.

Nana, she knew, had always had a reason for everything she did. Pilar suspected that she was about to embark on an unexpected journey for which she was in no way prepared. With uncharacteristic urgency, she tore open the envelope and began to read the letter inside, inscribed in her grandmother's beautiful handwriting.

September 9, 1987

Mi querida nieta:

  It has taken me years to begin.

  The fact that you are reading this means that I have passed away. After my death, your mother has instructions to give you these books.

  To your sister, Ana Carla, I have left the contents of my jewelry box. To you, my dearest granddaughter, I leave my diaries, the treasures of my heart.

  When you have finished reading them, I know that you will have many questions. This is my intent, for it is only by asking yourself such questions and carefully considering the information you have that you will come to form your own opinions. Because they spring from the depths of the soul, difficult questions often possess a greater power than their actual answers.

  I will do my best to satisfy your curiosity, to answer your unasked questions and share with you the meaning of our costumbres, those special ways of doing things that are so long established that they often carry the weight of law. This will help you understand why I did what I did and why I am choosing to tell you of it now.

  You will want to know if your mother has any knowledge of what happened. She was only ten years old when these events occurred, and you may well imagine that the late discovery of the truth would be almost impossible for her to comprehend, much less accept, even with the benefit of time. I am sure it has not escaped your notice that your mother and I are two very different women. There is a reason for that difference.

  Moreover, I am quite convinced that as my grandchild, by

virtue of the position you occupy in my life—being removed by a generation—you will be better able to cope with certain kinds of information than your mother, who was directly affected by the events I will share with you.

Please do not let the less-than-admirable nature of some of these lessons dissuade you from further reading. Back then I was able to see the picture quite clearly, but not my own hand in creating it. For years I waited for a clue, a revelation that would impart to me the meaning of it all. And in fact, as I wrote the story down for you, I finally began to make some sense of it myself.

I am an old woman now and have nothing more to lose. I have resolved to share my story with you in the hope that you will choose to live a life of no regrets, because in the end it is you, no one else, who must live your own life.

Even if you are paralyzed by fear, even if you are reluctant to hurt others' feelings, when you find your orchard of truth, you must find a way to enter it because if you don't, you will regret it for the rest of your days.

Con cariño,
Tu nana

When Pilar had finished reading, her eyes filled with tears. Nana was gone, but the letter had somehow brought her to life again and made the young woman feel as if she had one more chance to speak with the only person in the world who had ever really understood her. This thought gave her some peace.

She reread the letter several times and then, with trembling hands, folded it, tucked it back into its envelope, and placed both the envelope and the leather-bound volumes in the brocade box, which she hid, after a moment's thought, under the ruffle of the bed. Curious though she was about the diaries, she had decided to put off reading them for now. She had a sense that whatever was in them might very well change her life forever.

And then, at last, she turned off the lamp and went to sleep in her oversized bed fit for a señorita.

Friday evening found Pilar getting ready for a small dinner party at the Uslars'.

The invitation to dine with Rafael's family had been extended earlier in the week, after he and Pilar saw each other at Gabriela's funeral. It was accompanied by Rafael's requisite seductive disclaimers: he would, of course, understand if she could not find the time to come, but would be enchanted to see her if she could; he did not want to be "selfish" or to impose on her when she was here for such a short visit and when so many other friends surely wanted to express their condolences on her nana's death. "But *por favor,* try," he added.

He had invited her mother and her sister as well: "Ana Carla and her husband are welcome to join us, of course," he told her.

Pilar marveled at how easily and how rapidly, in her country, the simplest dinner invitation could expand into a fiesta. Even after living for several years in the States, where such formalities played little part in her life, she still felt inexplicably bound by them here.

She had confided to Rafael that with the stress of the funeral and her having to return to Chicago in a few days, it would be best if they could have a not-too-formal dinner limited to the Uslar family, herself, and her mother. In accepting his invitation, she was swayed once again by charm and protocol, only to realize, later, that she should have trusted her instincts in the first place and offered her regrets.

Ana Carla appreciated being included, but she said, "Really, *hermana,* there's no need to put Doña Carolina to all that trouble." Much as Ana Carla loved to be involved whenever there was even the slightest hint of intrigue, she was also one of the most considerate people in the world. Pilar was grateful that her sister had declined, for she wanted to keep her visit to the Uslars' as uncomplicated as possible. Ever since her arrival in Caracas for Nana's funeral, she had been spending most of her time trying to manage everyone's expectations about her supposed return to Venezuela.

As she inspected her appearance one last time in the mirror, a voice in Pilar's head told her to change out of her pants, which were both practical and very American, and put on a dress: *What were you thinking? Showing up for a dinner party in pants!* She scolded herself, while she changed, for giving in once again to Rafael's charm. Oh, well, it's just for a couple of hours, she finally told herself, trying to settle her thoughts. She could hardly wait to get back to Chicago on Sunday, even though it meant returning to the dizzying frenzy of the newsroom at the *Chicago Tribune*, where she worked as a business reporter.

When they were about to leave the house, Cristina looked at Pilar, reproachfully shook her head, and said, "Do you really intend to go out without wearing lipstick? Are you deliberately trying to ruin your chances with Rafael?"

Not wanting to antagonize her mother, and confused about her own feelings for her former fiancé, Pilar took a deep breath, went back up to her room and put on some lipstick, and came back downstairs to the front door. At that point, had she been able, she would have kept walking all the way to Chicago.

On the drive to the Uslars', Pilar had to admit to herself that she had accepted Rafael's invitation because, despite the fact that it was she who a few years back had broken their engagement, she still found him attractive and was disarmed by the ease with which he always seemed to insinuate himself into her life. She had to acknowledge, too, that deep down, she was afraid of disappointing her mother by making the wrong choice.

Pilar also thought about all the ties that bound their two families.

Don Fernando Uslar had been her father's dearest friend, and as the editor and publisher of *El Nacional,* one of Venezuela's leading daily newspapers, he had given her her first job as a reporter. Cristina and Rafael's mother, Carolina, were also good friends. Both women sat on the board of the Teresa Carreño Foundation for the Arts, one of the richest such endowments in Latin America.

It was when Pilar was in her second year at the Andrés Bello Catholic University that Rafael had embarked on a serious courtship of her that would culminate, a couple of years later, in a formal engagement. But long before that, their families had had an unspoken understanding that one day the two of them would be married.

Tonight, the moment she and her mother entered the Uslars' house, Pilar was welcomed with open arms, hugs, and kisses by Rafael's amiable and beautiful sisters, Paulina and María Celeste. "So happy to see you!" said María Celeste, the younger of the two. "How have you been, Pilar?" Paulina asked fondly. "I have heard great things about you from Doña Cristina." Pilar returned their kisses and hellos and prepared herself to greet the lady of the house.

Elegant as it undeniably was, Carolina's house barely escaped being ostentatious. Complementing the carefully chosen period furniture were oil portraits of every member of the owner's immediate family, tastefully hung in prominent locations. Had any of them been even one square centimeter larger, Carolina could have been accused of being pompous.

Gracefully authoritative and always the perfect hostess, Carolina herself now emerged from the living room to greet her guests. If they had been anyone else, she would have waited for a servant to usher them in, but Pilar was, after all, Juan Carlos Castillo's daughter, and to her, Carolina paid due respect.

By her manner alone, the matriarch made it clear that in the Uslar household, everything ran according to her seemingly benevolent directives, which must be unquestioningly obeyed. *Rebellion* was a word

unfamiliar to any of her children. If she never seemed less than conge-
nial, it was only because neither her daughters nor her son had ever given
her any reason to be otherwise. For as long as Pilar could recall, everyone in this family, especially Rafael, had always done what Carolina
said. Even her husband had no say in domestic matters: he and every
other Latin man had learned early on, either instinctively or through
painful experience, that there was no use in arguing with their women.

And so it was for all the family. Pilar knew—she remembered
all too well—that the other Uslars might as well be puppets, ready to
be manipulated through the evening's elaborate choreography by
Carolina's deft and commanding hands. She'd had ample proof, a
few years back, that this woman would do anything within her power
to ensure that her only son always got what he wanted. For this reason, Pilar, rather than feeling the feigned warmth that Carolina made
a show of exuding when she came to greet her at the door, sensed
instead the chill of the señora's shrewd appraisal.

But disguising her own reaction, in keeping with the etiquette of
the occasion, Pilar said, "So happy to see you, Doña Carolina," and
returned her hostess's welcoming smile.

"I am so glad you could come, Pilar. You look wonderful."

"*Muchas gracias*, Doña Carolina. You look very well, too."

Pilar now wished that Ana Carla had accompanied them to divert
attention from her. She was already tired of all these tedious pleas-
antries, and the evening had hardly begun.

Once they were all in the living room, Pilar noticed for the first
time how much Rafael had come to resemble his father. Both men
had an almost polished complexion the color of nutmeg, and slicked-
back, blue-black hair. Like his father, Rafael was tall enough to be
called handsome, though not so tall that he could pass for distin-
guished. From his mother, he had inherited an appreciation for elegantly tailored, impeccable clothes.

But it was not only Rafael's appearance that made people take notice; he also had a magnetic personality that drew others to him. And his every movement suggested that he was not unaware of his appeal.

In observing Rafael's father, Pilar immediately identified the source of all his son's charm. Nana used to say that superficial charm could be tested, and Pilar was about to see that firsthand.

Señor Uslar had a reputation for marital infidelities, which everyone in their circle knew about but no one ever mentioned. Hearing the sweet nothings that flowed so effortlessly from his lips, Pilar wondered why perfectly accomplished women of her mother's generation put up with such insolent behavior from their childlike husbands. "If you want to have a lasting marriage, you need to learn to pass lightly over things like that": this was Cristina's answer when Pilar once asked her why.

She could tell by the way her mother looked at Rafael that she more than approved of him as a potential son-in-law. Even though their engagement was long over, he was the sort of man who always kept fighting until he was certain—really certain—that he had lost. Accordingly, he had continued to visit Cristina from time to time despite her daughter's having moved to Chicago. And as far as Pilar herself was concerned? True, Rafael was handsome and well groomed, she would give him that, but a few years in the States had taught her that there was more to people than dress and address. *So why, then, did she still have feelings for him?*

From his two coquettish sisters Rafael had learned enough about the exhausting details of being a woman to charm Pilar, in front of everyone, with the first genuine compliment of the evening: "*Mi vida*, you've changed your hair! You look *divina!*"

Embarrassed to find that all eyes were now on her, she could manage only a simple "*Gracias*" and a flustered blush.

Even when his flattery seemed contrived, it was difficult to resist, the more so because it poured out of him with the lulling constancy of a running stream: if it ever stopped, its murmur would immediately be missed. But Pilar was smart enough to know that she had not been the first, nor would she be the last, object of Rafael's affections. In Venezuela, it didn't matter how perfect or devoted a wife one was; husbandly flirtations with other women were to be at once expected and dutifully ignored. The more women a Latin man seduced, the more macho he was considered, and the more highly regarded. This cultural norm had been nurtured for so long that everyone took it for granted. For her part, after a three-year absence from it all, Pilar felt sure that she could never be the sort of woman to turn a blind eye as her husband flirted shamelessly with another woman—even if he promised, as Latin men are so fond of doing when caught, "I will always come home to you, *mi vida*. You're the one I truly love."

The more closely she studied the attractive man before her, the harder Pilar found it to reconcile the detached formality of Rafael's address since her arrival this evening with the spontaneous ease with which he uttered his charming compliments. It was all part of the Latin man's seduction game, a means of keeping a woman off balance so she'd never be too sure of him and would become, as a result, intrigued by his pursuit. She had often thought that when such a man set out his snare, it was like talking with two men at the same time, one of whom was lying.

In the end, everything about Rafael, from his well-pressed suits to his well-polished arguments, proclaimed an assurance that, while not without its appeal, was really arrogance: he thought himself clearly superior.

Just as the pendulum clock that hung on the living-room wall tolled eight, the doorbell rang. A minute later, one of Carolina's maids showed in Archbishop Mariano Fermín del Toro, who had said Gabriela's funeral Mass and who, in keeping with a common practice in some South American homes, would be joining the Uslar family for dinner.

A solicitous Carolina greeted him effusively: "*Buenas noches, Su*

Eminencia. We feel blessed that you've decided to grace us with your presence."

As it would turn out, however, even the presence of one of the highest-ranking members of the Catholic Church would not be enough to change the course that Fate had laid for the evening.

Had she not been provoked during dinner, Pilar would probably have kept her opinions to herself. Certainly her mother would have preferred that. But even though she would later be aghast at her own conduct, the truth was that Don Fernando had left her no other choice: not to have spoken up would have been tacitly to concur with his implication that a woman's place was in the kitchen, and with the even more painful suggestion that her own father had felt the same way. She couldn't allow that to pass.

As soon as everyone was seated at the table, two members of Carolina's domestic staff began to serve what ended up being a very formal and elaborate dinner after all. About halfway through the meal, Don Fernando asked Pilar a question that was intended as a tease.

"*Dime,* Pilar, do the Americans pay you to put down on paper those pretty little words of yours? Rafael tells us you're a reporter for the *Chicago Tribune.* Is that true?"

Where a few years ago she would have taken this as a harmless and even mildly amusing bit of banter, her new understanding of women's issues now made it impossible for her to bite her tongue.

With a curt "That's true," she partially answered him. She could not comprehend how this man, the supposedly enlightened publisher of one of the most powerful newspapers in the country, could still entertain the Byzantine notion that a woman should do only "pretty" things.

Retreating a little, Don Fernando asked her what Americans thought of the current situation in Venezuela, to which her reply was, "You mean the *actual* situation, or the situation as it's being presented by the government and the media?"

Noting that the tenor of the conversation had shifted, and trying to avert a potential eruption, Carolina broke in to express how "delighted" they all were to have Pilar back home, and to propose a toast, a *brindis*, in her honor.

But Don Fernando would not be challenged, especially by a woman. After the *brindis*, in an effort to restore the balance of the conversation in his favor, he asked Pilar, in a tone somewhere between puzzled and patronizing, "What do you mean, 'as it's being presented'? Please don't tell me that after just a few years away you have turned on us."

Rafael was the only one who seemed to observe this interaction between his father and his former fiancée with something like bemusement.

Pilar took a sip of water and said in a high, clear voice, so that everyone could hear, "It's not a question of turning or not turning, Señor Uslar. It's more a matter of the liberties that are being taken with the rights of the people."

"And what rights might you be referring to, my dear?"

"Well, for one, the right to an objective press that doesn't lie. I'm sure you'd think nothing of tearing up an old document drafted by Simón Bolívar, a document called the constitution, and tossing it in the trash can in your office. Or at least that's what this morning's paper leads me to believe."

Fernando Uslar was obviously not impressed, but his tone remained paternally convivial: "Come on, Pilar, what does a young girl like you know about the constitution?" Then, trying to make her feel even more inadequate, he added, "I advise you to become better informed before you open that beautiful mouth of yours again. What would your father say?"

Sensing disapproval on all sides, Pilar narrowed her eyes and glared at Don Fernando with blind rage, too angry to respond. Then, to everyone's silent shock, she rose from her chair and announced to her mother, in front of all the pursed-lip company, "Mamá, I'm leaving. Are you coming or staying?"

Carolina, desperate to make the best of a hopeless impasse, walked Pilar and Cristina to the door, but not without the following parting words:

"Pilar, I'm surprised at you. Fernando would probably have taken that argument from a man, but *querida,* don't forget, you're a woman. What on earth were you thinking?"

This Pilar could not let pass. "How could I forget I'm a woman when the entire evening has been one long reminder of it? It is you who should be more respectful of our kind, Doña Carolina."

As soon as the front door had closed behind them, an outraged Cristina demanded to know if Pilar had lost her mind, exclaiming that she had likely ruined a decades-old family friendship.

For Pilar, it was incomprehensible that neither Carolina nor her mother perceived how their generation's outdated views on women's roles had contributed to keeping down their own. And Rafael—she was furious with him for not even trying to defend her. At the same time, she felt a little guilty about her outburst. She had surely embarrassed her mother, though she hadn't meant to.

When they got home, Pilar found a note from Hortensia, Cristina's housemaid, on her bed.

PLEASE CALL SEÑOR RAFAEL. HE OFFERS APOLOGIES FOR THIS EVENING.

She put the note on her nightstand and opened the windows and took some comfort in the cacophonous sounds of the night. Lulled by the chattering of crickets and drained by the evening's events, she lay down on the bed, on top of the covers, barefoot but otherwise fully dressed.

The clock on her nightstand put the time at 11:30. Still searching for a way to ease her anxiety, she thought of the brocade box. She got up off the bed, pulled the box from its hiding place, and lifted its lid. Carefully she took out volume I and made her way back to bed with it. After Pilar took her clothes off and slipped under the covers, she looked for a long while at the closed book before her, remembering her grandmother. Then she opened it and began to read.

I

The *Lady*

Even the most ordinary person, in the
presence of a Lady, suddenly acquires
brilliance.

—ANONYMOUS

Secrets *of* the **Living Room**

Mi querida nieta:

I will first share with you a few stories that capture the nature of a lady. The nuns at the San José de Tarbes School for Girls imprinted on me from a very early age an exquisite code of civility that has served me well in every social situation I have ever encountered.

Common courtesy is formally known as etiquette. Etiquette is a lot like art. While it can take many forms, depending on the surface on which it will ultimately be displayed, all truly great art is founded on the same underlying principles.

The Carmelite nuns took manners so seriously that I often thought civility must be second in importance only to religion. The code of conduct we were taught in school covered every challenge imaginable, from sitting in a chair properly to hosting a party for an ambassador. What I aspire to pass on to you through these stories is more modest in scope, but it will accomplish much in shaping your life as a lady. There are, of course, perfunctory rules of protocol that you must endeavor to learn and put into practice. I trust that your mother will have made sure you learned those at the appropriate time.

Etiquette is actually a very simple skill that requires little more than the ability to put oneself in someone else's place and to observe what is needed of one in any situation. Think of it as a way of living inspired by thought-

fulness, consideration, and respect for others and for oneself under any circumstances.

To this day, I can hear the Mother Superior admonishing me for not "sitting in curves." She would tap me gently on the shoulder, look at me with a smile in her beady eyes, and say, "Gabriela, you could improve your posture. A lady always sits in curves."

Even as I was being taught the strict tenets of good society in school, I was simultaneously learning about native beauty rituals at home. It is this very combination of modern civility and primitive lore that makes South American women so captivating.

In the pages that follow, I hope to honor both our beguiling traditions and the gentle manner of the women who showed me how to move majestically through the world. If you apply the principles set out in these stories, mi querida, you will save yourself from having to experience many unpleasant things.

First I will reveal to you our native beauty rituals and explain the art of seductive conversation, the meaning of courtship, the importance of good society, and your influential role as the mistress of the house.

Once you have mastered the art of being a lady, I will give you a taste of the kitchen, so you can learn the recipes that stir a man's desire. As you indulge your senses in the essence of what it is to be a chef, you will discover what makes some women successful in the kitchen and most others not.

Finally, I will entrust to you the key that unlocks the bedroom door. With this you may gain access to a world that men long to enter. Seduction and submission will tempt you, but behind closed doors, you will discover the difference between courting mere desire and satisfying ravishing lust.

Although these rules guided my life and often provided me with comfort, they also brought me great pain. Eventually, from a retrospective vantage on an entire life's experience, I acquired an equal respect for the rules that were meant to govern my actions and the forces that took them away. This is why I have chosen to pass on to you what I know of each.

And should you be fortunate enough to have a daughter, it will be your duty to see to it that these gifts are in turn handed down to her.

Con mucho cariño,
Tu nana

uno: YAMILA

Yamila was a mestiza.

She grew up in Canaima, a beckoning place in the middle of the Amazon where nature yields an unfamiliar bounty and where the native Yanomami Indians and the Spanish conquistadores once intermingled to produce the most primeval beauty.

Canaima is also home to the black puma, a cat whose predatory gaze forgives no prey and to whom many ritual dances are dedicated in hopes of appeasing its spirits.

As if the bounty of the Amazon forest were not enough to lure the senses, Yamila's homeland is also blessed with the tallest waterfall in the world, Angel Falls, whose waters descend proudly and majestically as if from heaven. The most extraordinary trait of *el salto Angel* is not its height, which is impressive enough, but the enormous pool below, where its rapid waters feed furiously into the Churún River, a tributary of the Caroní.

It may be such awe-inspiring natural surroundings that instill in us South American women our almost cultlike reverence for beauty. *La belleza* is the name given to the scrupulously cultivated sensual attitude that we are taught to nurture from an early age.

As the Spanish aristocracy began to settle in Caracas after the *Conquista,* it begat a social class that was to be known as the *criollos,* or *mantuanos.* The latter name for these Venezuelan-born descendants of the Spaniards referred to the *mantas,* or drapes, that their women wore over their dresses to cover themselves.

Over time, some members of the ruling class interbred with the indigenous population; their offspring were labeled mestizos.

The ethnic majority of the Venezuelan population was and still is identified as mestizo. The remainder is known as *indígena,* or Indian. This smaller group lives predominantly in the Amazon region and, as a discrete entity there, has maintained its traditional, national, and regional customs as well as its language, Papiamento.

When she was still a young girl, Yamila, as was customary, was brought to Caracas, where a family from the capital was expected to educate her in exchange for her services as a housemaid.

Back then, large families typically had two kinds of live-in maids. The first would cook and do the cleaning, while the second attended to the señoritas of the house as a maidservant. Yamila was my personal maid. Mayra was our resident chef.

Thanks to Yamila's knowledge of magical rituals and rare native concoctions, I soon learned to transform my body from a natural canvas into a walking work of art. With her help, I became an icon of eroticism.

dos: BEAUTY RITUALS

Beauty of the sort that incites desire is the currency of the fantasy world into which our men wish to be admitted.

In South America, beauty is an attitude that goes beyond physical appeal. Sensuality and the art of eroticism are inextricably bound up with it. As well as being encouraged to cultivate her natural beauty, every woman is urged from an early age to develop her sensuality in sophisticated ways.

Girls begin to learn about certain beauty rituals when they are still quite young—in their girlhood, or *niñez,* which officially lasts until they turn fifteen. Alongside academic skills such as reading and writing, the habit of personal grooming and the careful safeguarding of virtue are among the vital lessons that must be patiently imparted to a *niña* during this critical time. The practice of manners that will enable a señorita one day to become the mistress of the house—*la ama de su casa*—is another highlight of her *niñez.*

My own education came from several sources. From my mother, I learned that the principles involved in a girl's becoming a lady must remain a woman's watchword throughout her life. While the lady is made in childhood, the woman must always be chaste: next to her beauty, her virginity should be her most cherished possession.

From my brother, Antonio, I learned that even as girls are experiencing puberty, their male counterparts are simultaneously pursuing the generally prescribed and calculated development of their own sexuality, usually at brothels.

Through the almost ritualistic study of the *género femenino,* our men acquire a dexterity that apart from being useful in the bedroom also gives them the upper hand when it comes to distilling *la esencia de una mujer.* It is as a result of these rites of passage that South American women typically come to discover their own sexual essence, not only through important beauty rituals but through the gentle manner of their men in bed.

A stroll on the streets of downtown Caracas, and even a casual observation of men who enjoy walking behind pretty women while keeping their eyes focused on their undulating hips, make it abundantly clear that the pleasures of sensuality and eroticism go effortlessly and shamelessly hand in hand.

Entry into the secret cult of erotic sensuality requires a woman to devote boundless time to the enhancement of her own beauty. For beauty, even more than sex appeal, is an art form, an opportunity to put a brush to canvas and immortalize the womanly gifts one was born with.

A man who is told that a certain woman is beautiful will search out every possible way to arrange a meeting or assay a touch.

Throughout my life, I have faithfully adhered to the rituals that helped me to paint the canvas of my womanhood, but in order to find my true essence, I had to hand over the paintbrush to a man.

My mother also taught me that beauty must be as natural as breathing, and that to make herself look beautiful, a woman must, every day, before she even gets out of bed, turn all her energies toward *feeling* beautiful. "Even when you are alone in your bed," my mother used to say, "endeavor to regard yourself with respect. Feel lovely inside. Caress your own hair and wear exquisite undergarments, even if no one but you will take pleasure in seeing them."

Once, when I was twelve, I saw Yamila collecting from our garden a fresh bunch of yerbabuena leaves. I followed her into my mother's bedroom and watched as she carefully placed a glass of water and the mint leaves on a small plate on the round table in the anteroom.

After she left, I asked my mother curiously, "What are the leaves for, Mami?"

She smiled and said, "For my breath, Gabriela—to make it scented, cool, and sweet." She chewed on a few leaves and then rinsed her mouth with water before sitting down on her boudoir chair to begin her morning beauty routine.

"Can I try?"

"Yes, you may." She offered me some leaves and another smile. Then, lowering her voice to hint at a secret, she explained, "You're not old enough yet to know this, but a woman's fragrant breath is like a small invitation to a kiss."

A few seconds of chewing was enough to make me want to spit out the leaves, but I couldn't admit that to Mami. Instead, I moved closer and kissed her on the cheek, my mouth full of yerbabuenas, before asking, "Like this?"

Smiling at me fondly, Mami said in the most natural of ways, "Yes, Gabriela, like that . . . and like when your father kisses me on the lips."

"How many kisses can you get in a day if your breath smells really, really nice?"

"Well, *querida,* that all depends. That's enough for now." She held a plate out in front of me, and I took the leaves out of my mouth with my fingers and gently deposited them on it.

As I continued to watch my mother, I noticed that before applying any color to her eyes, she put some drops of water in them.

"What's the water for?" I asked her.

"To keep the inside of my eyes clear, Gabriela."

Originally used by Egyptian women for medicinal purposes, *el colirio,* or collyrium, gives the eyes a penetrating yet faraway quality. Now I knew the secret behind the spellbinding, gemlike shine in Mami's gaze.

I remained by her side, transfixed by her process of transformation.

My mother's perfectly oval face was the glowing canvas for her lovely, shifting expressions. I studied her as she applied to her cheeks a powdery mix of cinnamon and araguay seeds, telling me, "The powder of these seeds is light enough to blend with my skin but dark enough to lend it a sunny glow. This is what you want."

When I begged to try the mixture, she admonished that on my young face it would make me look like a prostitute. I must wait until I was older.

Next she reddened her full lips with a mixture of crushed bucare seeds and sticky honey that shone like glass.

The entire ritual culminated with the careful inking of her already full black lashes with a blend of *manteco negro* and water, after she first twisted them using a silver spoon. This, she explained, holding up the small spoon for me to inspect, "allows the lashes to curl upward and stay that way all day. See?"

When she was finished, I sighed. I could hardly wait until it was my turn to perform these magical rituals on myself.

Perhaps the most important lesson I learned about the perfecting of natural beauty was that anything applied to a woman's face should merely hint at the mysteries beneath its surface rather than obscuring them with unnecessary artifice.

Beauty was part of my mother's character; in fact, it *was* her character. It was the single overwhelming, thrilling thought that entered one's mind the moment one saw her. Like the beauty of a flower, Mami's beauty was sufficient unto itself, but to enhance her allure, she always dabbed the scent of rose petals and sweet almond oil behind her ears, between her breasts, and at the back of each knee. Having seen her do this, I dreamed of the day I could do it myself. Perfume seemed a kind of instant sensuality. I was now doubly entranced, by my mother's loveliness and by her intoxicating scent.

Our country is blessed with the largest variety of exotic plants and flowers to be found anywhere in the world. When you are old enough to discern what your own senses find appealing, you should have no trouble in securing the right combination of ingredients from which to create your own fragrance. Once you have concocted a fetching scent for yourself, keep the formula a secret, for your fragrance will become your feminine signature, recognizable and always unchanging. It will announce your presence even before you arrive in a room and recall it after you leave. Such a lingering reminder can be one of a woman's most seductive traits. This is why you should wear the same perfume throughout your life.

For my own personal scent, I still mix six drops of orchid water with three drops of geranium oil and a few drops of purified spirits.

WHEN I STUDIED MY MOTHER'S REFLECTION IN THE *espejo,* I longed to grow up. I wondered if my face would have the symmetry of hers, the full, moist lips, the sweetly sloping brow, and indefinable air of repose.

As I regarded with a daughter's pride the finished work of art before me, Mami addressed me in a way that let me know she was about to say something of great importance. "Gabriela, as soon as you are the right age, every single day at sunrise, after imagining your own glow in your mind's eye, you must leave your bed and begin to make your beauty your own by following these routines without fail."

I nodded to indicate that I understood, but her words sounded ominous to me at the time. I later realized that the formality with which she imparted this advice had been equal to the weight of its import.

As I followed her out of the room, I could not help but notice that in addition to her beauty, my mother also had a palpable air of self-possession, a gentle manner, and the elegant poise that merited her status as a "great lady." This was how I would always remember her moving through the world. Her walk was a sensual sight, reverent to her position in life: stately and elegant, head always held high, chin up. Her evanescent gait and extraordinary carriage reminded me that beneath the finery of her garments there lived and reigned a real woman.

It was from her that I learned that besides seemingly effortless beauty, a genteel manner, and a natural inclination toward sociability, extraordinary composure begins with a woman's graceful walk. At least once a week, for what seemed like hours, my mother would make my sisters and me walk a straight line with a book on our heads. Once we could do this easily and with grace, she taught us how to pick items up off the floor without hunching our backs.

From the way people regarded my mother, I learned that there are few things in life that earn so much favor and indulgence as privilege and beauty. I was certain that it was her bearing, her beauty, and her manner that had caused my father, Dr. Mario Grenales, a man widely acknowledged to be possessed of an untamable disposition, to fall madly and inexplicably in love with her.

Above all, my mother impressed upon her three girls—Constanza, Jacinta, and myself—that a woman must mind her beauty rituals without fail, but *never* within sight of a man.

As she started downstairs to take her morning coffee with my father, Mami's parting words were, "Gabriela, a man has no interest in what it takes to make a woman beautiful. Men prefer to believe that we have come just so into the world. Showing your secrets to a man will break the spell."

She blew me a kiss and left me standing at the top of the staircase, mesmerized and not yet quite able to grasp the significance of what she had said: witnessing the rigors of a woman's beautification will take away its hidden pleasure for a man by rudely unveiling the mystery behind the allure.

LATER THAT DAY, I WENT TO CONSTANZA'S ROOM and asked *her* how many kisses a girl could get if her breath smelled really nice.

"Whom have you been talking to?" she demanded.

"I watched Mami get dressed this morning. She told me about the green leaves, and the kisses!"

Always eager to prove that she knew more than anyone else, Constanza gave me what seemed, at the time, to be a very complicated answer: "Forget about the leaves. If you expect anyone to kiss you on the lips, you must first learn how to pout properly."

Seeing my puzzlement, she closed her eyes, raised her chin toward the ceiling, and stuck out her lips. "Like this," she said. "Come, I'll show you."

She grabbed my hand and led me toward the kitchen, where we crushed hot green peppers and mixed them with honey. After applying the mixture to her own lips, she urged me to do the same.

When the peppers touched my mouth, I felt like screaming, but because Constanza had resisted, I simply pursed my lips together and waited for the pain to subside. The honey was supposed to curb the sting of the peppers, but at that moment, I could not imagine why anyone in her right mind would want her lips to swell. Not terribly impressed, but still curious, I asked my sister to teach me more—*after* the sting had finally faded.

Ever the chemist, she showed me how to mix baking soda, water, and lime juice to make the shine of my smile glow brighter.

"Here, try it. It's not so bad," she offered. I wanted to spit out this chalky-tart concoction as soon as I tasted it, but trying once again to be brave like her, I rinsed my mouth with water instead.

When we were done with making potions in the kitchen, Constanza smiled a wicked smile and motioned me to follow her. I giggled as we tiptoed down the back stairs and toward the rear of the house. When I asked her where we were going, she put her right index finger to her lips.

"Shhh," she said. "It's a secret."

rough the meandering hallway and in a few sec-
selves in the part of the house where Mayra and

as Constanza shut her right eye and with her left
gh the keyhole in one of the two adjacent doors.
eered in, I worried that we might get caught, even
though ... d no idea whether what were doing was good or
bad.

Finally she stepped aside so I could put my own eye to the
keyhole. Most of the room was blocked from my view, but
straight ahead I could see Yamila on her bed. She had a towel
casually draped over her, as if she had just taken a bath.

"What is she doing?" I asked Constanza.

She clapped her hand over my mouth, and I remember that
her eyes looked as big as the whites of Mayra's fried eggs.

I kept on watching for a few more minutes, wondering what
it was that Yamila was rubbing between her legs. I also noticed
how different her manner with herself was from my mother's
gentle self-regard.

When we were safely upstairs again, Constanza told me it
was *aceite de yuquillo*. "It's an oil that is supposed to make men
swoon," she said.

From Yamila, I later learned that yuquillo oil came from a
rare plant of the same name that grows only near the delta of
the Orinoco River, not far from where she grew up. The much-
sought-after substance gets its light-red tinge from the color of
the earth near the river's *manglares*.

On the day that I first became aware of all these intricate
beauty routines, my confusion was infinite. I had no idea why I
had to start getting out of bed earlier as I grew older, when sleeping in was so much fun. Or why purposely making one's lips
sting for no good reason was a desirable thing. Or why rubbing
tart chalk against one's teeth should feel anything other than

sticky, especially if there was nothing wrong with those teeth in the first place. But I needed only to look at the luminous smiles of all the women in our family to know that my sister's concoctions truly worked.

By the time we returned upstairs and finished cleaning up the mess we had left in the kitchen, it was almost time for my afternoon bath, which Yamila always drew at the exact same hour each day, lest Mami reprimand her. When she came to my room to fetch me, I felt so ashamed of having spied on her that I wanted to cry.

As she did every afternoon, Yamila had prepared for me a bath of warm water, arnica flower, and cinnamon oil. When I was old enough to learn more about plants' properties, I realized that Yamila had added arnica to my bathwater because of its ability to quench the skin's thirst.

After my bath, I obediently followed Yamila back to my bedroom, where a white linen towel awaited me. The linen would quickly drink up the water from my dripping body while leaving the remaining oils to caress my skin.

Every few weeks, Yamila would scrub me thoroughly with *tierra de ceiba* to encourage the emergence of new, virgin skin. This rare substance from the banks of the Orinoco River is found only in Venezuelan soil.

Then, with a pleasure that I now believe was not entirely chaste, she would massage my entire body with warm almond oil while watching my reflection in the mirror. She encouraged me to love and admire myself as if a man were caressing me, all the while telling me, over and over, in a blend of her native Papiamento and Spanish, that it was impossible for a man to love a woman who did not know how to love herself.

We South American women have many more rituals and routines meant to ensure that throughout the years our skin will remain our most precious asset. The desired result is always a silky smooth surface, an irresistible elixir reminiscent of youth. I considered myself lucky to have earned one of the most coveted terms of endearment that a man can bestow upon a woman who has perfectly luminescent, light cinnamon skin: my charming childhood friend Jorge Armando Caballero used to address me in correspondence as *Querida piel de canela* or "Dear cinnamon skin."

From Yamila I learned that cutting a crest of the sábila plant makes it open abruptly like a cactus to emit a white, slick liquid: pure collagen. The women of her native Canaima apply the sticky, lathery substance instantly to heal any open wound. Señoritas from Caracas use the liquid for a different purpose: mixed with a few drops of water, the sábila's essence will give skin a youthful tone. As the years passed, every time I tried this rare substance, the result was always a radiant face on which a man's lips must ever want to rest.

When I was old enough, Yamila showed me to how remove all my pubic hair with warm honey and beeswax. She told me that men loved virgins and that the combination of beeswax and honey would keep this tender part of me forever immaculate. She was right.

My mother used to say that one could judge a woman's upbringing by looking at her hands and feet. Thanks to jojoba oil, which I still use nightly, mine have always had a natural, inviting luster.

Toenails, of course, must be painted. And the hue of one's fingernails and toenails must match the shade one wears on one's lips. "If you change one, you must change them all. If colors don't blend, you will look unladylike"—these were Mami's final words on the subject. "The blending of colors," she said, "must be flawless."

A woman's décolletage is one of her most important allurements. Coffee beans contain the highest concentration of caffeine of any plant in our country; mashed with ripe avocados and spread on a woman's breasts, they give the bust a wonderful lift that one should always endeavor to sustain. After I turned seventeen, both Mami and Yamila became obsessed with my following this messy ritual weekly.

Once a week, my hair would be treated with a mash of ripe bananas. I would then wash it several times, after which Yamila would detangle it. Afterward my black locks would tickle down my back, looking as soft and shiny as black silk.

But my favorite hair routine took place every night, when my mother would instruct me, before I got into bed, to turn my head upside down so she could gently brush my hair in this position. This seemed to me nothing more than a loving game between us, but its real purpose was to draw out my hair's natural oils from their source on my scalp and allow them to coat the rest of my wavy mane.

"Never cut your hair shorter than the curve of your shoulders," Mami warned. She explained, "Men desire women whose hair undulates in concert with their walk. Short hair is for boys."

Later in life I would recall her wise advice when the only man I ever loved told me, with desire in his eyes, that my luscious hair reminded him of the sea waves of Macuto.

Many years after my escapade with Constanza had faded into a tender childhood memory, I learned to massage yuquillo oil between my own legs to keep the area moist, warm, and tingly. I smiled when I realized that my sister had been right, not only about the yuquillo oil but about all the other beauty rituals she had so generously shared with me that day.

tres: RITOS FEMENINOS

On this special day when I was thirteen, I was given a white brocade box and a detailed explanation of the ritual of immersion.

Beside myself with excitement, I ignored everything and
everyone else around me. Mami seemed delighted to see my girlish grin.

From the contents of the box, I derived the greatest pleasure.

Both of my grandmothers were in attendance, and my
mother's sisters, my own sisters, my cousins Clara, Corina, and
Ercilia, my older brother, Antonio, and my proud papi. I was
immersed in an ocean of loving hearts.

Dressed in a beautiful red peasant dress that Mami had had
made especially for the occasion, I ran around the living room
showing everyone the gold *medalla* of the Virgin Mary that hung
delicately from the bracelet around my wrist—my first piece of
jewelry, a gift from my father.

"Gabriela, I know you're excited, but you need to pay attention to the ceremony now," my mother said. "At the end of this
ritual, you will be enlightened about the sacred rites of being a
woman."

Amid all these familiar faces, I could see only my mother's.
But in keeping with tradition, it was my grandmother Doña
Victoria Contreras who welcomed me into the world of a
woman's secrets.

As my grandmother spoke, I must have looked puzzled, for my
mother acknowledged my confusion: "Don't worry, Gabriela—
tonight, when you go to bed, I'll make sure that it all makes sense
to you." As she whispered these words in my ear, she caressed the
top of my head with her gentle hand.

Once my grandmother had finished speaking about the two kinds of cleanliness, we all went outside for the actual ceremony. One at a time, the women of my family poured water over my head in a symbolic act of purification.

Doña Victoria explained that this ritual served as a symbolic rebirth, my emergence from the cleansing waters of new beginnings. In this ceremony, she said, a woman moved from one state of cleanliness, the physical, to another, the ritually pure.

In the Bible, the canonical site for ritual immersion is a natural body of water, whether a river, stream, pond, or lake. On my special day, the purified liquid came from the rivulet that coursed through the tropical garden in back of our house.

After the ceremony, traditional Venezuelan music was played as everyone clapped, leapt around, and swayed in honor of my coming-of-age. Roasted pigeons, wonderful sweets, and breads and fruits were brought from the kitchen as I received an abundance of good wishes and hearty congratulations.

At day's end, my mother took me up to bed, and as she brushed my hair, I finally got to open the brocade box. Inside was a red silk ribbon to remind me of my first blood; from now on, if I wished, I could tie my hair proudly with it. Also in the box were three white cotton cloths onto which that loss of potential life in the form of blood would seep, a small mirror in which I could observe the first bloom of my womanhood, and a tiny bottle of perfume to mix with my natural scent.

After a few minutes, Mami instructed me to place the box on my night table, and then she read me a passage from the Old Testament:

> . . . *the Lord spoke to Moses saying: When a woman has had a discharge of blood, she shall count off seven days, and after bathing in flowing waters for every one of the seven days, she*

shall be purified. On the eighth day, she shall take two pigeons to the priest. The priest shall offer the one as a sin offering for there is, for a short time, the loss of potential for any new life being conceived, loss of life itself, and the other as the potential for the creation of life. . . .

The next few days would flow by like the gentle waters of a stream. I would cleanse my body each day in preparation for life's cycle to begin again.

Before putting out the lights and kissing me softly on the cheek, Mami asked me to give thanks for my gift, the gift of knowing that life would one day spring from the tender place between my legs.

cuatro: FANNING DESIRE

The rite of passage through which I became a woman was eventually followed by a lesson in feminine wiles, whereby I learned that few things increase a man's desire for a woman more than having to wait for her.

One afternoon when I was still thirteen, Santiago, our next-door neighbor, came to our house to call on me. As soon as I heard the doorbell ring, I suspected it might be him, and wanting to go outside and play, I rushed downstairs to open the door before Mayra or Yamila could get to it.

Breathless, I was dismayed when I got to the bottom of the stairs and found my father waiting for me with a serious look on his face.

"Gabriela, what exactly do you think you are doing?"

I explained that I was expecting Santiago and that we were going to go outside and play. To this my father sternly replied, "*Aprende a darte tu puesto*"—"Know your own worth." He ordered me to my room and went to greet Santiago himself.

Mortified at the notion of my father's talking to my young friend, I didn't go to my room; instead, I stayed at the top of the stairs and tried to eavesdrop on their conversation.

"*Buenas tardes,* Dr. Grenales."

"Good afternoon, Santiago. What brings you to our home today?"

"I am here to ask Gabriela to come out and play."

"Won't you have a seat? I will go and see if *la reina* is available."

From my post at the top of the spiral staircase, I heard my father's words, and impatiently I thought, Of course I'm available! What does he mean? I'm right here. Then I hid so Papi wouldn't see me there.

When my father got to the top of the stairs and caught a glimpse of me, he raised an eyebrow and with his matador stare sent me to my room without saying a single word. Once I was in my room, I understood: he had never intended to fetch me. His walk upstairs had been a ruse to keep Santiago waiting.

He went back downstairs, thanked Santiago for his invitation, and told him that I was "indisposed for the day" but would be pleased to have him call tomorrow. And with that, I heard the sound of the front door closing.

After that incident, I was upset and convinced that Santiago would never again ask me to play. As I was getting ready for bed that night, I told Mami how horrible Papi had been and complained that no boy would "ever, ever" want to have anything to do with me if I made him wait.

While they were well suited for each other, in me my father and my mother had managed to produce a child who was constantly besieged by a divided self. I spent most of my childhood wavering between my mother's vigilant eye and my father's insatiable appetite for life. Eventually, however, I deduced from the way my father received other men's affections toward his daughters that having grown up around men and knowing what they were capable of, he had decided early on that adventure and excitement were to be exclusively a male province. He would do everything in his power to keep his daughters from wading in those waters.

At twenty-nine, my father, Dr. Mario Grenales, had been one of the most desirable bachelors in Venezuela, just returned from Madrid, where he had completed advanced studies in medicine and surgery. But if medical science had taught him discipline and imparted a certain tendency toward fastidiousness, my father also had his artistic side: he was an accomplished dancer, and no one was better at improvising "Blue Moon" on the piano or attracting a roomful of people to hear his stories. Seeing him on such occasions, one would have thought youth eternal.

I once asked him what he would have wanted to be if he weren't a doctor, and he told me he would have been Enrico Caruso. Although he could not sing, Papi did have the commanding voice of a tenor and was a natural musician, playing piano strictly by ear and without any formal training.

His music was sacred to him; none of us was allowed to go anywhere near his records lest we scratch them with the phonograph needle. He got musical gifts from his friends in Europe and from the American ambassador, who gave him big-band recordings by Tommy Dorsey and Artie Shaw.

As a legacy of his Spanish heritage, my father enjoyed overindulgence. Much like his conquistador ancestors, he had a passion for all things rich, including delicious food, delectable wines, and devastatingly beautiful women. And despite the fact that he was a doctor and should have known better, he had a weakness for Romeo y Julieta cigars, which led people to believe that he was actually Cuban instead.

Women always succumbed to my father's charm, even though they knew he was happily married, and made fools of themselves in their eagerness to be in his presence.

Although he was so accustomed to having women throw themselves at him, Mario Grenales fell without resistance for my mother's quiet charm the moment he first saw her, gliding like a dove out of the cathedral one Christmas Eve.

One of his most endearing traits was his abiding belief in premonitions, apparitions, and the power of saints to answer his prayers. He was fond of saying that it was San Agustín who had placed my mother in his path that night after Midnight Mass.

My own childhood curiosity on any subject was always fueled by my father's predilection for drama and my mother's obdurate strength, which most of the time served as a tonic to his love of excess.

His family background stood in sharp contrast to my mother's strict yet delicate upbringing. She often said that his seven brothers, though full of seductive charms, had few manners and seemed to feel that society's rules applied to everyone but themselves.

Many times I had heard my mother remark that she had married my father because they were complete opposites, and opposites attracted. But when she put me to bed that night, I realized that Mami and Papi were one and the same. I would always vividly recall the look on her face when she gazed into my father's eyes, a look that suggested not only that they knew each other very well but also that on all important matters, they were in complete agreement.

I could have continued to protest, as was both my nature and my style, Santiago's unfair dismissal, but my mother's firm yet gentle tone in supporting my father's decision was all it took to persuade me that they were united on this matter.

As she was about to wish me good night, Mami cupped my chin in her elegant hand, as if she were holding a tiny bird with broken wings.

"*Mi vida,* your name is Gabriela Grenales. You must always remember what that means. You are a señorita. What would Santiago think if you were to throw yourself at him like a commoner whenever he felt like calling on you? Your father has done you a favor. You must thank him when you have the chance." And she gave me the sweetest of pillowy kisses.

Much later, after I became a mother myself, I remembered that night and understood that having two parents who are *de acuerdo* makes any child feel safe.

I still went to bed confused, too young to comprehend the significance of what I had just learned. But in time I would come to appreciate that, in addition to teaching him regard for a woman, anticipation fans a man's interest and strokes his ardor.

During my formal courtship it became clear to me that it was not only customary but necessary to make a man wait, and I saw then that men are but simple creatures who find the dance of flirtation quite alluring and whose greatest aim in life is to show the world the meaning of a conquest.

Santiago called on me promptly the next day. But this time, when I heard the doorbell ring, I felt a little disappointed that anyone could be so easily predictable.

cinco: LAS PIEZAS

Shortly after my younger sister, Jacinta, celebrated her own immersion ritual, she, Constanza, and I were invited up to my mother's room.

Entering my mother's chamber was always an invitation to bask in the glory of femininity, excitement, sensuality, and delicacy.

Atop the hand-embroidered Spanish bed covers lay the objects of her affection and the delicate subjects of our next lesson: a luxurious crepe de chine peignoir set, a smooth silk camisole, an age-defying cut-velvet corset, a whisper-thin chiffon baby-doll nightgown, and an exquisite, hand-laced merry widow.

Our mother began our tutorial by listing the colors of lingerie that, once married, every woman should have in her *armario* and informing us that all these *piezas* had a single purpose: to seduce one's beloved on any and every occasion.

Although the word stems from the French *linge,* meaning linen, lingerie has come to be associated with dreams of silk and satin, elegant and seductive underpinnings made not just from linen but also from sensual lace, silk, chiffon, and crêpe de chine.

Enraptured, Constanza, the oldest of us girls, sat at attention on the blue velvet boudoir chair next to my mother's bed. Jacinta, for her part, seemed puzzled by all the designs. And I? I could not wait for the opportunity to discover for myself the allure behind every piece.

"These are your most intimate garments," my mother began. "They are a personal and secret expression of the mood that you will wear from the bedroom to the ballroom. Your choice of lingerie will affect your behavior throughout the day and set the tone for the evening to follow." This was our first introduction to the secret world behind the seams.

She then proceeded to show us the soft bisque peignoir set, a classic Italian silk ensemble featuring a long, flowing slip with a luxurious matching robe that she wore, as was customary, to entertain our father after we children had been put to bed.

The white silk camisole with the thread-thin straps was to be worn underneath a dress, she said, to accentuate the contours of a woman's figure. Choosing a dress to wear was the least of it, however, because women were required to don the proper foundation garments—including layers of undershirts, half-slips, and petticoats—before they even gave a thought to their choice of frock. The camisole could be midthigh length or longer, depending on the dress. Also referred to as a corset cover, or petticoat bodice, the flirtatious camisole was the favored undergarment of the day.

My own favorite on my mother's bed was the red velvet corset, so obviously complicated and exciting. So fascinated was I by the close-fitting vest that I traced its ribs with my fingers.

The corset family includes the basque, in which a section of the bodice falls below the waist to shape the wearer's hips; the bustier, basically a long-line brassiere; the girdle, a lighter-weight corset that extends from waist to upper thigh; and the corsolette, a tubular garment combining brassiere and girdle, fitted with shoulder straps and suspenders, which enhances a womanly silhouette beyond recognition.

While the ostensible object of the tightly laced piece was to ensure the perfect waist (sometimes two or three inches smaller than a woman's natural waistline), its real mission, according to Mami, was to enhance sexual fantasy and eroticism by drawing attention to the breasts. The upward push it effected produced in men less than immaculate thoughts. I suppose it must be considered a miracle that any woman ever managed to make it out of the bedroom at all when wearing a seductive, show-stopping corset.

The ulterior nature of the *cotte* lent itself readily to passionate prints and flirty fabrics. Some time later, right before Constanza's wedding, we went to buy her trousseau. I advised her to buy a tartan-patterned corset that caught my eye and looked like fun—at fourteen, I imagined that one would play with the piece itself! My mother, always graceful, quietly explained that "looking like a French prostitute should not be one's idea of fun in the bedroom."

In sharp contrast to the meretricious merry widow next to it, the innocent sky blue baby-doll nightgown was the quintessentially feminine trifle. A baby doll is meant to be worn to sleep, and if it does not carry the weight of a corset, it is nonetheless a powerful example of beckoning femininity.

As Mami was about to tell us about the entrancing black merry-widow ensemble, there was a knock on her bedroom door. It was my father, asking her if she could come see him in the study in a few minutes.

"*Por supuesto*, Mario," was her reply.

As if she had been summoned by the Holy See, my mother immediately gathered up her lingerie from her bed, tucked each piece carefully into its proper box, and told us that our lesson was over for the day, adding, "*Niñas*, when your husband calls for you, no matter what you are doing, your response should always be 'of course.' Husbands must come first."

In her haste, my mother had left her merry widow on the bed. As I stared at it, hypnotized by its intricate patterns of lace, strings, and stays, I thought dreamily of the day when a man would lovingly unwrap *my* body from a similar confection.

seis: EL CORTEJO

When I was fifteen, I had the honor of participating in one of the most rewarding rituals to which a young woman in our society can aspire. I became eligible for courtship.

For as long as I can remember, the transition from childhood to womanhood has been one of the most significant passages for adolescent girls in South America. Throughout our own country, this passage is marked by the *quinceañera* ball, or fifteenth-birthday celebration. This occasion is a way to acknowledge that a young woman has reached her sexual maturity and is thus marriageable.

As part of this ritual, a *joven,* or young woman, must learn how to be courted. Courtship, in turn, is an essential part of being treated like a woman while yet remaining a señorita. The señorita may receive and respond to love letters, accept visits from potential suitors, and attend parties with a *chaperona*—never alone. This is the time in a girl's life when her reputation and her virtue must be most jealously guarded. Being alone with a member of the opposite sex for any reason at all is considered in poor taste and worthy of serious social recrimination.

In advance of courtship, a young man usually calls on the aspiring señorita and arranges a visit with her and her parents. During this scheduled visit he is expected to express his desire to become a formal suitor once the young lady has been introduced to society at her *quinceañera* ball.

HERE IS HOW IT IS SUPPOSED TO GO: AS SOON AS the *joven* communicates her desire to spend more time with a suitable candidate, her parents are to make every effort to orchestrate a meeting between the two families and bring about the union.

During this first meeting, she must be on her best behavior. No matter how giddy she may feel, it is essential that she not giggle or engage in any childish antics that might give her future family or her potential husband the impression that she is lacking in what it takes to be a good wife.

A MONTH BEFORE MY OWN *QUINCEAÑERA* BALL, Jorge Armando Caballero, the brother of my best friend, Carmela, called on my parents to arrange a first visit. They agreed, but only reluctantly—which puzzled me because I had thought they would be delighted at the prospect of receiving my first formal suitor. On the appointed day, I secretly hoped that my parents would like him, for in my prayers I had begged God to let Jorge Armando be not only my first dance but also my first love. My prayers, though, were to be only partially answered.

Despite my parents' rather chilly demeanor toward him, I found it difficult to conceal my joy. I knew this visit was the first step in my debut at the *quinceañera* ball at the Caracas Country Club, and I was dreaming of a first kiss.

The thought of being a *quinceañera* had been on my mind ever since I saw my mother's scrapbook from that time in her life. Taking her as my role model, I decided early on that one of my life's goals would be to have rich experiences that would lead to wonderful memories. In the end, memories are all we have.

In preparation for the event, it became my mother's main concern to dress me exquisitely so that I could be seen by as many eligible suitors as possible. Accordingly, the making of my *quinceañera*'s dress was one of the highlights of the entire courtship experience for both of us, though for different reasons. I wanted to impress just one young man.

When it is your turn to go through this rite of passage, you should aim to wear the most beautiful gown you can find, because an object that is not attractively decorated will not

attract any buyers. A man falls in love through his eyes first; after that it is the woman's job to captivate his other senses.

I remember going to my mother's seamstress in the Avenida Urdaneta for fittings. The place had a decidedly French-couturier feel to it, with two enormous dressing rooms each closed off with a red velvet curtain. It was like shopping for a wedding dress, except that there was no groom.

After looking at various dresses, my mother and I settled on an elegant hand-beaded gold gown that hinted at my budding décolletage.

The second step was deciding when and where I was going to be presented. I had no say in this decision; my parents had already chosen the annual ball at the country club.

When saying yes to a potential suitor, whether it is yes to a dance at the ball, or yes to a follow-up visit, you must keep in mind—yes, even now—the five pillars that hold up any marriage. Without virtue, good family, a shared desire to have children, wealth, or a common religion, even the most magical of unions will be hard-pressed to succeed.

So important are these elements, in fact, that the moment a suitor is discovered to be lacking in these criteria, he must be promptly discarded. I would not know this with such certainty had I heeded my own advice: because I married for all the wrong reasons, it was inevitable that I would find *mi gran amor* elsewhere.

You must know that it is not easy for me to pass on this advice, especially because throughout my life, I myself found some of it very difficult to follow. But with the passage of time, I am better poised to offer counsel, having learned from my mistakes.

In terms of pure discipline, however, these core tenets have been my greatest salvation. They served me well when good judgment failed me and when I could not find it in my heart to do the right thing of my own accord. At such times I used to wonder how I could possibly honor the treasures that had been entrusted to me.

At any rate, after that initial courtship meeting, I had a better sense of my interest in Jorge Armando, and I also learned, to my delight, that my feelings were reciprocated. But when I confessed as much to my mother, she brushed off my confidence, for no reason I could see. My curiosity regarding her response would later turn into preoccupation, and later still into despair.

Before relating the events of the months following my *quinceañera* ball, I want to impress upon you that it should be your prerogative, as much as your potential suitor's, to marry for love, all other things being equal. Keeping in mind that the connection between two people is primal and unprompted, and that no one knows better than they themselves whether it is fantasy or reality, the ideal is to marry someone within your circle, with whom you are also in love. While I say that is the ideal, this was nevertheless not my own experience.

From the way things turned out for me, I learned instead that passion alone is seldom enough to sustain an otherwise unsuitable union. I also learned, much to my surprise, that with time, patience, and determination, it is indeed possible for a carefully arranged union to bear fruit—fortunately or unfortunately, depending on one's point of view. I further came to understand that there is a remarkable difference in taste between the fruits of a prescribed marriage and the fruits of real love. But ideally, as I have said, love and marriage should be one and the same.

As you try to make up your mind about who it is you wish to share the rest of your life with, your parents will no doubt encourage you to enter into a marriage of equals out of which love will in time grow. This is exactly what my parents did with me, but at the time of their decision, it was impossible for any of us to foresee what the future would bring. Arbitrary actions can sometimes wreak havoc on our lives, and the consequences may pursue us to the grave.

On the night of my *quinceañera* ball, I experienced nothing but pure joy. When I entered the grand ballroom, the chandeliers were lit, the orchestra was playing, the glasses were clinking, and my father was escorting me, his arm linked with mine. The other *quinceañeras* and I, some of them my good friends from the San José de Tarbes School for Girls, were to be presented after dinner.

When it was my turn, a male voice called out: "Gabriela Grenales, descended from Carlos Alberto Grenales of Spain."

At that moment, I understood that aristocratic blood flowed through my veins. At the mention of her name, every *quinceañera* was reminded of her duty to preserve her heritage by ensuring that her ancestral line and honor were upheld. Little did I suspect, that night, how great a challenge that would prove to be for me.

Sadly for me, not even the riches of the love that I would later find, would nourish the desperate feeling of dishonoring my family's name. So powerfully imprinted was the concept of honor in my mind, that even in the midst of the most consuming passion, I would later imagine the faces of my parents drawn close together at the dinner table: their laughter and delight in each other, and in me, turning to disappointment. Flashes of my mother, Ana Amelia Contreras de Grenales, who proudly told stories of the Contreras family of Trujillo, would flicker through my mind.

The theft of my heart would be the cruelest tragedy of my life. But my loss would never compare to the tragedy of tarnishing my family's honor because the loss of one's good fortune pales before the loss of one's good name. The Grenales name still courses through my blood, hot and never still.

I smiled and made a deep curtsy toward the evening's sponsors. Just then, the music started to play. My father, *el Doctor* Mario Grenales, grudgingly offered my arm to Jorge Armando Caballero, the young man who had already touched my heart and who would now lead me in the first dance of my life.

siete: MY FIRST KISS

A few days after my *quinceañera* ball, I got my hoped-for first kiss, in the shade of a mango tree.

In Venezuela, mango trees grow like mirages. It's the sweltering equatorial heat that does it.

Perhaps as a defense against the heat that gives it life, the sweet and juicy mango packs its rich juices into a thick, polished skin that ranges in color from deep green to vivid, yellowish red. And after its contours have led one into temptation, to eat it after all, there is an even more succulent surprise waiting inside. Peeling a mango is like peeling the sun itself, the bright orange-yellow flesh a fresh reminder that only vibrant tropical sunlight could be the source of this fruit's life.

No matter how one approaches the lascivious mango, its slippery flesh always drips in an unending gush of sweet liquid drops that are impossible to catch with one's mouth; the hands must come to the rescue, making the eating of a mango a messy enterprise from which no one ever emerges unsoiled. Much to my delight, every bite of my first experience with the fruit lived up to this ambitious promise.

Nearly every afternoon, I used to walk to the fruit stand near our house to buy Constanza a little bag of *torontos,* a sort of irresistible chocolate with an *avellana* in the center. (A local delicacy, these nuts fall unbidden off the trees.) Knowing how I loved adventure, my older sister was always able to persuade me to go happily off in search of whatever might satisfy her craving.

On this occasion, however, as I made my way homeward from the fruit stand, I noticed out of the corner of my eye a young man walking in the same direction. I got flustered and quickened my pace, not turning to look. A minute later, when he caught up to me, I saw, to my secret delight, that it was Jorge Armando. He was carrying a jute sack full to bursting with something I could not identify. Trying to mask my excitement, I asked him with feigned impatience, "What's in the sack?"

"Ripe fruit. Ready to be eaten. May I offer you one *muñeca?*"

He pulled out a mango and presented it to me with an inviting smile. Despite my better judgment, I was unable to resist. I knew that my even talking to him was a terrible breach of custom: if I were ever caught alone with a man, I would certainly be punished.

All the same, I felt my temperature begin to rise as a disconcerting and urgent new sensation spread over my lips. He moved closer, and a sudden rush of blood seemed to invade my face. My mind tried to argue against what was about to happen, but my body was weak, ready to surrender to desire. We hid behind a tree, I praying all the while that Constanza would not come looking for me.

As I held the mango to my mouth, its juice began to drip slowly down my neck, and toward my elbow, his tongue catching every meandering drop. I stood before him, perplexed, but obedient as a soldier, fighting not to relent to seduction. I continued to bite the sweet flesh of the mango, entranced, surprised at the excessively familiar taste and why I had such a craving for it.

Strangely, each taste seemed different than the one before. And, caught up in the experience, I welcomed the promise of each tender bite and the warmth of Jorge Armando's breath, in complete silence and with an uncontrollable hunger that lifted me to a new plane where the rigors of self-awareness vanished, as if by magic. His eyes, tugging urgently at mine, made me forget where I was and invited me to a forbidden place I would know only in his presence, in another time in my life.

That night, as I lay awake, wracked with guilt, I wondered if I should tell Constanza about what had happened under the mango tree. But as I drifted into the dreamy sleep of a fifteen-year-old girl just hours past her first kiss, I decided that if magic moments were to retain their charm, one must resist the temptation to explain them.

Having promised to meet every afternoon after school under the mango tree, Jorge Armando and I, unbeknownst to anyone, would steal many more kisses.

ocho: PIANO LESSONS

The year of my first kiss was also the year I fell sick with love.

One night soon after my debut, when my entire family was seated at the dinner table, I brightly remarked that it would not be long, now, until my suitor came calling.

My mother looked surprised. "Who is this lucky young man?" she inquired.

"Why, Jorge Armando, of course—Carmela's brother. Don't you remember, he asked you and Papi if he could court me?"

On hearing his name, Mami searched for my father's eyes and

went so pale that I thought she must have taken ill. When at last she spoke, her tone was icy: "I am afraid that such a courtship will not be possible, Gabriela. I expect you will understand why."

But I *didn't* understand—not one bit. Nevertheless, it was clear that as far as she was concerned, the subject was closed. My father, too, wore a grave expression, and he was slowly shaking his head. It was all I could do not to burst into tears.

My sister Jacinta gave me a glance of pure, distilled compassion, and my brother, Antonio, with his gift for empathy, looked in my direction as if to acknowledge that at that moment, my young dreams must be slipping away before my very eyes.

Not another word was said at the dinner table that evening on that or any other matter.

It was only through talking to Constanza later that night that I learned why my parents would never permit Jorge Armando to court me. "Don't you see?" my sister asked. "We're *criollos,* and he's practically a *mestizo.* You can't marry him—what would people say?"

In my parents' view, Jorge Armando was no more worthy of my hand than a servant. Although his father, Don Manolo, owned a lucrative import business whose profits enabled the family to live in La Laguna, people of our class dismissed the notion that an immigrant with no background, however rich he might be, could ever win admission into the privileged world of the *Mantuanos.*

"It is common knowledge that Don Manolo bought his way into the country club," Constanza confided.

And there it was: Jorge Armando's father may have made large financial contributions to the country club and succeeded in getting his family invited to various social functions, but that hardly meant that the Caballeros' presence was welcome in elite society.

I was desperate to refute my sister's irrational explanation, but with so much evidence pointing to its accuracy, how could I? So I opted instead to protest, "I don't care what people say—we *like* each other!"

"You may not care about the gossip, but our parents do. Put him out of your mind, *hermana*. It will be easier for everyone that way."

I stood there in her room and watched her braid her hair and get ready for bed as if nothing had happened—as if the world were not coming to an end. Then, matter-of-factly, but in a tone that banished any faint hope I still clung to, she added, "Besides, who says it's up to you? You will marry the man our parents *allow* you to marry."

After my talk with Constanza, I went back to my own room, feeling desolate and completely alone. That loneliness would continue to haunt me for years to come.

Unable to sleep, I lay awake for most of the night, trying to figure out a solution to my predicament, until finally a potentially workable scheme began to take shape in my mind.

Delirious with the fever of the forbidden, I resolved that Jorge Armando and I would henceforth seize every opportunity we could find to speak with or see each other. This would be no easy task, for in those days, young women were under the supervision of an adult at all times. In school, the spying nuns never took their watchful eyes off us, and at home, if Yamila wasn't with me, Mayra was—though mostly I was under my mother's vigilant care until dinnertime. Needless to say, such a life permitted few distractions for a girl of fifteen.

The next morning, I set in motion the first part of my plan. In science class, I pretended to be taking notes but instead wrote a brief missive to Jorge Armando in my school notebook, laying out the nature of the situation and my thoughts on how to get around it. During recess, I folded the piece of paper, explained my plight and my ploy to Carmela, and asked her to please give the letter to her brother after school.

If Carmela did not yet know what it was like to be in love, she had nevertheless always had a vocation for intrigue, and besides, she adored her brother. Neither she nor I could imagine anything better than our being sisters-in-law one day. Ever since we were little, I had been marrying her off to Antonio in my mind, and she had been doing the same for me and Jorge Armando.

The following week, under the pretext of occupying myself with better things, I told my mother I wished to begin piano lessons. "I could not have come up with a better idea myself, Gabriela!" she exclaimed. "A proper señorita *should* know how to play the piano."

From then on, Carmela and I would spend every Thursday evening from four to six learning to read and play music at the home of Isabel Valladares, a neighborhood spinster who lived with her seven cats and her three unmarried sisters. Señorita Valladares had been a celebrated pianist in her youth, and she was said to be a gifted teacher. But as it would turn out, my acquaintance with her would teach me a lesson I had not intended to learn.

Each week Jorge Armando would walk his sister to the home of Señorita Valladares a good fifteen minutes before our lesson was to start, so that he and I could have a chance to be alone together. The perfect accomplice, Carmela offered our suspicious piano teacher the persuasive possible excuse for her early arrival: "Señorita Valladares, I need more time to practice my octaves." Our arrangement worked, at least for a while.

It was during this brief, idyllic period that I fell in love with Jorge Armando's way with words. For almost a year, we secretly exchanged letters on a weekly basis. Back at home after my piano lesson, I would lock myself in the bathroom and get lost in what he had written to me.

Because we had so little time together, our mutual passion, as is usually the case in such situations, intensified, and our clandestine correspondence grew more and more impatient. Our letters were increasingly filled with pledges of eternal love, until one memorable Thursday afternoon, Jorge Armando handed me a note asking if I would marry him someday. Although I knew in my heart that my parents would never allow it—even now I don't know what I was thinking, or where I expected this childish exchange to take us—I was so excited that I tore a small piece from a page of sheet music and scribbled the following words: *Yes, Jorge Armando, I will marry you one day. The only condition is that you not make me eat split-pea soup.* On my way out of Señorita Valladares's house, I hastily folded the scrap of paper, tied it with my red silk hair ribbon, and handed him my fifteen-year-old's acceptance of his marriage proposal.

THEN IT HAPPENED. THAT NIGHT, WITHOUT ANY warning, my father burst into my room and commenced a frantic search. I could feel the blood drain from my face and flood my heart, for the look on his face made it all too clear that I was in serious trouble. I prayed that he would not notice my trembling hands or the fear in my eyes; I did not want to confirm whatever suspicions he might be harboring.

"Where are they, Gabriela?"

"Where are *what*, Papi?" I begged.

"The letters, by God—tell me where they are, this instant."

Terrified of his rage, I pointed to the bottom drawer of my dresser, where I kept my school socks. And there they were, all of my suitor's innocent pledges of endless love, hidden inside my white brocade box, organized by date and lovingly tied with white linen strings. I knew when my father's hands found them that I would never see Jorge Armando's letters again. I knew, too, that I would never forgive him for robbing me so callously of the treasures of my heart. After that night, I no longer wanted to be his *reina*.

Clutching the bundle of letters so tightly that his knuckles went white, my father said, "The only thing worse than suffering a death in the family is having a daughter with loose morals."

I did not dare say a word. I had courage enough, but I knew I would lose any argument with him.

"You are never to see him again, Gabriela. Do you understand?"

I felt nauseated, but still I could not give up. I tried to plead with him: "But Papi . . ."

"Not another word from you. Neither your mother nor I will permit you to carry on with a young man who doesn't think enough of you to protect your honor. Especially since we have already informed you that he is not suitable."

I tried to speak again, but my father raised his right hand so quickly that for a moment I thought he was going to hit me.

"And the biggest tragedy of all is not your insolent disobedience; it's that you think so little of yourself that you allowed this disgrace to happen in the first place."

With that, he left the room, before I had a chance to reply.

My mother never came to say good night.

THE ONLY LETTER I MANAGED TO SAVE WAS ONE THAT Jorge Armando had written to me the year before, after a trip to Macuto, about the chirimoya fruit. Because of its compromising contents, I kept it tucked away in the back of my science notebook.

I later learned what had happened from Yamila, who earlier that evening had answered the phone and then overheard my parents talking.

Isabel Valladares had called my mother to tell her that she

could not continue to teach a student who was so obviously uninterested in studying the piano: "Gabriela is too busy tearing up her sheet music and exchanging notes with the other student's brother," she reported. My mother must have assumed, as any woman would, that I had saved these messages. (Among the larger lessons of that night was how naive I had been to think I could forever keep such a thing secret from my parents. At the time, however, I remember being convinced that they must be either magicians or spies, for I had told no one else about the letters.)

In the weeks that followed, Yamila heard from Rosa, Carmela's housemaid, that my father had called on the Caballeros. I never did learn whom he went there to see, or what his purpose may have been, but I recall feeling a pang of regret at not having warned Jorge Armando that we had been found out.

SHORTLY AFTER OUR LOVE HAD BEEN FORBIDDEN, Jorge Armando sent me, through Yamila, a small silver milagro sweetly wrapped in street vendor's paper.

Milagros of special significance are sometimes called ex-votos, meaning "from vows." When they are offered as gifts of fashion, they are called simply *dijes,* or charms. But I could tell as soon as I unwrapped it that Jorge Armando's gift was not a mere charm: inside the wrinkled tissue paper was a medal depicting the Virgen del Valle, and when I turned it over, I saw that there was an inscription on the back.

I strung the *medalla* on a chain and wore it around my neck from that day forward. But it was not until many years later that I realized how clever a choice the gift had really been. First, because it was a medal of the Virgin, I could wear it without being questioned by my parents, for every young Catholic woman of the day was supposed to show her devotion in such a manner. Second, in the context of our lost love, it signified both a vow and a miracle. And finally, there was the inscription on the back: "Find music." When I first read it, I assumed it must have something to do with the piano lessons. I was only partially correct.

In the weeks after my father confiscated Jorge Armando's letter, I gradually lost my appetite and all desire to do anything other than cry. When I wasn't locked in the bathroom weeping, I spent entire nights either staring at the ceiling or tossing and turning in my bed. Soon I began to have fainting spells because I wasn't eating, and my disorientation became so severe that I could not attend school.

Frustrated at his inability to diagnose me himself, my father called one of his colleagues at the Algodonal Hospital, then another. But neither of the doctors whom my father brought home to see me could find anything physically wrong. After performing various examinations and asking me a series of tedious and intrusive questions, they could only state the obvious: I had no fever, though my pulse was weak; I was pale but seemed not to be in any pain. They were right on all counts except the last, for the affliction of my heart stabbed me so sharply that the only two things that I craved were a solitary place to cry and the desperate desire to die.

Having nothing more to lose, I took a step in that direction.

nueve: THE RIGHT WORDS

Around the same time I started taking piano lessons, my parents gave a cocktail party at our house that proved to be my first real opportunity to practice the art of intelligent discourse.

It is expected of every young señorita that behind the allure of her beauty, a man may be able to discern an articulate, literary, and highly educated woman. Through the art of conversation, your clever mind should make others crave to know your thoughts on matters great and small. You may ensure this by devoting time to studying and cultivating speech as an art form. It is the powerful combination of feminine beauty and a cultivated mind that drives men to distraction.

When a man enters the mind of a woman so trained in the art of dialogue, he must feel intrigued at exploring the uncharted territory that, in conjunction with her physical charms, makes her both a mystery and a challenge to him.

You must always remember that real skill in conversing demands a kind of fearlessness, the ability to balance on the razor's edge of wit. Do not be afraid of it; it can be a thrilling undertaking.

I learned to hold my own in conversation in part from Molière's amusing plays, of which my father was especially fond, and in part through my always tantalizing Thursday-afternoon exchanges with Jorge Armando.

"A true gentleman, *piel de canela*," he once told me, "is able to handle even the most offensive person without giving offense."

"I'm glad I'm not a man, for then that is a test I would surely fail, *cariño*," I said coquettishly.

"Nonsense, *muñeca*, you could never offend anyone. What I mean is that the real test of a gentleman is not whether he manages to behave properly in the presence of a lady—any man can manage that—but how he behaves in the presence of a boor."

I never knew for sure where Jorge Armando acquired his gentility of address, for his father was always traveling, and was brusque of manner. If I had to guess, I'd say it came perhaps from his mother, Marina, who, while not a great lady, was not without poise or grace; either that, or from the strict Franciscan priests at the San Ignacio de Loyola, where he attended school.

From Jorge Armando I learned that a gentleman opens doors for others, both literally and figuratively. I deduced that the same quality must be no less important for a lady, for the one can hardly exist without the other.

So, too, must there be a certain gentility, an etiquette, in conversation. In my day, young women were encouraged to attend social gatherings with their parents and actively to participate in discussions with other adults, particularly of the opposite sex, so as to acquire both conversational dexterity and the skill of flirtation, or gender play. Such exchanges were like fencing matches, with good parrying encouraged as a means of defending family honor.

On the night of that cocktail party at our house—my formal introduction to the game—my father presented me to a gentleman with whom he was acquainted. I was still fifteen then, and my heartbreak over Jorge Armando lay in the future. I was eager to intrigue this man, impress him, and thereby make my father proud.

"This is my daughter Gabriela," Papi told his guest, nodding at me with a confident smile. "*Mi reina,* have you met Señor Rodolfo Betancourt?"

Early on, young women in South America learn to be addressed, especially by men, with a carefully woven net of terms of endearments. My father was very much given to using such terms: I was his *reina,* or queen, Constanza was his *preciosa,* and Jacinta was his *encanto.* My older sister was indeed impossibly beautiful, and my younger sister could charm anyone.

I tipped my head slightly to acknowledge Señor Betancourt's age and his status. Then I held his gaze for a moment before offering my own greeting.

"*Encantada de conocerlo,* Señor Betancourt," I said, and boldly raised my chin.

Holding a man's gaze is a nearly fail-proof way to disarm him. It also establishes the balance of power in the conversation that is about to commence.

"*Encantado,* Señorita Grenales."

When addressing anyone on first acquaintance, you must always use his or her last name. You may suggest familiarity through your body language, but never through your speech. Such informality is considered impolite and impertinent.

My heart was pounding so in anticipation of the upcoming challenge that for a moment I wished I could wrench it out of my chest and set it on the side table while I spoke with Señor Betancourt. Then I realized that this sudden surge of excitement was part of the appeal of entering another's mind. So I began.

"How did you manage to get yourself into this situation?" I asked flirtatiously.

"To which situation are you referring, señorita?"

"Putting yourself in harm's way by conversing with my father's favorite daughter."

"Is that so? You are a confident young woman, for your age."

I have always liked, from time to time, to test the boundaries of politeness in order to gauge men's mettle and reactions. With that end in mind, I now prepared my next response, doing my best to conceal a mischievous smirk that would have betrayed my true intent.

"Despite the difference in our years, Señor Betancourt, I believe you will find yourself outnumbered tonight."

He seemed a bit taken aback by my charming insolence, but he smiled gallantly nonetheless, as a gentleman should always do. So far, he had passed the test.

"Well, in that case, I consider myself fortunate to have made your acquaintance, however briefly," he said.

Recognizing that he was about to end the conversation, which would mean I had lost the match, I tried to engage him again by graduating to flirting's next level. I asked him an almost indecorous question, both to assay his vulnerability to it and to see how far he would take it. A gentleman should take comments of this kind from a woman far enough to acknowledge her wit, but not so far as to offend her or make her uncomfortable.

"Giving up so soon, Señor Betancourt? What would my father think of your lack of endurance?"

Obviously not knowing quite what to say, and trying to buy time, he replied to my question with one of his own: "And what do you suggest a man should do upon finding himself, as you say, 'outnumbered,' Señorita Grenales?"

"Isn't that every man's obligation? To fight to the bitter end? But I guess it depends on the man, doesn't it?"

I let this sink in for a moment before shamelessly continuing, "The trick to developing staying power, or so I'm told, is to take the trouble to discover what the other person wants."

"And I imagine you have such knowledge, señorita." He spoke these words in a confidential tone that led me to believe I might be getting in over my head. Feeling slightly uneasy, I backtracked a little, moving the conversation to the literal subject at hand and away from the metaphorical one.

"My mother says it is the job of a good hostess always to know the motivation of every one of her guests," I offered.

Without giving him another chance, I then cut the conversation short, as a woman always must if she wishes to leave a man wanting more. "It has indeed been *un placer*, Señor Betancourt. If you will be kind enough to excuse me, I must now greet our other guests. I do hope we will meet again."

I spoke these last words with a hostess's smile—the sort of smile that must rest permanently on a lady's lips, somewhere between engaging and determined, to prevent any one guest from lingering in her company to the exclusion of others.

"As you wish, señorita," said my first fencing partner. He smiled, bowed slightly, and looked a little lost for a moment, until he saw my father's satisfied grin.

When Papi winked at me, I knew I had won the match.

After the last guest had departed, I replayed my success back in my mind so as to identify what I had done right and ensure that I would be able to repeat it the next time. In so doing, I realized that in addition to the treasures of my mind, the benefit of a hostess's home turf, and the bloom of youth, I had a secret weapon: the knowledge that men always want to be the ones to begin and end every interaction. When a woman gets the upper hand, her male opponent will inevitably seek a second opportunity to establish himself as the victor.

Señor Betancourt didn't know it yet, but he was due for a rematch.

LEARNING HOW TO ENTER A MAN'S HEAD AND PLAY there is only half the battle. As in any other sport, to win consistently in conversation, one must be familiar with the rules of engagement.

Before she can fully enthrall a man through discourse, a woman must first make peace with the fact that good conversation is a reciprocal exchange, during which both sides must take turns talking and listening.

The link between two minds begins with good listening skills. In much the same way that we learn to write by reading, we learn to speak by listening. But the truth is that the great majority of people do not do it well. Impatience is always pulling them out of the conversation: either they're trying to improve the situation inside their mind, or they're busy preparing the entrance they'll make when the other person steps off the stage. Here is what I know: more than anything else, most people want to pour their hearts out to someone, so when they find a willing listener, they are grateful indeed. More than you may realize, it is an honor simply to be listened to.

How, then, can one become good at *both* listening and talking?

Good listening involves being able to draw another out without prying, being empathetic and understanding, not giving advice unless one is asked, and being capable of inspiring a response to one's own thoughts. All dialogue has two elements: irritants that hinder conversation and specific skills that enhance it. The trick is to avoid the irritants, such as interrupting others in midsentence or speaking when one has nothing to say, while practicing the skills that can actually improve discourse.

If you take the trouble to become a good listener, others will crave your company. And if you can fulfill the following requirements of an accomplished conversationalist, everyone will be eager to hear what you have to say. You must:

1. control a vast store of information;
2. learn to capture others' interest; and
3. have both the desire and the determination to please.

The first of these requirements is of an intellectual nature and one that you will satisfy through good schooling, good society, and purposeful reading. Your parents and teachers will offer you a wealth of knowledge far beyond what you believe your brain can possibly retain. It is your job to absorb this information with a strong disposition of mind. For every bit of knowledge you acquire, ask yourself, what aspect of it might be of particular interest to others? Your aim is the application of the knowledge, rather than the knowledge itself.

Learn much, judge it well, and form strong opinions so that you will be able to converse with elegant simplicity, and so that when people speak with you, they will feel as if they were reading the most fascinating of books. Without a higher purpose to guide your erudition, you will be no more than a walking encyclopedia, and others will promptly dispense with your company after learning what they need from you.

Erudition requires, among other things, that you read the classics—including the works of Sophocles, Euripides, Locke, Rousseau, and Chateaubriand—and memorize a good deal of poetry. You must become acquainted with Pedro Calderón de La Barca's *La Vida es Sueño* and with Dante Alighieri's *Divine Comedy. The Little Prince,* by Antoine de Saint-Exupery, will also hold you in good stead, for it invites analysis and introspection. Machiavelli, Ariosto, and Tasso should be on your reading list as well. By becoming acquainted with these literary giants, their views, and the contradictions among them, you will learn the meaning of intellectual discourse and achieve a healthy equilibrium in your own opinions.

In addition to reading the classics, you must become intimately familiar with various Spanish and Latin American authors. Our heritage is rich with the wisdom of many fine men, among them the Venezuelan author Rómulo Gallegos, the Spaniards Calderón de la Barca and Lope de Vega, the Chilean poet Neftali Ricardo Reyes Basoalto, better known to the world as Pablo Neruda.

Neruda's poems are filled with his homage to the world, to love and to its essence. He was an *orfebre de la poesía*, crafting love poems and sonnets as if from gold.

Because my life was equally touched by love, ecstasy, sadness, and nostalgia, I came to appreciate poetry as one of the most magical media for conveying the raw emotions that inevitably besiege the human condition.

I have copied out one of my favorite poems, one of the many Jorge Armando wrote for me, and ask that you please keep it close to your heart, for it has had special meaning for me. Every time I read "Tu Ausencia a la Luz de Luna," the embers between its lines offer me a tender warmth:

> *There is only one star in my moonless sky tonight*
> *Strangely it gives no light*
> *I wonder why?*
> *I lower my gaze*
> *And when I look in my own direction*
> *In the onyx of night*
> *A frozen tear turned to ice*
> *Tells me there will never be light*
> *In the incandescent silence of your absence.*

When reading poetry, try to immerse yourself in its lyrical rhythms and the hidden meaning behind the words. I hope that in your lifetime you may be blessed with true love, as I once was— passionate, desperate love, the kind of love that threatens to burst through your veins, the kind of flame that burns like an obsession when you finally meet that one person without whom, you sadly realize, your own precious life is not worth living.

To enter the mind of a man is no small thing, but to remain there with the force of unrelenting desire—that is even more suggestive, and much more erotic, than anything you can ever hope to express in conversation.

Finding the right words is but one aspect of inspired conversation. A woman's refusal to submit will also capture the fancy of an interested suitor. At times you must give the impression that you have already rightfully won the match, though you must not seem overconfident or boastful about it. Your aim is to enrapture a man's questing mind by turning a casual conversation into an adventure.

If you observe carefully, you will notice that in conversation, men rarely feel the need to flaunt their accomplishments. As if by some birthright, they assume ownership of terra firma, even when they are walking on tenuous ground. Women find this quality entrancing.

Finally, in order to claim a decisive victory over another's mind, you must be determined to please but not allow yourself to seem subservient. Pleasure is to be carefully meted out through a genuine interest in your subject. What man can resist such devotion? To the tender male ego, few things seem more intoxicating than a woman enthralled. The measured uncovering of your mind's hidden treasures, combined with your seductive regard for him, will arouse in a man a desperate longing to seize your mind with his hands as if it were a land to be conquered.

So indomitable, so ferocious, and so well versed must you be in the exigencies of conversation if you are to frighten a man with precisely that which he most desires.

The ultimate secret of good discourse lies in holding up a mirror to a man's face, as an enchantress might, and allowing him to see only one reflection: a better image of himself.

diez: THE VIRGIN BRIDE

In time, and through the example of another's misfortune, I would learn that no amount of good conversation can help a woman talk herself out of a sullied reputation.

At Friday-morning Mass at the San José de Tarbes, Father Alfonso used to tell the single señoritas that virtue was an indication of both a woman's moral excellence and her basic goodness. In his sermons, he vehemently insisted that virtue was exemplified by the ability to remain a virgin, untouched and unsullied by any man. This in itself should have been enough of a warning for us—for how can a man who has never been married know anything about a woman's virtue? But we were no more than twelve or thirteen at the time, so we blindly accepted the priest's definition and were outwardly proud of our own hymeneal innocence: *"Yo soy virgen,"* we used to brag to one another during recess.

The details of my Catholic education will offer you some insight into certain aspects of my character, which I myself later learned to recognize, with complete sincerity of mind and heart, as sometimes the good and sometimes the bad effects of a religious education. As a result of this skepticism, I never became absolutely pious but have always tried to maintain a healthy orthodoxy, one that allowed me to acknowledge the possibility of holiness even if I was myself not directly touched by the experience. Over the course of my schooling, I began slowly to accept that various features of the religious edifice are essentially irreconcilable.

After giving the issue of virtue much consideration over the years, I decided that I disagreed fundamentally with Father Alfonso. Such dissent from the word of a member of the Curia is no trivial matter, but in order to avoid the annihilation of her intellect, a woman must learn to be of her own mind.

By Father Alfonso's definition, any woman would be sullied after matrimony—that is, after losing her virginity. This meant that my own mother, my aunts, and my grandmothers were not women of virtue. How could that be, when in my eyes they were the very icons of good behavior and irreproachable character?

Later in life, I would give some thought to those traits that are often wrongly confused with virtue, and I would come to two conclusions: on the one hand, a woman can, in fact, retain her physical state of virginity without necessarily being pure; and, on the other hand, a woman may be considered chaste so long as she remains pure in her heart. Virginity thus becomes merely the physical condition of being untouched by a man and has nothing to do with moral excellence or goodness.

In our culture, the rare quality of purity of heart, at the outset accompanied by the physical condition of virginity, is called *pudor*. This is that shy demeanor, that girlish appeal, which makes a man fiercely desirous of a union with the woman who possesses it. It is possible for a woman to maintain her *pudor* throughout her life, even when she is no longer a virgin.

I will never forget the day when I rushed into the bathroom as my mother was getting ready for a dinner party. I was very young, and I had to go, so I did not knock before entering. My mother, who was standing there in her beautiful silk camisole, girdle, and stockings, hurriedly reached for a towel to cover herself. She smiled patiently at me, but I could tell from her sudden blush that something was not quite right. Only years later, when she lectured me about the need always to preserve one's *pudor*, did I understand about that day in the bathroom, when she suffered a moment of quiet embarrassment at the unnecessary exposure of herself to another.

Closely tied to virginity is the concept of the *luna de miel*, or honeymoon. The term is derived from the notion that the first month of matrimony is when a man is permitted to taste a woman's honey, her pleasant yellowish nectar, which is to be released to him for the first time during this period.

A shocking tale I heard as a child helped solidify in my mind how imperative it was that a woman remain chaste until marriage. Conzuela Moreno, a beautiful young woman who lived on our street, was returned to the house of her parents after her new husband discovered, on their honeymoon, that she was not a virgin. No sooner had our mother heard the story of Conzuela's misfortune than she called all three of us girls into the living room and shared it with us as an example of what might happen if we did not safeguard this sacred gift.

As Mami told it, Juan Alberto Guzmán, the bridegroom, dragged his wife back to her parents' home by her hair, creating a public spectacle. This was especially humiliating for her father and her three brothers, for it revealed that they had not been men enough to protect her honor in the first place.

The only thing left for a father to do after his daughter so disgraced her family's good name was to try to salvage his already damaged reputation by taking the girl out of circulation. Even though Conzuela was well born, beautiful, and well read, she would not marry a second time, because no man wanted to share his bed with a woman who had permitted herself to be so misused.

My mother's aim in recounting this incident to us was to impress on our young minds the truism that once a woman's virtue has been soiled, there is nothing she can do to recover from the ensuing poverty of spirit.

How, then, should a bride-to-be prepare for her *luna de miel*?

During your first night together, the man you marry must, to some extent, defer his own pleasure. Thanks to their experience in the brothels, our men generally know that if they can be patient during this critical time, the rewards will be worth the wait, as eventually their brides will awaken to the true nature of erotic pleasure. The secret is this: once a woman has been loved by a man who knows how to please her, she will never leave his bed, provided he is able to unleash her passion each and every time.

You, meanwhile, must be kind to yourself. Remember, this will be your first night ever away from home, and that alone is likely to make you feel unnerved and ill at ease. You will doubtless miss your family.

For my part, the memory of my own wedding night still brings tears to my eyes. I was hopelessly ill prepared for what ensued, and it was not until many years later that I fully understood that a woman's first encounter with a man has consequences for her identity that reach far beyond the physical.

As I heard from my own mother, during the first three or four nights following your nuptials, you should spend most of your time talking, strengthening your bond with each other, and relaxing together. Your husband should know that any action on his part that is too abrupt may cause you to withdraw and make you react negatively to anything connected with him. For a sensitive woman, such premature advances may be tantamount to an assault. Instead, he should try to win you over with gentle love games, amorous touches, and tender words. Most men in our culture have carefully cultivated the art of seduction and instinctively know that their brides are fragile at this time and need support to help them overcome their anxiety.

The first real embrace should take place only after a few days, the preceding nights having been spent with the couple's sleeping side by side, without any insistent touching. In order to avoid offending you, your new husband should embrace only the upper part of your body, and even that only in the dark or semidark.

Even if you are feeling eager, let him take the lead, acknowledging that he is more experienced than you.

During his eventual attempts fully to embrace you, endeavor to remain calm and pleasing to him. If you particularly like something he is doing, nod your head to give him an indication that you enjoy his touch. This will increase his confidence and invite him to proceed. A well-trained lover will understand your reaction to his touch and know when the time has come gently to part your legs. He will start by massaging the area between your thighs, loosening your garments, and then will move on to gently caressing your most private self with his fingers. If you resist him now, he should realize that this is only natural and simply means that he needs to do more to help you overcome your shyness. Our men know that if they are to succeed with us, they must neither accede to our every wish nor oppose us completely. They also know that a woman can fall in love with a man only after gaining both confidence and respect in his ability as a lover. If your husband should make the mistake of dismissing you as too timid in the bedroom, the price will be that you will either come to hate him or turn to a more understanding lover.

On or around the tenth day of your honeymoon, your easy acquiescence to his touch will signal to him that you are ready to accept him into your body. At first you will feel uneasy as he penetrates you; this is to be expected. Open your hands, relax your feet, and listen to the sound of your own breath instead of his. This moment will feel like a burglary unless he has first made every effort to explore your inner world with the lightest of touches and soothed your mind with gentle words, letting you know how much he cares for you.

You are now ready to learn that there are two types of men, those who take a short time and those who take a long time to achieve their own sexual fulfillment. This means that it will not always be possible for a husband and wife to reach their climax at the same time. Climax, or orgasm, is a spasm resulting from the pleasure that erupts from one's inner core. A powerful spasm, while not usually a common occurrence during a woman's first experience of lovemaking, can momentarily blind her as the ripples of energy move consecutively through her body. Because it takes most women a long time to reach this state, a man who is slow to climax will be amply rewarded for his patience. One who takes his pleasure too soon will deprive his wife of her own delight, and she would be justified in rejecting him until he learns to treat her as he should.

A man who is fit for your bed will understand that your desire does not end with his. If he is a careful lover, he will also know that while the friction of his body against yours may satisfy you, it is his kisses and caresses that will calm your heart and cause you to fall in love with him.

When celebrating your union with your husband, keep in mind that your mutual aim should always be the same: you are sexually united in order to give and to receive. Once you have consummated your union, you should both feel complete in every way.

Through long, sleepless nights in later years, I would ponder how it was that these tenets had come to be so carelessly violated in my *own* nuptial chambers.

But of my parents' three daughters, the one who entered those chambers first was my older sister, Constanza.

once: CONSTANZA'S WEDDING

Daily, the echoing toll of the oldest bell tower in the country calls to the citizens of Caracas and invites them to stop their routines and listen. Simón Bolívar, the national hero of Venezuela, was proclaimed its *Libertador* within the walls of this historic monument.

Built in the second half of the seventeenth century, the Caracas Cathedral stands proudly before the Plaza Bolívar in the bishopric Curia, located in *Monjas a Gradillas.*

This was the place where, three years before my own walk down the aisle, my older sister, Constanza, was married.

The First Book of Baptism, dating back to 1583, the Books of Matrimony of 1615, and the Books of Death, of 1625, are all archived here. Within these records, curiously enough, one can also find original birth and marriage certificates of local Indians commingled with those of people of other social strata. You may think me old-fashioned for suggesting this, *mi amor,* but if you can ever spare an afternoon to visit this impressive national landmark, you will be glad you did.

A life-sized *Parable of the Loaves and Fishes,* painted by the revered Venezuelan artist Arturo Michelena, covers the main entrance wall. I think you will agree that it is most impressive. Above the gilded high altar and spanning nine bays, stunning frescoes grace the cupola and chapel ceilings, looking as if they were painted only days ago, not centuries. And around the perimeter, the stories of Genesis, from the Separation of Light from Darkness to the Drunkenness of Noah, are represented in the vertical forms of colorful hand-cut stained-glass windows. Throughout the day, natural light glows gently through the glass, making the biblical figures seem to come to life. Thus animated, the rich array of folkloric blues, reds, greens, and yellows casts a myriad of distorted shadows inside the church and lends it a divine grace that contrasts sharply with the Gothic architecture.

On the side walls, five prophets alternate with the same number of sibyls, so that each prophet is paired with a sibyl on the opposite wall. Taken together with the other group and featured single figures, these depict the forty generations of Christ's ancestors, as described in the Bible.

A fervent Catholic obsessed with *la sociedad Caraqueña* and devoted to the rigorous observance of every one of the seven sacraments, my sister Constanza Grenales married Mauricio Cisneros in this hallowed cathedral on July 30, 1940.

On that day, Constanza and Mauricio stood together before the high altar. Moments before my sister was to walk down the aisle, the lights had been switched on to illuminate it, and streams of light now poured diagonally over the exquisitely gilded altarpieces, the hand-carved columns, and the sculpted Virgin who stood, arms spread, above the tabernacle containing the consecrated host and wine for the Eucharist, the communion with the body of Christ, one of the most revered of sacraments.

Once the couple had said their vows and professed their love for each other according to Catholic custom, Mauricio cupped his hands to receive from my sister seven gold coins, symbolic of her dowry. The two of them then knelt before the altar and crossed themselves "in the name of the Father, the Son, and the Holy Spirit"—one last blessing before the powerful divinity of their union carried them through the chapel and out of the cathedral, into the world.

After the ceremony, which had been personally conducted by the archbishop of Caracas, a traditional Venezuelan *fiesta de bodas* was held at the country club for the two sets of parents' three hundred closest friends and acquaintances.

The Cisneros family was extremely well connected and had occupied the land surrounding the country club for several generations. This fact was not without significance in my sister's decision to marry Mauricio, and when his father insisted that the newlyweds must live in one of the four adjacent houses he owned, Constanza rejoiced. For the couple to buy a home of their own would have been not only a breach of etiquette and an insult to his parents but a detriment to the preservation of the family's wealth.

If this marriage had not, strictly speaking, been arranged, it had most certainly been "encouraged." And my sister had figured out early on that life was a great deal easier for those who were inclined to follow rather than lead. In the end, all her aspirations were circumscribed to living in a paradise of banality where people would address her as Constanza Grenales de Cisneros and pay homage to the snaring web of frivolities that came with the right address.

But despite the pledges of eternal love that we all heard in the cathedral, my mind, in replaying my sister's wedding and the carefully orchestrated actions of those around her on that day and afterward, eventually meandered toward a most uncomfortable truth: what some brides took to be love was really, it seemed to me, nothing more than an illusory desire for worldly comfort. And society paid tribute to the false merits of that arrangement by insisting that in marriage, a man's name was fair exchange for a woman's hand, with the indecent assurance that love would follow.

My own future matrimonial experience would bring me further disillusion with the invalid notions of ordered happiness and with the misguided wisdom of running a household that never managed to feel like a home. I would grow resentful of some of the traditions that bound me and would conclude that in the end, it must be the *illusion* of security to which women assigned value when they entered into marriages of convenience. This illusion was hardly an opponent of real love.

I can attest to this with certainty because I was the daughter who married next.

doce: MIS NUPCIAS

My eventual decision to marry would be influenced by an array of complex and competing feelings: the remnants of heartbreak from my abruptly ended courtship with Jorge Armando; a childish desire to trade my innocence for experience; and guilt over my most recent debacle, a misguided attempt to join the convent. But the luxury of insight is usually retrospective.

By my eighteenth birthday, my strict Catholic upbringing at San José de Tarbes had all but preordained my views on chastity by strongly endorsing the merits of virtue. I had been taught to believe that the surrender of one's virginity could be safely accomplished only through the sacrament of matrimony. It did not occur to me that given my fevered longing to explore and to measure lived experience against intellectual ideas, I was gambling with my own life.

So, too, had I been reckless some months before, when I resolved to take my vows as a nun. I had known all along that my temporary flight toward the vocation was in fact an effort to escape a broken heart. My parents, for their part, were happy to support me in what I had persuaded them was my "calling." But did they really believe that? Perhaps they simply hoped that a period of time at the convent would mitigate my infatuation with the young man they judged to be so far beneath my station.

Every single minute of the five months and twenty days of my stay at the Abbey of Santa Teresa was devoted to killing time.

Although I had imagined that the opposite would be true, within the convent's walls, the regimen imposed on me was as strict as the one that bound me at home. Mealtimes were prescribed, reading hours at the convent's library were prescribed, prayer times were prescribed, music instruction was prescribed, even Bible study was prescribed. It didn't take me long to realize that I had merely exchanged one set of constraints for another.

I dreaded the agonizing boredom of daily Mass, the disingenuous servitude of my fellow novices, and the imperious rule of Mother Francisca, mistress of the abbey. What most frightened me, however, was the chilling shrieks of desperation that could not be heard but only be felt reverberating through the numbing silence of the walls. I knew this was supposed to be a spiritually enriching experience, but after a time, it began to seem to me that nothing could be more tainted with spiritual poverty than the insincere and distorted existence of these young women who had willingly resigned themselves to a life term in prison.

For a brief interval, the abbey did provide me with the solitary place to cry that I had so yearned for following the sudden rupture of my ties to Jorge Armando, but after several months of unbearable solitude, I could stand it no longer.

Repentant for my transgressions, I now hoped that through my act of contrition I might be granted a second chance, and eventually I convinced myself that God would not have given me life only to let me squander it in the wrong place. I vowed that if I was allowed to leave the convent, I would embark on a more useful and fulfilling journey and cease all manner of impetuous and irresponsible behavior.

With this in mind, four days before Christmas, I expressed to Mother Francisca my desire to return home. I was surprised to find her completely accepting of my change in plans: she immediately said that she understood and that I must not remain at the abbey unless my heart was truly in it.

At the time, I failed to account for yet another factor that I now believe played an important role in my decision: without realizing it, I was being ineluctably drawn by the forces of tradition toward the exalted ideals of marriage, motherhood, and home.

At this crucial juncture in my life, my subconscious desire was fueled by my parents' diligent efforts to marry me off to a man whom they supposed to be the perfect match for a Venezuelan señorita well trained in every aspect of being a lady and the finer points of etiquette.

That year, I celebrated Christmas at home. Curiously enough, upon my return from Santa Teresa, no one even asked me any questions about my leaving; it was as if everyone had expected me to do just that, and welcoming me home after my temporary bout of insanity was a routine business.

On New Year's Day, my father knocked on my bedroom door, came in wearing one of his invincible smiles, and handed me a letter. Unable to make out the handwriting on the envelope, I asked him whom it was from.

"*Mi reina*, a gentleman is waiting downstairs to call on you. You have my permission to accept his visit."

Puzzled by this announcement, especially coming from my father, I placed the letter on my nightstand. As Papi stood there grinning with anticipation, I thought how disingenuous it was for him to presume to serve as love's envoy after so perfunctorily destroying Jorge Armando's letters to me not so long before. And then I did the unthinkable: I spoke disrespectfully to my father, and in such a way that neither one of us quite recognized the vitriol or the woman behind my sarcasm.

"I guess letters count only when they come on fancy paper, Papi. Please tell the gentleman that I cannot entertain him because I find myself 'indisposed'—isn't that what you taught me once?"

My father suffered my impertinence without blinking an eye and proceeded to expound on my caller's many virtues. "I cannot understand you," he said. "Any woman with a shred of common sense would be honored to win the affections of Jonathan Knowles. You are making a mistake, Gabriela."

After he left my room, I picked up the letter from my nightstand and examined the gold crest on the back of its starch-stiffened envelope and the precise fountain-pen handwriting on the front. I then carried it into my mother's sewing room and cut it into tiny pieces with her scissors. I had never for a moment intended to read it.

My parents had met Mr. Knowles at a war briefing given at the American embassy by Ambassador Frank P. Corrigan. In our house, the ambassador was known simply as Francis Patrick, for he and my father were good friends. On the rare occasions when his schedule permitted it, he could be found in my father's study holding forth on the two men's favorite topics, politics and medicine.

Unlike others in his position, Ambassador Corrigan was not a career diplomat but an eminent physician, like my father; he had even assisted in the first blood transfusion ever performed in the United States in the early years of the twentieth century. He had been appointed ambassador to Venezuela at the beginning of the war in Europe and would hold the post until two years after the war's end.

At the time, our country was the primary producer of oil in

the world, though it had neither a state nor a private national industry. This meant that the principal national resource was being exploited solely by foreign enterprises. And because oil was the main commodity driving the war effort, you can imagine how frenzied was the courtship of foreign governments on our behalf. It was as if Venezuela were the last single woman in the Caribbean, with dozens of rich suitors flying in from all over the world to ask for her hand.

Because my father was a respected doctor and a pillar of the community, very little went on in Caracas in which he was not invited to participate. In addition to serving as head surgeon at the Hospital Algodonal de Caracas, he was the president for life of the medical college and one of the founders of the city's art museum. I often heard people say that Dr. Mario Grenales was as dedicated to his duties as a civic leader as he was to healing those in pain. His involvement with so many causes meant that it was quite common for us to have, at any given time, a number of guests at our house from various countries and diplomatic posts.

Like most wars, this "reasonable war"—so called by World War I victors England and France—was being fought in the press no less than on the battlefield. Because of Venezuela's role as the major supplier of oil, the foreign press kept a close watch on the government of President Isaías Medina Angarita and its stance on the war in Europe. This was how Jonathan Knowles had come to be present at Ambassador Corrigan's briefing: when my parents met him, he was a foreign correspondent for the *Times* of London.

He paid his second visit to our home two weeks later, in mid-January, after the holiday season had passed. This time, instead of waiting, he simply left the letter with Yamila, who brought it up to my room on the small oblong silver tray that was used to deliver correspondence to every member of the household.

His second missive, like his first, went unread and unanswered.

Then, on February 13, I received both a visit and a letter. This time Yamila came to my room and said, "Señorita Gabriela, there's a gentleman downstairs to see you. He said to tell you that he will wait for your response." She then handed me a small card with the name *Jonathan R. Knowles* embossed on it in black.

I could not fathom how anyone could be so ill mannered or so vain as to impose himself on a stranger in such a way, but knowing that he was an acquaintance of my father's, I resigned myself to his unwelcome presence.

Even if he had not been announced, I would have recognized him at once. His eyes were crystal blue, and in them I could immediately read volumes. His gestures were precise and refined, just like the three buttons on the front of his silver brocade vest, the hands on his gold pocket watch, and the handwriting on the letter that he now presented to me along with a small box, tied with a violet silk ribbon embroidered with the word *Harrod's* in gold thread.

"I've been misinformed," were his first words as I descended the stairs.

Ignoring the formality of the occasion, I said the first impertinent thing that came to mind: "Regarding?"

He was unfazed, as if he had been awaiting just such a reply.

"I was going to say your beauty, but perhaps I mean your disposition, señorita."

I was suddenly curious to know what he had been told about either one, but I didn't want to reveal my interest. Instead I said, "So have I been misinformed, Mr. Knowles, so have I."

"And may I inquire as to which aspect of my person *you* are referring to?"

"Your manner, Mr. Knowles. How do you expect to win any-one's affection if you insist on insulting her on first acquain-tance?"

"Well, that's a matter of opinion, señorita. Others might well disagree with you about my charm."

Was I mistaken, or was he boasting of his other conquests? What arrogance! In the coldest tone I could manage, I remarked, "I'm sure a man of your stature must be aware of the effect opinion can have on reputation. And of reputation, Mr. Knowles . . . there are only two kinds."

Amused and intrigued by my inborn haughtiness—or per-haps challenged by it, I never knew which—he smiled and held his ground in the entrance hall, obviously expecting to be asked in.

After staring at him for a minute or so without saying a word, I finally gave in, but only partly. "I would invite you to sit down, Mr. Knowles, but my parents are not at home. I will, however, endeavor to read your letter, and I thank you in advance for your gift."

I then offered a purposely short curtsy and extended my hand toward him without taking off my lace mitt glove. Both gestures were intended to signal to him that our acquaintance remained on very formal terms. While I didn't admit it to him, or to any-one else, his self-possession intrigued me.

After he left, I went up to my room and carefully unwrapped his gift, which turned out to be a small and delicate bottle of lavender perfume. I then opened the letter, just as I had told him I might do.

Had I not met him first, I would have been surprised by the wording of his courtship proposal:

February 13, 1943
Dear Señorita Grenales,

As you may know, our countries are allies in the "reasonable war." Your indifference to my entreaties seems to me a most unreasonable affair.

Yours truly,
Jonathan R. Knowles
p.s. . . . But I have my theories on the subject, if you're apt to discuss them.

After reading the letter, I smiled at its cleverness and imagined myself playing word games with this man for the rest of my life. Who could resist such a ferociously intelligent mind, or decline his daring invitation to respond? He had engaged me.

I immediately sent Yamila to buy some fancy stationery, ink, and wax, and while awaiting her return, I began to compose a reply in my mind.

Before joining my parents for dinner that evening, I went to my father's study to write out my letter. I could not bear to do it in my room, which was sacred in my memory as the place where I had once inscribed my heart to Jorge Armando.

When I was satisfied with what I had written, I folded the letter, tucked it inside an envelope, sealed it with royal-blue wax, and wrote Mr. Knowles's name on the front in black ink that shone like crude oil on the cream-colored paper.

At the dinner table I handed the envelope to my father, who gratefully took it from me with a knowing smile. They had finally worn me down.

February 13, 1943
Dear Mr. Knowles,

It is you who seem indifferent to the fact that you are courting trouble. But if you insist on it, a meeting may be arranged

between our two countries so you may speak to my father about
a Peace Treaty.
    I capitulate.

                    Gabriela Grenales

p.s. I am more than prepared to address your theories when next
we meet.

The next week, a meeting took place between my father and
Jonathan Knowles. It was followed months later by a formal dinner at our house to celebrate our engagement and announce that
we would be marrying in August.

Our courtship of six months was considered brief in those
days, but my parents agreed to it joyfully and without insisting
on a chaperone. To my surprise, during that period, Mr. Knowles
came calling almost every day at his will, without eliciting even a
raised eyebrow from my mother or father.

It was over those few months that my doubts started to vanish and I became better acquainted with the man I was going to
marry.

      JONATHAN KNOWLES HAD SPENT THE FIRST THIRTY-
five years of his life in cerebral solitude and isolation, preparing
for what he wanted most in the world: one day to thrive in the
highest echelons of the *Times'* hierarchy. He would finally
achieve his ambition in 1957.

Born in Oxford, England, to a good family that ensured his
exacting education in at least three languages, your grandfather
had a punctilious upbringing that was an excellent complement
to my formal training as a South American lady. As soon as I met
him, I knew he would accomplish important things. His enviable
self-possession immediately gave others the impression that his
destiny had been preordained and that throughout his life he
would remain, first and foremost, true to himself. For a woman

who wanted a reliable husband, there could be no candidate more appealing. During our many long conversations, I also learned that he took his work very seriously. At the *Times,* he was in turn highly regarded as a superb journalist with impeccable news judgment and a luminous mind.

As our courtship drew to a close, I felt certain that I was marrying a respectable man (almost twice my age) of great integrity, who would be both a faithful husband and a devoted father. But what I failed to foresee in my clairvoyant flash of maturity was that the price I would have to pay for the much sought-after commodity of a predictable marriage was my own life.

AUGUST FINALLY CAME.

Three days before my wedding, on the pretext of looking at some bed linens I fancied, I asked my mother to allow Yamila to accompany me on a shopping excursion. After she agreed, I instructed my father's driver to take us to a jewelry store in the commercial district of Sabana Grande, where I purchased a small milagro almost identical to the one that still hung around my neck, though this one was made of gold. I then waited inside the shop while the jeweler, at my request, engraved on the back of the medal the two words *In Silence.*

When he was finished, I paid him, and he handed me the milagro nestled inside a miniature blood-red velvet box. When we got home, I wrapped the box in newspaper, gave it to Yamila, and begged her to keep it in her room until I asked for it again.

Our wedding was a sumptuous affair of champagne and roses.

I wore an evanescent organza gown with a long train and an elaborate pearl tiara. (I had left all the details to my mother and Constanza, who organized the event with the exactitude that

two generals might bring to the planning of a military campaign.)

It was with a determined mind and a divided heart that I
walked down the aisle of the cathedral on the arm of my father,
who looked as confident and as self-possessed as I had ever seen
him. Toward the end of the ceremony, which was presided over
by both the bishop and the archbishop, I began to worry that my
soon-to-be husband would see the secret sorrow in my eyes
when he lifted my veil. But then the moment came, and the fragile alabaster smile I had managed to plaster on my face fooled
everyone—everyone but myself, that is.

During the reception afterward, the thought of what lay
ahead pricked at me more than the stays of my corset. I could
not stop thinking that after the last of the five hundred guests
had gone home, the matrimonial bed would offer scant shelter to
a virgin bride who had married a man she didn't love.

WHAT NO ONE ELSE EVER KNEW WAS THAT ON THE
morning of my wedding day, I had sent my housemaid on an
errand that could well have cost me my future.

I called Yamila into my room and asked her to stand by the
door in case anyone tried to come in. I didn't think anyone
would, since everyone was too busy running around and receiving the flowers and gifts that continued to pour into the house,
but I couldn't be too careful.

I can still picture her standing there, patiently waiting for me
to finish the note I was writing, with that look of understanding
in her eyes that conveyed her faithful, quiet friendship.

When I was done, I licked the back of the envelope and asked
her to please deliver it, in absolute secrecy, only into Jorge
Armando's hands, along with the small box I had asked her to
keep in her room.

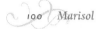

Mi viejo querido:

    On this day, I will marry. But my heart belongs to you.

    Now that I know what you meant, I will try to Find Music, In *the* Silence *of your absence. At least I think that is what I am doing, but still . . . I hope you will be able to forgive me.*

    Your gift will grace my neck until the day I die, for even though we have been split in half, our love is the most magical milagro of all.

Siempre tuya,
Piel de canela

After Yamila left my room that morning, I remember thinking as tears rolled down my face that there was no crime in this world worse than being an accessory to the breaking of one's own heart.

In the end, I was the radiant center stone set amid paste imitations, adorning a wedding that had been carefully arranged yet whose crowning glory was not the bride's happiness but the sacramental confirmation of tradition and the order of the day.

trece: MY SISTER JACINTA

It was now my little sister's turn for vows—but in this instance, as a nun.

I had asked Constanza and my mother to wait outside while I spoke with Jacinta; Antonio and my father were already in the *sacristía* with Father Ferro, our family priest.

My secret mission earlier that day had been to dissuade Jacinta from making what seemed to me a grave mistake. I had convinced myself, three years after my own wavering walk down the aisle, that she could not possibly want to pursue the course she was about to embark upon. But now, in her room, I hadn't the heart to speak my mind. My sister's happiness mattered a great deal to me, and I suddenly became aware how selfish I was being.

As I watched her prepare for her special day, I sensed in her the peace that emanates from those who have clarity of heart.

THE CEREMONY TOOK PLACE IN THE MAGNIFICENT Chapel of Santa Teresa, inside the centuries-old Church of Santander.

His Eminence the archbishop was in full churchly regalia, wearing miter, cope, stole, cassock, cross, and ring. I fell silent at the sight; to this day, I cannot begin to describe the splendor of the dress of the archbishop who presided over the ceremony.

I could surmise the feelings of the bride-to-be. I tried to put myself in Jacinta's place, and it seemed to me that she must be experiencing something close to panic.

As the novices prostrated themselves before His Grace, nearly formless in their black velvet palls, I felt that Jacinta would soon die to this world. Having a nun in the family was a source of great pride for most Catholics, but I could not help thinking of this as the day when I would lose my beloved little sister forever. I prayed to be forgiven for my blasphemous thoughts.

As Jacinta waited to take her perpetual vows, every day of my own months at the convent flashed before my eyes, and I shuddered at the thought that I had once been a postulant myself. Were I to live an entire other lifetime, I would never be able to undo the embarrassment and humiliation I knew I had caused my Catholic family by so impetuously entering and then departing the vocation. Since my marriage, I had at last admitted to myself that my calling had been less than genuine, but I had never shared that hard truth with my parents or my sisters.

Earlier that day, believing that the time had come for a confession of sorts, I had broached the subject with Jacinta. Seeing her pious devotion made me feel all the more guilty for having promoted such a fiction, and I tried to tell her so. But she would not entertain my apology. She loved me, she said, and urged, "Please embrace peace and serenity, *querida hermana*. God loves you no matter what."

I so admired my little sister, who was always composed, visibly calm, and uncannily able to find the right words. That was why Papi called her *Encanto*. But I supposed these were all requisite qualities for someone who intended forever to renounce the pleasures of the flesh.

I felt ashamed that before such a kind, reverent young woman who was about to celebrate the happiest day of her life, the only emotions I'd been able to manage were remorse and regret.

Now, inside the church, confined with my own unease, I felt the sudden desire to escape. And perhaps I was not the only one: one of the novices fainted, and another screamed as she realized what it would mean to be a bride of Christ forever. Jacinta, however, was steadfast.

Before the altar, she knelt, put her hands together, and, with the obeisance she had exhibited as a child, vehemently repeated her vows after the archbishop:

> *Virgin Mary, guide me, protect me so that one day I may present myself before your Jesus, not with empty hands but with a brimming heart. I, Sister Jacinta, vow to honor your name on this day of my perpetual vows and each day from this day forward, until the day of my death, when I shall join in the Glory of the Lord Jesus Christ.*

As the black pall was lifted from each novice in turn—a sign that she had been reborn in Christ—the church bell began to toll. The novices, their faces wet with tears, were at last given their new names, before Jesus Christ, by the archbishop.

The mistress of the abbey, Mother Francisca, had already cut off locks of the postulants' hair in preparation for the ceremony. Now she smiled encouragingly at them, possibly in an effort to soothe their frayed nerves. She gave them their new clothes and entrusted them to the care of another nun, who would take them to a side room and shave their heads.

His Holiness blessed the nuns, now dressed in their new habits, and the ceremony was over.

Tonight was Sister Jacinta's wedding. I wondered how she was feeling. Would a divine embrace be as warming as a human one?

As soon as the last novice had taken the veil, I tried to slip quietly away with the rest of my family, but I would not be spared: Mother Francisca met my furtive glance and locked her eyes on mine. She knew my ways too well; after all, I had been under her care during my brief religious career. She motioned for me to follow her.

As we walked toward the abbey together in deafening silence, I realized that I did not have a map for this journey. But once we were in her office, she lit a candle and kindly invited me to sit down.

Without her even asking, I informed her that I had found happiness outside the convent walls. I told her about my wonderfully accomplished husband and my charming daughter, Cristina, but I could see that she did not believe me. She simply stared at me as I continued chattering away.

In the gloom of her chamber, Mother Francisca strained to look at me and gently said, "My poor child, if you believe what you are telling me, why must you try so hard to convince me?

One thing you mustn't do, Gabriela, is keep the truth from yourself."

"*Madre*," I said, feeling the tears well up in my eyes, "what makes you say such a thing?"

"My dear, a pleasant glow always graces the face of a happily married woman."

"With all due respect, Mother Francisca, how would you know that?"

"Living in a convent does not make us nuns blind to the world. Your heart will not find peace until it finds its home."

I considered her words for a moment and wondered what I must do next.

As I was about to leave her company, Mother Francisca closed her eyes piously and with her right hand held up her rosary, a figure of Christ carved in mother-of-pearl, and gave me the blessing of the cross.

With her blessing in my heart and a prayer on my lips, I walked out of the Abbey of Santa Teresa for the last time, fervently repeating to myself the last lines of the Our Father:

Thy Kingdom come, thy will be done, on earth as it is in Heaven. Give us this day our daily bread. Forgive our trespasses, as we forgive those who trespass against us. Lead us not into temptation, and deliver us from evil . . .

Deep in my heart I hoped that this prayer would be enough to protect me from the jagged rocks of the sins I would later commit.

catorce: THE MISTRESS OF THE HOUSE

All the time I was growing up, I had the privilege of learning through my mother's good example that my only duty in life was to discover how to please a man in every way, and that my greatest ambition should be to become the perfect mistress of the house.

Back in those days, before she married, a young woman was expected, even as she pursued her intellectual development, to acquire practical knowledge about running a household and being a good wife and hostess who would make her husband proud. Any deviation from this ideal had to be repressed, and every unpleasantness borne with a smile; a husband must never be able to detect any competing claims between his wife's commitment to their marriage and her past.

This knowledge assured me with unequivocal certainty that my role in life had been predetermined, and that living for my husband, even at the risk of self-abnegation, would be the ultimate expression of my good standing as a wife.

My upbringing was based on the premise that because men are not fully capable of molding to matrimony, it is necessarily incumbent upon women to guide them through it, usually by bending compliantly. My mother was fond of saying that men were like babies—"That's why we must learn to anticipate their every need and satisfy it for them. It's as simple as that."

This dynamic was never more evident than when, early some morning, my father would call to my mother, "Ana Amelia, *dónde está mi café?*" This seemingly straightforward question could hardly, in fact, have been *less* so.

First of all, it meant that my father had woken up earlier than usual but that Mayra had not divined this and therefore did not have his coffee waiting for him in the study. It further revealed that my father had not the slightest idea of where anything was kept in his own house, especially in the kitchen, and so could not possibly be expected to make his own coffee. A husband wandering around in the kitchen could signify only one thing: his wife had failed miserably in her duties. And ridiculous though it may seem to us now, no man would ever have known whom to address such a request to anyway. It is entirely likely that my father never had any notion which of our two maids did what in our home. Had he asked Yamila for his coffee, he would have unwittingly offended Mayra, whose province the kitchen was, and thus set off an irreversible cascade of events culminating in one of my mother's vexed looks. For while my father agreed that he had no business meddling in the intricate chain of domestic duties (nor indeed any skill in this area), he still told my mother that this was her only job: "Ana Amelia, why can't my *café con leche* be ready when I get up? I cannot understand it." But it was not about the coffee; it was about its being on time, in the right place, at the right temperature, and served by the right person. Nothing was more disconcerting to my mother than to find my father's coffee cup left untouched, for this could be interpreted in only one way: his coffee was less than perfect, and she would have to fix it, somehow, without having to ask what was wrong with it. On those occasions when she *did* ask, my father would merely reply, "I don't know. It's just not the same." At that point, without getting her back or her temper up, my mother would quietly remove the offending cup, take it back to the kitchen, and tell Mayra to start over.

In my own marriage, I took pride in the fact that just as my mother had done, I made our home a castle in which my husband was always king. I was and remain especially proud that even though the fire of passion never burned in our bedroom, I was nevertheless able to maintain my stature as the mistress of the house by adhering to the conventions I had been taught—at least most of the time.

When doing so became a challenge for one reason or another, I would replay in my mind the childhood experiences that lent support to this expectation.

One of the most vivid of these was the routine every day when my father came home after work. As soon as my mother heard his voice, she would rush to greet him, always radiant and smiling, always elegantly dressed, always ready with the same question: "What can I get you, Mario?" This conveyed to him not only that he was the ruling monarch but also that she was pleased to see him and eager to grant his every wish from that moment forward. She would then gracefully relieve him of his black leather doctor's bag and stow it in the study while he went upstairs to freshen up before dinner.

What my father never knew, or even suspected, was the madhouse that preceded his peaceful sunsets at home.

Each day by midmorning, every decision involved in the smooth running of the household had to have been made, including the coordination of the day's meals, the cleaning of the house, the making of the beds, the polishing of the floors, and the setting of the table in accordance with the rules of etiquette. But despite such careful planning, most late afternoons still found my mother rushing about giving orders to everyone in frantic anticipation of her husband's arrival. Mayra was to have dinner ready at exactly six-thirty. Yamila was to have bathed and dressed the four of us—Constanza, Jacinta, Antonio, and me—and we were to be cheerful but quiet after Papi got home, or else. These were the only times, as far as I can remember, when my mother ever let slip her usual grace and poise. She never raised her voice or lost her temper, but she could make it clear with a single ominous look that my father's homecoming was a serious business and had best go according to plan.

One of the most important daily rituals was getting an elaborate dinner to the table. My mother used to say that serving my father a delicious meal was a way of letting him know she had been thinking about him all day: "Nothing is more flattering to a man," she noted.

This did not mean, of course, that she did the cooking herself. It simply meant that she planned every detail, including making up the menu and telling Mayra what to buy each day, right down to the flowers that ought to be placed in vases around the house and the produce she wanted from the fruit and vegetable vendors who came to the door from dawn to dusk.

Even as she supervised Mayra in the timely completion of all the kitchen tasks, Mami also had to see to it that Yamila took care of the four of us children and did her other chores, including ironing and folding the linens, polishing the silver, and watering the plants. My mother discharged these duties with the pious devotion of one answerable to the Holy Father.

Closer to the time when our father was due to arrive, after checking to make sure that nothing had been left undone, Mami would go up to her room to touch up her face, brush her hair, and put on a pleasant smile. She used to tell us that on coming home, a husband "must be greeted with nothing but smiles and good news"—his just reward for a hard day's work. Last of all, she would inspect each of her children, military style, to ensure that we, too, were ready to welcome Papi.

You might guess that by virtue of being a boy, Antonio would have been spared some of these lessons, but in fact, his participation was a lesson in and of itself: Mami insisted that he pay attention to what she told us girls so he would know what to expect of his wife once he got married himself.

Before dinner, we children generally stayed in our rooms playing until we were called to the table; we were strictly forbidden to go outside to play after having our baths. On special occasions, Mami would invite us to perch obediently on one of the sofas in the living room while she and Papi talked.

When he first sat down, my father mostly spoke about his day; Mami seemed happy simply to sit there and listen to him go on and on. When I got older, I would realize that he hadn't been sharing any specific information he wanted her to hear; he'd just been clearing out his mind, as one might do with a closet overstuffed with unwanted clothes. So my mother listened closely, but not to his words: she once explained to us that a wife must pay close attention "to what her husband *doesn't* say, and to the tone of his voice," because from these two things, "any intelligent woman should be able to deduce what her man really needs and what he's really trying to say."

As if divining the pronouncements of an oracle, Mami knew that the moment Papi's tone softened, it meant that "his closet was cleared out" and he was ready for dinner. If we were in the room, she would nod in our direction with a slight upward tilt of her chin, our signal to begin marching toward the dining room and cue Mayra that it was time for dinner to be served.

As our father went to take his seat at the head of the table, Mami would pull out his chair and stand next to it for a few seconds, her amber-colored eyes gazing at him with a look of admiration and approval that no man could have found in his power to resist.

There was never a day in my mother's adult life when she didn't go to any length to put her husband and children first. She was completely dedicated to the difficult and thankless jobs of being a wife and mother and running a household. Doing the latter well—indeed, perfectly—was, she believed, the only way for a wife to keep her husband from straying. "Your aim in homemaking is to anticipate and satisfy your man's every need," she advised us girls. "You must never give him any reason to seek comfort elsewhere."

From observing my mother at work, I learned that *"la ama de la casa"* was much more than an empty title; it was a badge of honor. The highest compliment a man could pay a woman was to entrust her, in a manner of speaking, with the keys to his house. But still, this was only half of a wife's job.

Beyond administering the household, Mami also taught us how important a role a good wife played in her husband's public life. From her I learned how to entertain my future husband's friends and colleagues and what to wear on every occasion so as to reflect well on him in the company of others.

Of course, there was more to being a lady than fine clothes and homemaking skills. "All the beauty routines in the world and all the smooth running of your household will do you no good if you don't manage to acquire the rare gift of self-possession," my mother used to say. Before she could be considered a lady, a woman had to acquire the manners that would make her behavior in public as predictable and precise as the movement of a clock's pendulum.

In this regard, I have found that one of the best things a woman can do for herself is learn to nurture her self-confidence. This alone will give her the self-assurance that will captivate a man time and again, the easy demeanor that will cause others to covet her friendship, and the unshakeable strength of character that will make her worthy of being a gentleman's wife.

In addition to her other duties, a wife must do everything in her power to protect her husband's good name, for his reputation can never be either better or worse than her care of it on his behalf. Because you represent him and are, in a sense, your man's public face, your behavior and manner, in the company of others and even alone before your servants, must be beyond reproach. Neither virtue nor wealth can be achieved in the absence of exemplary behavior.

While opinion is a flexible notion of which there are various kinds, reputation is not. Take, for instance, what a society calls scandal. In some cases, it is not scandal at all and nothing more than someone's opinion based on an arbitrary convention, which usually varies from time to time and from place to place. But even with that being the case, you must always aim to respect prevailing conventions so as not to court scandal and sully your reputation, of which there can be only two kinds: good and bad.

The rewards for your decorous behavior will be your husband's pride in you, his devotion, and his support. Such loyalty on his part will in turn ensure that you will never need to worry about his taking a mistress.

Irreproachable deportment requires a courteous manner in all situations. Among other things, you should show genuine interest in your husband's work and learn to be gracefully tolerant of his views so he will seek out your advice and value your good judgment.

Friends are an important influence, for good or ill, in nearly every marriage. While old friendships may be the most cherished and the most enduring, new attachments may be formed throughout your life. Always endeavor to preserve those ties that stimulate your highest ambitions and help you understand the meaning of unselfishness, one of the hallmarks of a lady.

In cultivating friendships, you will need to strive hard to make yourself worthy of having good friends. The ability to mix well

with others is an admirable and very desirable trait, as is the capacity to acknowledge your own imperfections as well as those of others and to be tolerant of both.

Even more crucial than the ability to adhere to the rules of comportment in the presence of your husband is the ability to do so in his *absence.* Difficult though it may be, when he is away, you must endeavor to pass the time attending to your home, occupying yourself with your children, going to church, and visiting with his family; the latter two constitute the only valid reasons for leaving your house. Additionally, until he returns, you should wear only black, so as not to give him any reason for worry or jealousy, two emotions you must never intentionally cultivate.

In looking back over my life, I sometimes wish *I* had been able to mind these rules on every occasion. Whenever I felt overwhelmed by the exigencies of matrimony, I tried to remind myself of the exacting standards that earned a woman the right to be called the mistress of the house. To my dismay, all my efforts would be in vain: by the time my heart had traveled elsewhere, all that was left for me to do was follow.

quince: LAS TENTACIONES

The threat of the upcoming thirtieth year of my life assailed me like a hungry beast. Raw desire battered my body with such violent blows that despite the gathering menace, I could think of little else.

Every night, I lay awake staring at the ceiling, desperately longing for some revelation, some flash of meaning. I felt ungrateful. I had a good life, a faithful and devoted husband of a dozen years, and a ten-year-old daughter. Jolts of hopelessness kept overwhelming me all the same.

Despite my good fortune, I was irritable and anxious. Life seemed impossibly complex: I felt as if I were being watched at all times, and I questioned everyone's motives, even my loved ones'. I experienced a constant, unquenchable thirst and began to have a recurring nightmare that I was choking on a throatful of dry sand.

Late on the afternoon of my birthday, the world broke over me with a vengeance. Life seemed to attack me physically and seize me by my nerve endings. Looking out my bedroom window, I felt aggrieved to see sap bleeding from the trunk of the mango tree in back, and resented the setting sun for smoldering the puffy white clouds.

I dreaded the evening to come. Despite my protests to the contrary, my family had insisted that a party would be just the thing to lift my spirits. They had also decided, unbeknownst to me, to invite my best childhood friend, Carmela Caballero, whom I hadn't spoken to in ages. And Carmela, without asking anyone—for her family had never been much for protocol—asked her brother to come along.

The moment I came down the stairs and spotted the two of them in the entrance hall, I knew that my recent depression must have caused my parents a good deal of concern, for it was highly unlikely that they would ever have sought Carmela out otherwise. If anyone else registered surprise at the presence of Jorge Armando, I was too dazed to notice it. Perhaps they all supposed that after fourteen years, twelve of which I had been married, he couldn't pose much of a threat.

After exchanging greetings, we proceeded to the living room,

where we had cocktails and first Jonathan and then my father made toasts in my honor. Jorge Armando must have sensed my discomfort, for at the first opportunity, he caught me by the elbow and asked in a low voice:

"What sad thoughts could be troubling such a beautiful face?"

Feeling *pudor* rise in my cheeks, I loudly suggested that we all go in to dinner.

I had already taken the maid aside and instructed her to set additional places for my unexpected guests. On entering the dining room, I found to my horror that the only two table settings without place cards were on my immediate left and right. All through the meal, I forced myself not to stare at Jorge Armando, even as he tried repeatedly to engage me in conversation. I wanted only to get away from him before my actions or my expression betrayed the desire that until this moment had seemed like a faint murmur from a faraway land.

But I had forgotten just how charming he could be. The qualities that had made me blush as a girl had only been enhanced by age: the effortless charisma, the irresistible swagger, and the seductive, mesmerizing, measured voice, an instrument of such extraordinary range that it was unforgettable to anyone who ever heard him speak, an instrument he used to address me, intimately, directly, by my own name.

Carmela, to my right, could only smile knowingly each time he bent his head close to mine. Now he whispered softly in my ear, his breath so warm that I wanted to throw myself at him like a common whore, "I have waited all these years to see you blossom into a woman. You are even lovelier than I imagined you would be, Gabriela."

My composure must have cracked a little, for he grew more and more flirtatious as the various courses were served, seemingly unaware that we were in the company of ten other guests and I was married to the man at the head of the table.

"Forgive my impertinence, but I find myself intrigued," he said quietly.

I waited for him to continue.

"How can a woman like you endure being married to a man who is obviously preoccupied with everything but her?"

So taken aback was I by this remark that I felt torn between slapping him for his daring familiarity and running toward his embrace at the same time. My impeccable upbringing, however, kept me from following the latter course, while the sweet memory of our stolen moments as adolescents together ruled out the former. Instead, I coolly replied that while no doubt any number of men might be fit for her bed, the mistress of the house had many other important matters with which to occupy her time and keep herself quite content.

But deep inside, I felt suddenly suffocated by what I now realized I had known all along: the man seated at the head of the table was not the love of my life. I only prayed I had managed to fool Jorge Armando, for I could no longer deceive myself. And with that, I caught my husband's eye and excused myself for the rest of the evening on account of an unforgiving headache.

Up in my room, I struggled with temptation and with the lessons I knew I must learn from it. Why, I asked myself, had my old love come uninvited back into my life?

While I suspected that my bid for existential self-possession would prove deadly, I was also all too certain that surrendering to desire would mean that one day, my heart would be not merely broken but shattered. And then my life would swing wide open, like a door through which love, betrayal, remorse, and regret would all have to pass.

The next morning, after a sleepless night of confusion, raw desire, and anxiety, I marched down to the living room, determined to figure out a way to put my mind at ease. But I was on my own: after my birthday party, Jonathan had left for London and I wouldn't have spoken of it to him anyway.

Increasingly agitated, I called my older sister and begged her to come see me, even though I doubted she would understand anything so ostensibly irrational as my desire for wild, illicit adventure. Almost as soon as she came through the front door, I blurted out the whole story, not even stopping for breath.

"He tried to seduce you?" Constanza asked, incredulous and judgmental as only she could be.

Intent on shocking her, if only momentarily to escape the misery of my situation, I said, in jest, "Who am I to deny a man so willing to rescue me from this menacing condition?"

As I had as a child, I now felt that somehow I had temporary immunity from harm and a permanent license to eschew all responsible behavior. I huffed impatiently like a child who knows she will not get her way and reminded my sister that in my house, the clock had marked the hour of thirty, an age at which women were ready for love. Perhaps I was *too* ready.

Constanza was duly shocked. Appalled that I could try to dismiss Jorge Armando's offense with what she called my "reprehensible disregard," she insisted that I must learn to exercise the restraint befitting my position in life.

A FEW WEEKS LATER, CONCERNED BY MY WORSENing depression, the family doctor ordered me to take some time away to rest. My worried parents offered their vacation home in Macuto, my childhood haven and paradise. My mother and Constanza would care for young Cristina in my absence.

I knew that my sickness ran deeper, and I was fearful that my desire would eventually defeat my good sense. I knew I must learn to conquer restraint, but I could tell it would never come easily to me.

Given the gravity of the situation, Dr. Castellano's orders seemed the perfect prescription for my racing heart. That is how I came to spend time in Macuto.

Nana's voice was like a shadow. Through her grandmother's journals, the reality of what Pilar would eventually confront was brought home to her. She knew that at some point, she would have to face her inner struggle, and that when that time came, there would be no way for her to shelter herself from the truth.

She thought again of Nana's letter to her: *In whatever you do, you must do what's right for you . . . because if you don't . . .*

Exactly a week after her grandmother's funeral, Rafael picked Pilar up at her mother's house to drive her to the airport. She assumed Cristina had arranged it, or at least agreed to it; it was just like her.

On the way, they talked freely about old times and cautiously about the future. It was like an old-fashioned dance, with Rafael attempting to sway her his way, and Pilar trying to lean away while still holding on to his hand. And every so often, during gaps in their conversation, she would silently wonder where, or whether, she would ever fit in.

Glancing over at her, Rafael asked, "*Mi vida*, do you really think you could live in a foreign country for the rest of your life? Without your family?"

One of Rafael's many talents was the ability to pinpoint with uncanny accuracy, and without being told, whatever was foremost on her mind. Pilar thought this skill must have something to do with his training as a lawyer. She marveled that with two simple questions, he had given voice to her plight, and admired his deft attempt to press her on the very issues with which she was now grappling. She knew there were worse things than uncertainty, but still, his queries mirrored her own wish for resolution. She hoped for hope.

Between her mother and Rafael, she couldn't decide who was more gifted in the art of persuasion. Pilar thought of her mother's invincible convictions and of Rafael's flattering insistence, and she worried that like the tiny drops used so effectively in Chinese water torture to obtain a prisoner's confession, their arguments might eventually wear her down. All week long, Cristina had busied herself with cultivating seeds of doubt in her daughter's mind. And it had worked: Pilar felt now more confused than ever.

By the time she checked her luggage, she felt sure that there wasn't a bachelor in all of Caracas more desirable, more attentive, or more eligible than Rafael Uslar. She knew that many other girls would have done anything to land him, but somehow he had always managed to remain tantalizingly out of their reach. He was like a piece of delicious chocolate cake that they could see through a bakery window but couldn't touch.

As they walked together to her gate, Pilar thought once more about Rafael's earlier questions. Was Chicago her home now? Or Caracas? Will I ever find my place? she asked herself.

Just as she was about to board the plane, Rafael caught her off guard yet again. "I'll be in Chicago on business at the end of the month," he said. "I'll give you a call and take you out to dinner—like old times, *sí*?" When he kissed her good-bye, she was surprised to realize that she was actually going to miss him. Trying to keep her composure, she pursed her lips and nodded. She wasn't sure that seeing him in Chicago would be such a good idea.

By the time she took her seat on the airplane, she felt like a traitor. Were a week and a few kisses all it took to turn her whole life around?

As the passengers on either side settled in for the flight, Pilar contemplated, for the hundredth time, the puzzling riddle that was her love life.

On the one hand, she was positive that there could be no happiness purer than that of strolling by Lake Michigan hand in hand with Patrick, laughing at his silly jokes and getting lost in his kisses. When she was with him, she felt lithe and ethereal, as if she could fly.

On the other hand, over the years, Rafael and all he represented had grown inside her like the roots of an old oak tree. In his presence, she felt that she was standing on solid ground and wouldn't stumble—and if she ever did, he'd be there to catch her. But she knew that this sense of security, however reassuring, was a well-dressed impostor that could never pass for real love. What had Nana called it? An "illusion of security."

Her thoughts were interrupted by the flight attendant's safety presentation: "Ladies and gentlemen, we need just a few minutes of your time. . . ."

Eventually, Pilar turned on her laptop to try to get some work done before going back in to the paper on Wednesday. She was glad she'd have the next two days off to decompress after her strenuous and emotional trip.

While the *idea* of working was a good one, she knew it was just a game she was playing with herself. She wasn't really thinking about work; she couldn't. Staring at the computer screen, she asked herself, Will I ever be happy? She certainly *wanted* to be. The problem was that whenever she thought about it, a torrent of fears flooded her: the fear that she would never get married, the fear that she would never have children, the fear that she would never *belong*.

During the day, she almost always managed to keep her mind busy with work, but sometimes at night, especially when Patrick was staying at his own place, she would curl up in bed and feel that she was all alone in the world.

She had done well in school and now had a successful career. She was a good sister and tried to be a good daughter. But the most important thing in life, happiness, had so far managed to elude her.

"Something to drink, miss?" The high-pitched voice of the flight attendant reminded her where she was.

"Do you have any apple juice?"

"Yes, I do."

Pilar took a sip of the juice, leaned back in her seat, and mentally traveled back to a time before she moved to Chicago.

They were both in their second year of college when Rafael began courting her in earnest. He was majoring in law, and she was studying journalism. Often, after class, they would stop at an old-fashioned ice cream parlor near her grandmother's house in Los Rosales.

Knowing, like all Latin men, that the best way to win a señorita's heart was to court every other woman in her family, Rafael used to suggest that they pay Gabriela a visit—"just to give her *nuestros saludos*. It's on our way, *muñeca*," he'd say, and his easygoing manner would inevitably persuade the exhausted Pilar to drop in at Nana's for a brief hello.

Having taken the trouble to note how much Doña Gabriela loved fragrant gardenias—the sort of endearing observation that proved he'd been raised to be thoughtful—Rafael would always pluck a blossom from the tree outside her house, and as soon as she greeted them with the words "*Adelante, mijos*," he would present the flower to her with such a grand gesture that anyone would have thought it was an entire bouquet. He would then nod his head, smile disarmingly, and say with an air of formality, "*Para usted, Doña Gabriela*." All of this pomp and circumstance constituted a formula for any man wishing to charm his girlfriend. Pilar's grandmother was properly impressed, and Pilar herself responded as expected, feeling proud to be the *novia* of "such a thoughtful and enchanting young man," in Nana's words.

Some evenings, they would go to Pilar's house, where they would spread out their books on the floor of the living room and study for their exams. Cristina, like her mother, became almost girlish in Rafael's presence; Pilar marveled at how solicitous she was, asking after his parents, talking with him about his college courses, even bringing him a glass of water herself, rather than having the maid do it.

After he left, Cristina would often say something like, "What an ambitious young man! And so polite!" While Pilar did not disagree, she was suspicious of her mother's motives, so she kept her own counsel.

On one occasion, Cristina engaged Rafael in a discussion about the law and what he intended do after graduation. In a friendly tone, almost as if making a statement of fact, she told him, "There's nothing standing in your way, *muchacho*. You can do anything you want; your only challenge will lie in deciding precisely what that will be. With your talents, you could make your mark in whatever career you set your sights on." Her comments infuriated Pilar. Why didn't her mother ever tell *her* that there was nothing standing in her way?

Genially, Rafael accepted Cristina's compliment: "Perhaps you are right, Señora Castillo."

(Although she had never said anything to him about it, Rafael's lack of modesty had always bothered Pilar, and this week's visit confirmed that little had changed in that regard during her absence. It was an arrogance all too typical of Latin men, who everyone assumed could, should, and would succeed at anything, almost as a birthright. It made her furious just to think of it now.)

Every so often, as if to cement in Rafael's mind the notion that he ought to marry her daughter, Cristina would mention some foundation project on which she and his mother, Carolina, were working together. If he ever detected the eagerness in her voice, he was too much of a gentleman to give any indication of it.

"Please give your mother my best," she might say as he was leaving, "and tell her I'll see her at the board meeting next week."

With a polite bow of the head, Rafael would always say, "*Sí,* Señora Castillo. I will make sure to give your *saludos a Mamá.*"

Pilar had often thought about those conversations between her *novio* and her mother. It seemed to her that each possessed a surprisingly detailed surface familiarity with, yet no real substantive interest in, the life and activities of the other. She used to wonder how a man Rafael's age could possibly be so fascinated by her mother's charity work.

Rafael often inquired, too, about Señora Castillo's childhood. "What was it like to grow up as the Venezuelan daughter of an Englishman?" he asked Cristina one evening. It wasn't that Pilar believed their mutual interest was feigned; it was just that it seemed to her so charged with ulterior purpose.

More than once, she sensed that Rafael Uslar was courting not the señorita Pilar Castillo but rather the future Señora Castillo de Uslar. And flattered though she was by that, as she now contemplated yet again the possibility of making a life with Rafael, she asked herself, Shouldn't love count for *something*? Thoroughly confused, she thought of Nana's advice that the point of courtship was precisely to try on a role. If that was so, then all was going according to plan. Wasn't it?

After Pilar graduated from college, Rafael's father offered her a job at *El Nacional*. With that, both Cristina and Carolina assumed that a wedding between their daughter and son could not be far behind. They were wrong: while the couple had talked about marrying, Pilar had reached the conclusion that they were still too young. "What's the rush?" she'd asked Rafael.

Whereas her sister, Ana Carla, always lived in the present, Pilar preferred to look to the future. She had found that it was almost never a good idea to jump into anything without first thinking it through. She had a larger vision of what she wanted to accomplish in her life, and an early marriage was not part of her plan.

Cristina was crushed to hear from her younger daughter's own lips that work, not marriage, was to be Pilar's first priority.

"Don't you want to get married?" she demanded.

"Of course I do, Mamá—one day. For now I just want to be successful."

"And don't you think marriage can be a success of sorts, *hija*?"

"Has it ever occurred to you that I might be happier having a career than being married? Besides, I haven't said I'll *never* marry."

"Well, let's just say I think you'd be happier if your future were guaranteed."

"You mean *you* would be happier, Mamá."

The week before Pilar was to start her job at *El Nacional*, she was on her way downstairs for a dinner date with Rafael when she overheard him talking with Cristina in the living room. The exchange would persuade her once and for all that it was up to her, and her alone, to look out for her own best interests, as neither her mother nor her boyfriend could be relied upon in this regard.

"I wish you would try to talk some sense into her, Rafael. Don't you mind the idea of her working?"

"Don't worry, Señora Castillo, it's only an assistant society editor's job—nothing to worry about," he assured her.

Cristina pressed the point and at the same time got in a plug for their marriage: "All the same, wouldn't it be awkward for an ambitious young attorney to have a wife working on a newspaper? Wouldn't it look as though he couldn't support his family?"

Furious that these two were making plans for *her* life, Pilar continued down the stairs, pretending not to have heard anything, and filed the information away for later.

As soon as they saw her at the bottom of the stairs, Rafael and Cristina both smiled. Rafael had never gotten the chance to answer

Cristina's last questions; Pilar wondered what his response would have been.

As they went off to dinner, Pilar felt puzzled. Rafael had been taking credit for getting his father to offer her the job at the newspaper, so why should he have been so dismissive of it? As it turned out, the truth behind the story was quite different. When Pilar had earlier mentioned the possibility of moving to the States to pursue graduate studies, Rafael had gone to his mother for help. It was *Carolina* who spoke to Señor Uslar about finding Pilar a place at the paper, not her son. And what made Pilar angriest when she found out was that it all had been a ploy to keep her from doing what she really wanted to do.

During their date that night, in a fit of amorous honesty, Rafael finally told her the real story. Pilar listened patiently as he explained that his mother had intervened and gotten her the job because it meant that when she wasn't with him, she would be under the watchful eye of his father. Although it was Rafael speaking these words, Pilar heard Carolina's voice instead.

"You're a catch, Pilar. I need to keep a close eye on you," he teased.

While she was more than a little uncomfortable with the thought that she had been deftly manipulated, at the time, she simply smiled at Rafael's confession and began her job as assistant society editor the following week. Two years later, however, everyone was shocked when she announced her renewed resolve to move to the United States and pursue her degree. That was when, to the dismay of both families, she broke with tradition and with full support from her grandmother, called off her engagement to Rafael, and shattered everyone's expectations for her.

But that was not the only reason for her decision to leave Venezuela.

While she had hoped even then to get a position as a business reporter, Pilar resigned herself, at first, to writing about engagements, weddings, and society parties. If nothing else, it would get her foot in the door until she got an opportunity to find her way into the business section and work on stories of greater substance.

She had been at *El Nacional* for a year or so when she saw her chance.

She was assigned to cover the *quinceañera* celebration of a young member of Caracas's elite society. Having enjoyed a flurry of success with her reportage of other, similar stories, Pilar mused that the prominence of the girl's family might allow her to do a longer piece on the tradition of the *quinceañera* ball and how it had evolved over the years. She wanted to write about something of more consequence than the debutantes' trips to Europe, their elaborate gowns, the equally elaborate guest lists, and the size of the chandeliers at the country club.

One day over lunch, she explained her idea to Rafael: "I think people may be tired of all this emphasis on high society. I'm envisioning a feature story that would address the real issues faced by women of our generation, something beyond the anxiety involved in trying to find the perfect dress. What do you think?"

Pilar could have scripted his reply.

Rafael commended her for her "smart idea," but he still had to qualify his response: "Sounds good to me—I don't see why you shouldn't do it—but I'll ask my mother what she thinks."

It was a matter of hierarchy and protocol, and something she'd have to get used to if she was going to marry Rafael Uslar. She had to play by these unwritten but all-important rules. So far, she had never had any trouble negotiating the intricate workings of the corset-tight society she'd grown up in, but she knew that one day, if she pushed the limits too far, all that could change. It was best to follow protocol from the start, because once she was Rafael's wife, this was how she would have to navigate through every decision, even in her own household. On some issues only her husband would have to be consulted, and on others just her mother-in-law, but on the most important matters, the patriarch, her father-in-law, would have to be brought in.

Pilar started researching her story that same afternoon. She put in a request for the paper's best photographer to work with her on the piece and set up an interview with young María Corina Cisneros Ayala, the *quinceañera* in question, hoping to get her opinions on the changing roles of women. It was her plan to include some background and a few photos of the Cisneros family home in the feature, rather than just the standard formal portrait taken of the *quinceañera* at the country club on the night of the ball.

A few days after that, she received a call from Carolina, asking her to lunch.

"Rafael told me about your story, Pilar," Señora Uslar said as soon as they were seated on the country club's terrace. "And I'm anxious to hear more."

Pilar described what she had in mind: "The piece will be about the evolution of traditions, Señora Uslar, and the hold they have on our society. I want to make my readers *think*. I mean, what possible reason can there be, nowadays, for throwing a dinner party for five hundred people just to introduce a young woman to her family's closest friends?"

"If you want my opinion," Carolina offered—which really meant that Pilar had better take her advice on the matter, or else—"you ought to stick to writing the *quinceañera* story the way it has always been written."

But Pilar persisted. "Really, Señora Uslar, don't you think it's an obsolete ritual? It no longer applies to the world we live in. It's just a system designed to preserve the old power structures."

"That's a curiously radical viewpoint, my dear. You will find that things will go easier for you when you change your mind on that point."

Pilar studied the woman across from her and was struck by the thought that in a few years, if she didn't stand up for herself, she would become a younger version of Señora Uslar. She shuddered at the idea.

Before responding to Carolina's remark, Pilar wondered how women like her could still believe they ruled the roost. Despite claims to the contrary, Venezuelan society was anything *but* a matriarchy. Even when they brought all the money into the marriage, as had been the case with Carolina Mancera, such wives were content to turn it over to their husbands in exchange for the privilege of administering the household and raising children. She felt a strange pity for Señora Uslar and vowed that she would never end up like her.

"With all due respect, Señora Uslar, can you give me one good reason I should change my mind?" she asked, sounding a little more impatient than she'd intended.

"I can give you more than one, but this should be enough." Then, speaking of her husband as if he were a perfect stranger to her, Carolina went on to declaim: "Señor Uslar is of the mind that there is enough social unrest in our country already, and that publishing photos of the Cisneros home in his newspaper would merely excite public envy. He thinks your story idea is irresponsible."

"But Señora Uslar, the point of journalism is to tell the truth and make people think. What kind of reporter would I be if I didn't question the things that I believe don't make sense?"

Seeing that she was not making any headway, Señora Uslar suddenly changed her tack: "My dear, you can hardly expect Fernando to agree that your little aspirations as a journalist are more important than the preservation of a tradition that has been in place since long before your birth."

Pilar left the country club frustrated. That night, she asked Rafael to meet her for drinks at their favorite restaurant so they could discuss her future mother-in-law's veto.

"Try to understand, *mi vida*," he said. "That stupid photographer went to the Cisneros home to snap some exterior shots for your story, and the next thing you know, my father gets a call from Ernesto Cisneros himself. Why don't you give it a rest, *preciosa*?"

When Pilar asked Rafael if there was any way she could appeal to his father, he gave her an irritated look and changed the subject, asking where she would like to go on their honeymoon. Pilar suspected that this was yet another of his mother's suggestions. She could almost hear Carolina's voice urging him, "Engage her in some diversion, such as the details of your wedding. That will make her forget all about her absurd story."

When she got home, she didn't even bother to mention the incident to Cristina. Instead, she started making plans. She called her nana for help, broke up with Rafael the very next day, and a few months later, long after the *quinceañera* piece had been reassigned to another reporter, Pilar tendered her resignation to Señor Uslar himself, giving as her reason her impending move to Chicago, where she intended to earn a business degree.

It was the most serious breach of protocol she had ever committed: delivering such news to a man first, without even the courtesy of an advance warning to his wife, the proper intermediary through whom to convey "information of a delicate nature." But Pilar was confident in her decision, especially since she had her nana's full support.

Not long after that conversation with Señor Uslar, Pilar found herself in the United States, a country that had always intrigued her and that had since, little by little, captured her heart.

Pilar's first year in America had been challenging, to say the least.

Thanks to her British maternal grandfather and her bilingual education at Saint Mary's Academy for Girls in Caracas, Pilar's English was nearly flawless, but nothing could have prepared her for the dizzying pace at which things moved in the United States.

The admissions process at Northwestern required more paperwork and letters of recommendation, it seemed, than applying for a job as U.S. president. She managed to get it all done with the help of an admissions counselor named Tracy, whose last name she never learned.

Once she had cleared that hurdle and gotten through the equally daunting visits to U.S. Immigration to obtain a student visa, she could finally look forward to her first day of school. But when that day finally came, it was not at all what she'd been expecting; the entire first week, in fact, was devoted to an initiation retreat for new graduate students, called the Ropes Adventure.

The program comprised a variety of outdoor exercises aimed at teaching the students how to trust one another. In one exercise, each participant was lifted into the air by a group of perfect strangers, his or her future classmates, and then passed from hand to hand through something that looked like a spiderweb, without touching any part of it. This was no easy thing for Pilar, who was not only self-conscious in front of other people but also quite poor at doing tasks that demanded any degree of physical dexterity. And in any event, she thought the whole notion of an "adventure" ridiculous and briefly wondered whether her move to the States had been a mistake.

Over the course of that grueling week, she did, however, bond with a few people, some of whom would later become good friends. Still, Pilar felt hugely relieved when the initiation ritual was at last over. When school started, she quickly realized that her customary high heels would be both a hazard and a liability on the spread-out campus; reluctantly, she bought her first-ever pair of tennis shoes.

One of the things that most surprised her was how thoroughly American culture was geared toward comfort, on campus and off. She could count on the fingers of one hand the women she saw wearing stilettos, and several of *those* seemed to be streetwalkers. (Still, when Cristina came for a visit, she was dismayed to see Pilar leave for the grocery store wearing tennis shoes. "Are you going to shop at the supermarket or clean it, Pilar?" she chided.)

During that first year of school, Pilar got a crash course in American culture via television. The commercials especially fascinated her because they were so different from their counterparts on

Venezuelan TV: there seemed to be almost no families shown in American ads, which were instead largely aimed at individuals concerned with personal improvement and consumption.

As far as she could tell through this informal research, half of the U.S. population was on a diet, and the other half was eating fast food at midnight, alone. She could not help but notice how much food there was on television, whether viewers were being encouraged to eat it or to *stop* eating it. Eventually, she, too, became obsessed with food and with her weight.

As is often the case, this change occurred gradually. It was only after almost an entire year of looking at emaciated models on magazine covers and seeing "perfect" bodies in workout videos that she began to think, *for the first time in her life,* that her generous hips were in fact fat and must be trimmed. Like they said on TV.

It didn't take a genius to conclude from watching even a few hours of television that Americans were a highly efficient, time-conscious group of people who on the one hand denied themselves food and on the other demanded that it be available to them twenty-four hours a day.

When at last Pilar began interacting with others, she realized how precise everything and everyone was in the United States. At first, Americans' specificity about time seemed unreasonable to her; she could not believe people were serious when they said, for instance, "I'll see you at twelve-fifteen." But eventually, she came to revere this respect for others' time and taught herself to stick to a schedule, buying a daytimer and then later a Palm Pilot (which now she could not live without).

She soon learned to love the freedom of movement and the comfort provided by her tennis shoes, and then one day, at the urging of a classmate who had expressed disbelief that she didn't work out, she joined a gym. In the beginning, exercising felt strange to her, but then she started to enjoy it just a little, and then before she knew it, she was addicted, like most of her friends, to working out on the stair-stepper three times a week.

Overall, the United States was definitely a more casual society than Venezuela, less formal in every aspect except punctuality, which seemed to Pilar yet another national obsession. But she approved of both of those qualities. She liked the way everything was so practical and casual, the fact that one didn't need to check with an entire family before invit-ing one of its members to dinner, and she thought that keeping track of one's time was the epitome of personal accountability.

During that first year of graduate school, she rented an apartment in nearby Evanston. While the keys to her own place opened the door to freedom, it was not a freedom that she felt ready for or even fully understood. That so many Americans left their parents' home before they were married seemed to her odd, and she was ill pre-pared to cope with the cruel loneliness of such a living arrangement.

Equally unfamiliar to Pilar was the concept of casually dating a series of men rather than being formally courted by one man. She had been raised with the expectation of becoming someone's wife, not everyone's date. Because of this, she took the few relationships she did have far too seriously, when they were really nothing more than casual dates. More than anything else in the world, she hoped that the next man she met would be "the one" so she wouldn't have to go through the heartache that went along with the cumbersome and often painful process of romantic elimination.

Over time, she learned to appreciate certain aspects of her newly acquired freedom and to take pride in the accountability that came with being on her own and making her own decisions. Still, every so often, she felt nostalgic for this or that detail of her Latin culture. She also missed her nana and sister terribly; on first moving to the United States, she phoned Ana Carla every Saturday, until the expense got to be too much. To her regret, she couldn't attend the baptism of little Luis Guillermo, Ana Carla's youngest son and Pilar's favorite nephew and godchild. After that, she reminded herself how important family was, and came to realize how quickly priorities could shift when one found oneself in a new environment—sometimes for the worse. She often looked into the mirror and did not recognize the person who looked back.

At Kellogg, Northwestern's business school, she made a few friends, all of them extremely bright women who took the time to educate her about the history of the feminist movement. In time, she began to understand and then to internalize the principles involved. She felt she had a lifetime—many lifetimes—of catching up to do: her Latin upbringing, her culture, had, in this sense at least, betrayed her.

One of Pilar's first experiences with expressing her own opinion came in Dr. Thomas Mueller's "Change Management" class. He had assigned a paper on the topic of organizational change, and Pilar had done a stellar job of researching every great mind's thoughts on the subject—only to learn, much to her dismay, that all her effort and sleepless nights were worth only, in Dr. Mueller's estimation, a B-minus. When she approached him to ask what was wrong with her paper, he told her, "There's nothing wrong with it. I just want you to stick your neck out a bit more."

"Stick my neck out? What do you mean by that?"

His comment was an instant education for her, both in American slang (she pictured herself sticking out her neck like a chicken) and in how women were regarded in her new country.

"Seems to me you went to a lot of trouble to document what everyone else has written on the subject. I'm interested in what *you* think," he explained.

Astonished, Pilar repeated, "What *I* think? What does it matter what *I* think?"

They had both been perplexed at this exchange for the same reason; Tom Mueller because he wanted her opinion, Pilar, because Dr.

Mueller wanted her opinion. Had he really asked her for her thoughts? She remembered thinking at the time that it must be some kind of joke.

As an undergraduate in Venezuela, she had been under the impression that women attended school to learn, not to argue their point of view. They were supposed to be educated, but that was as far as it went. To her, this seemed to be one of the fundamental differences between the two countries—differences that lay beneath the surface and that one could not grasp merely by watching television.

Her own acceptance of feminism as a powerful and positive social force was gradual. First she learned about the celebration of the individual; then she combined that knowledge with an awareness of America's emphasis on First Amendment rights. Add the freedom of the press and the right of political expression, and there it was—a simplified view of the women's movement. It all began to seem so obvious to her, so *right*.

After their conversation, Pilar asked Dr. Mueller if she could rewrite her paper and this time include her own views and opinions, in the hope that she might be able to do a better job. He agreed, and when she turned it in, he was evidently impressed, not only with her determination to get it right and to work twice as hard as everyone else in the class, but also with her writing ability, her keen journalistic eye. In the end, she got an A-plus on the rewrite. She almost cried with joy on seeing her grade, and fell in love on the spot with the very American notion of the meritocracy.

Just before her graduation, Dr. Mueller suggested that she call Dan Grossman at the *Tribune*. The two men were old friends and sat on the boards of several charities together. "Feel free to mention my name. I think you two might hit it off—and in any case, it's worth a try," he said.

Dr. Mueller was right: Dan Grossman and Pilar Castillo *did* hit it off. In fact, they made a perfect pair. He was as demanding as a

Supreme Court Justice and would have easily broken any stress meter; she was equally hardworking but as steady as a surgeon's hand. Dan loved good writing and was obsessed with deadlines and well-researched stories; Pilar had a passion for words, was compulsive about turning work in on time, and reveled in the minutiae of good research. So long as she didn't have to get up in front of a group of people and give a talk, she thrived.

Her student visa was up, and U.S. immigration law prevented her from earning a wage, so after Pilar met with Dan and he offered her a position as a reporter, she had to find a way to accept it without getting either of them in trouble. A fellow student told her she might be able to turn her job offer into a one-year Practical Training, one of the few programs under which foreigners could work in the United States.

Despite the enormous bureaucracy and extensive paperwork involved in getting a Practical Training approved, Pilar was determined to succeed. When the approval came through, she was thrilled. Best of all was that she had gotten this on her own merit, without some Don Fernando making her feel he was doing her a favor by giving her a job for which she was more than qualified. The only problem with the Practical Training permit was that after a year she'd have to go back home. But she couldn't worry about that now; all she could think about was doing well in a job she deserved.

After just a few days at the *Tribune,* she began to toy with the idea of staying, of actually making the United States her adopted home. But when she mentioned this in a phone call to her mother, Cristina was horrified: "You don't know what you're saying, *hija*! You want to live in another country? Permanently? What about your family?" Then she got on the next plane to Chicago, intent on talking some sense into her wayward daughter.

It was around this time that Pilar moved out of her apartment in Evanston and into a fifty-story highrise on the Gold Coast, practically in the middle of downtown Chicago, so she could be nearer the *Tribune*'s offices. An added benefit was its proximity to Lake Michigan, which looked to her more like an ocean.

She liked almost everything about the *Chicago Tribune*, starting with the almost baroque architecture of its building, which reminded her a little of Caracas, and the way it seemed to just sit there like a spaceship atop the Chicago River. But it was the people *in* the building that she liked best.

The other journalists she met there were a lot like her: well read and quietly dedicated, often possessed of strong opinions but duty-bound to convey to readers a balanced view of the issues. Most of them had simmering passions that, like her own, came to a boil only when stirred by the wrong people.

The appeal of her job at the *Tribune* was magnified further on the day she met Patrick Russo.

He caught her completely by surprise.

"Some story you must be working on—you've been chained to your desk since this morning."

Those were the first words Patrick spoke to Pilar. Even before she looked up, he set a bright-red apple on her desk and added, "I bet you're starving." He smiled a mischievous, boyish smile.

It was her second week on the job, and though she had noticed Patrick coming and going, cameras in hand, on what she assumed were various assignments, it had never occurred to her that he would ever take an interest in her. Just watching him walk by had been enough to make her pulse race.

Now, as she saw the color of his eyes, her breath quickened.

"C'mon, Dimples, go for it! You know you want it." He was referring to the apple, of course, but his teasing encouragement made her think of something else.

"Dimples?" was all she could manage by way of a reply.

"Yeah! Dimples, to remind you to smile. And by the way, I'm Patrick—Patrick Russo. I'm a staff photographer here. It's nice to meet you."

"Patrick?"

In a daze, she kept staring at his perfectly square teeth, thinking that they must have been cut this way, to order. The more he smiled at her, the less inclined she was to say another word.

"I'll take it personally if you don't eat that apple," he said with a wink that made her blush.

She had goosebumps as he walked away. Too distracted now to think straight, she had to set aside the story she'd been working on until she could collect her thoughts again and regain her concentration.

With a shock of embarrassment, she realized she had never introduced herself, not so much as said, "Hi, my name is Pilar." But his materializing before her like an apparition and placing that red apple on her desk like an offering had been enough to make her forget her own name. Oh, no, she remembered, I didn't even thank him for the apple. He must think I'm so rude.

At home that night, she replayed their entire exchange over and over in her mind until she was exhausted. She finally settled on sending him a thank-you e-mail the next day.

The following week, they were assigned to the same story. Patrick insisted on driving because all his equipment was in his Jeep, and "it would be a hassle to have to take it out."

Already, Pilar could sense that this man moved through the world effortlessly and had a natural and uncomplicated approach to every situation. Once they were in the car, he began to tell her about himself. He was a New Yorker, he said—"born and raised in Queens. You learn to be practical in New York."

Mostly she just listened as he talked.

On completing their assignment, at Patrick's suggestion, they went to Pete's Grill for burgers and beers. "It's a dive," he admitted, "but you'll love it! Best burgers in town."

Pilar had never been to a "dive" before, and she ordered wine instead of beer. But somehow, everything Patrick presented to her came tied in the red ribbon of his enthusiasm. She had never had as much fun with Rafael as she did with him that night. Shortly after that, they started dating.

His appetite for life was contagious. Urging her on, he often said to Pilar, "Dimples, let's go bite the world in the ass!" And looking forward to the next adventure, she would happily go along.

She especially loved listening to his stories. During the many walks they took along the river and the lakeshore, he told her about his childhood, about his sister, Karen, and about his mother, whom he loved "more than anyone in the world."

She learned that his favorite pastime growing up had been jumping subway turnstiles with his best friend, Eric. He laughed as he recalled their antics, that infectious laughter that was all Patrick. "I was a bad boy," he said. "But we never got caught, not once!"

And he told her about his first love, little Annie.

When Patrick was in kindergarten, his mother got a worried call one day from his teacher. It seemed that during recess that morning, when all the children were outside on the playground, Patrick had pulled down Annie's panties. "They were pink and had those little ruffles, you know?" he explained to Pilar. "What was I supposed to do?" He spoke these words with all the innocence and bewilderment of a naughty four-year-old who still, after all those years, could not comprehend the reason for the reprimand. Was he being serious? Pilar wondered.

When they had been seeing each other for a few weeks, he invited her back to his place, and with some trepidation, she went. To herself, she thought she would never get used to this business of being alone with a man in his apartment. But he wanted her to see his collection, he said, and she was intrigued.

"I have a lot of neon signs," he said. "The odder they are, the better I like 'em."

Even as a boy, Patrick said, he used to collect things: Yoo Hoo bottles, baseballs, torn ticket stubs from Yankee Stadium. When he grew up, his collector's habits remained the same, but his interests changed: now he sought out neon signs, especially from diners. "In this country, you have to go to a diner to get a really good burger, and to the ballpark for a hot dog," he lectured Pilar with all the gravity of a connoisseur.

His apartment wasn't like anything she had ever seen before. An efficiency basement with the feel of a warehouse, it had exposed redbrick walls out of which rolls of seamless black and gray paper spilled like waterfalls. Almost all of his work for the *Trib,* as he liked to call the newspaper, was done at the office using digital technology, but he did his hobby and freelance work at home, the old-fashioned way. To that end, he had converted his entire apartment into a photographer's studio in which he also lived. The tripod stands for his lights shared a corner with a rudimentary kitchen made up of a sink, a tiny fridge, and a two-burner electric hot plate. Because the bathroom had the only other sink, it served a dual purpose as well, as his darkroom. When he was developing film or prints, he put a towel under the door to keep out the light.

Right outside of the bathroom was a black and red futon where Patrick crashed after working late. But despite everything in it, the room was not without some artistic appeal, which Patrick had managed to achieve through the strategic use of light. Intended to cleverly hide some of the imperfections of the room, the casting of shadows resulted in a style he liked to call "accidental hip."

One of the things Pilar came to like best about going over to Patrick's was that every time she walked in, there was a different CD playing, depending on his mood. When he was working, he preferred early jazz, which filled the background without distracting him. And when he had to stay up late, Massive Attack would reverberate through the small but powerful speakers on the wall, Patrick's one true extravagance.

His much-cherished neon signs were carefully arranged on the floor on one side of the room. The only one that was lit up was his pride and joy, advertising Armour Hot Dogs, the food of choice at Wrigley Field. This was the sign that had inspired his whole collection, and he loved telling the story of its acquisition.

Driving by the ballpark one early-spring day, he'd spotted a pair of construction guys lugging an odd-shaped coil toward a Dumpster. He screeched to a stop and yelled to the men, "How much?"

Puzzled, they looked at each other for a second before one of them yelled back, "You mean this?" He hefted the twisted coil waist-high.

"Yeah—I'll take it from you," Patrick said, and then he asked again, "How much?"

"It's trash, man," the second man replied.

Taking that as his cue, Patrick leapt out of his Jeep, pulled two tens from his wallet, slapped one into each guy's hand, and, before they could object, sped off with the neon Armour Hot Dogs sign in the back of his Wrangler.

When he got home that night, he plugged in the sign and was thrilled to discover that it still worked. As the garish colors came to life, the neon tubes made an intermittent buzzing sound, as if there were a bunch of insects flying around inside. Patrick traced the shape of the hot-dog bun with his finger and marveled that from a distance, yellow and red neon could look almost like real mustard and ketchup.

After this coup, he was hooked. Addicted to hunting for signs to buy, photograph, or both, he seized every opportunity to travel to out-of-the-way places in search of examples from old diners. From time to time, he also came across other interesting signs that he described as relics. His red, white, and blue Esso was one of these, and Pink Martini was another, with its electric-green olive that had become a favorite photographic subject of his.

Captivated by these colorful displays of moving lights, with a child's sense of wonder, Patrick had taken photo after photo of each sign until he perfected his technique. After printing the pictures, he would hand-tint them with watercolors, making them look like old-fashioned portraits of the forgotten places he had visited.

"Patrick, they're wonderful. Have you ever exhibited them?" Pilar asked.

"No, not formally. Not many people have seen them—I really just take them for my own enjoyment." He thought for a moment, then said, "I do gigs for *American Photographer* every once in a while. Maybe I'll try to get some of these published in there one day."

Pilar nodded, but she couldn't help thinking that more than creating these photographs, what seemed to excite Patrick most was traveling to those faraway places and hunting down his unique collectibles. In most cases, the signs weren't for sale, and he'd have to convince the owners to part with their neon "relics." It was a true test of his persuasiveness and charm, and he loved every minute of it. He rarely left empty-handed.

Pilar would always cherish the memory of their first evening together at Patrick's apartment, when she sat on his futon and listened to the stories of some of his greatest finds. She had never met anyone like him, so eager simply to pick up and go without having any specific plan, without even knowing where he was going or when he would be back, clearly finding some thrill in the uncertainty of it all.

By the time he finished talking, Pilar knew she was falling for him. That night was the first time they made love.

The next morning, she learned of yet another of his talents when, still dreamy from the fantasy of the night before, she opened her eyes to see a shirtless Patrick standing beside the futon in his snug-fitting jeans. There was a paper towel draped over his arm and a plate in his hand, which he now presented to her with a proud smile and a little bow, as if he were both chef and waiter at the best restaurant in town. The ham-and-cheese omelet was one of the most delicious things she had ever tasted, even though she was not usually a fan of omelets. As she savored it, she thought of one of Patrick's favorite sayings: "If you wanna eat an omelet, Dimples, you gotta break a few eggs."

With Patrick, for the first time since she was a child, Pilar felt free to laugh, to be herself, to drop her guard. In her heart, she thanked him for that gift, as she would thank him for others in the months to come.

Indeed, the list of endearing things he did on her behalf would grow longer than she had ever imagined was possible. Some weekends, he even did her laundry for her because she disliked going down to the cold basement in her building, where the washers and driers were located. It astonished her that an American man would even do his *own* laundry, let alone his girlfriend's. Every time Patrick made the offer, she couldn't help thinking that a Latin man would slit his wrists before he would touch *anyone's* soiled clothes.

Then, too, Patrick delighted in taking her picture. The most exquisite were his photos of her face after they made love. He pointed out to her the "unusual shine" in her eyes in these portraits, and how happy and beautiful she looked. She was too modest to say so, but she agreed. It was more than just his skill as a photographer, though, for what he had captured was the luster that glows in the heart of a woman in love. His personal favorite among these pictures was the result of a bit of an ambush: one evening in bed, he had tried to photograph more than just Pilar's face, and she had grabbed the sheets to cover her naked body, and it was at that exact moment that the flash clicked. The portrait showed the most content and most shocked expression Patrick had ever seen on a grown woman.

Some evenings after work, he gave her foot massages. One at a time, he would take off her high heels, after much deliberate teasing:

"I don't see how you can even walk on these stilts. They're the reason your feet hurt." Holding one shoe by its instep, he would then use its skinny heel to softly caress her calves all the way up to her knees, at which point he would put down the shoe and continue on with his hands, which he moved like a guitar player's. Pilar would soon become so engrossed in his touch that she would forget all her self-consciousness over the foot massage.

Still, despite all the attention Patrick showered on her, Pilar always had the impression that there was something missing. It wasn't anything he'd said; he said a lot and spoke enthusiastically about almost everything. It was what he *hadn't* said that bothered her.

First of all, she'd noticed that he never used the word *we*; for Patrick, it was always *I*. If a coworker asked what he'd done over the weekend, for instance, even if he and Pilar had gone to see a movie together, he'd give a vague answer along the lines of "Caught a movie—how 'bout you?" She told herself it was because he wanted to keep their relationship private and not invite office gossip. But then there was the issue of special occasions, such as his birthday, which Patrick spent with his "buddies," and did not ask her to join him there, even when he knew she wasn't going home to Venezuela. After giving it much thought, she finally concluded that it must be one of those American things she didn't yet understand.

The night she got the call from Cristina about her nana, Pilar was a wreck. Immediately after hanging up with her mother, she dialed American Airlines and booked a round-trip ticket to Caracas. And then she phoned Patrick and asked him to come over, something she was generally too shy to do.

"I'll be right there, Dimples," he promised. "Just give me thirty minutes."

Before he arrived, Pilar tried to figure out what to pack for Nana's funeral, but she didn't get very far: less than half an hour after her call, the doorbell rang, and there was Patrick, wearing his usual suede jacket. "I'm sorry about your grandmother, Dimples. When do you leave?"

"Tomorrow morning."

"Need any help packing?"

She gave him a languid smile. "No." She shook her head. Then, "Maybe. I don't know."

They stood there hugging, the door barely closed behind them. Patrick cleared strands of Pilar's hair from her face until he uncovered her eyes, then softly kissed their lids, one at a time.

He followed her to the couch, where they sat and held each other for a few minutes. Then, slowly, with a questioning look in his eyes, he undid the first button of her blue silk blouse and gave her another kiss, this one on the lips. This kiss was deep, like an ocean; she could dive into it and forget everything else. With expert hands, he undid another button, then another, until she was aware of nothing beyond the fluid movement of two bodies that fit together like one. And with every movement, Pilar felt her sorrow ebb a little. Patrick's touch was like a poem: with every caress, he made her feel that each part of her body was a beautiful word meant to rhyme with every other. He traced the sloping curves of her breasts with the cadence of a verse. And then, with the barest touch, his fingers brushed her nipples lightly one more time before moving down to draw a line on her belly, then a pause, then on her waist, then all over. When he had strung all these words together, Pilar awoke from her dream and was able to read the poem he had written on her. Over the days to come, every time she thought of it she would fall in love all over again.

Afterward, she rested her head on his chest and took in that sweet smell of languorous love. She could imagine nothing more blissful than being in his arms.

Some time later, Patrick retrieved his T-shirt from the floor and offered it to her: "Here, you must be cold."

She took his shirt and put it on, and then she got up off the couch and started for her bedroom. "I guess I'd better pack," she said with a smile. "But you're welcome to stay if you'd like."

"You're sure you don't need any help?"

"I'm sure."

"OK. I'll hang out for a while."

Idly, Patrick picked up a thick hardback copy of *Don Quixote* that was sitting on the coffee table, opened it to the first page, and went to put his feet up. As he did so, he almost knocked over a crystal vase filled with pink rosebuds. "Phew," he exclaimed after Pilar leapt halfway across the room to steady it. "That was close!" Eyebrows raised, she nodded and headed back toward her room.

But she never made it there. Before she reached the door, she turned around, and there he was, standing right behind her, so close she could feel his breath on her forehead. In one fluid move, he pulled her over to a chair, sat on it, and lifted her onto his lap so she was facing him.

She looked into his eyes, intense, returning her gaze, then at his body, hot to the touch, making her rock, slowly at first, then the first drops, feeling like mist, followed by wriggles, it felt so sweet, her eyes tightly shut, she rode his rhythm, refrained, searching for something, fluid like rain, climbing again, her eyes still shut, she hid nothing, he fondled her breasts, she moaned, then held her breath, just for a moment, and then she bit her lips, searching for something she couldn't find, heaving, urgently now; she strained, arched and clutched, looking for more, slipping again, her eyes still shut, another sigh, a surge, her nipples now hard, her head thrown back, backward, then forward, euphoria, then the grip, the grip between her legs, the flushing heat; she dipped, rose, lingered . . . then plunged again, and in a thrall, pulled her own hair, a riot of movement, eyelids still closed, hungry still, thrusting up, another rush, longer this time, lashes squeezed tight, lifting once more, please one more time, his hands tight around her waist, holding her spasm, she wasn't alone, another moan, a small explosion, and before she collapsed, exhausted, into his arms, a last frantic aftershock, her eyes, opened at last, looked at the vase, that like crushed ice, lay scattered on the floor.

II

The **Chef**

There is no one who would have me—
I can't cook.

—GRETA GARBO

Secrets *of* the **Kitchen**

Mi querida nieta:

As a result of an earthly encounter, I learned the roundabout routes by which the fruits of the garden make their way into the kitchen, and discovered the answer to the question, *Why do we cook in the first place?*

Back from Eden, I craved to teach your mother about her past and her beginnings by sharing with her the recipes that had marked some of the most important events of my life. But my return to the kitchen was not easy. I wanted to show my daughter how to roll the perfect golfiados. I longed to tell her about how a woman finds her essence, and I yearned to share with her the heartwarming tale of my favorite cousin's wedding. But I never did. I had no taste for any of it. I wanted to feed him and him alone. It was in the absence of his nourishing love that I became acquainted with the other meaning of hunger.

One day, I realized that if I were ever to cook again as I had done in Macuto, I would have to forget. And at the same time, I would also have to remember. I would have to remember the love with which my favorite childhood meals had been prepared.

Through the loss of my appetite, I discovered the answer to my own question. Aside from cooking to ease our hunger, we cook to make those whom we love happy. When you concern yourself with the person who will consume your food as much as with the ingredients themselves, you will fill his heart as well as his plate.

From the memories I left behind, I also found that a big part of indulging another is to be able to transport that person through time and space with your food. Think about this for yourself. Isn't there some taste you can't forget? Isn't there some food that brings back a childhood memory and puts a smile on your face? Find out what your lover's favorite childhood taste was, and make it appear on his plate as if by magic.

To succeed in feeding another, you must also know that there are three ways to sate hunger: through the eyes, through the stomach, and through the heart. Now that you know this, with your own special touch, aim to feed your lover what he craves. Make use of all your senses, but pay special attention to your imagination, for it is the most powerful aphrodisiac of all.

Display a sunny mango on a plate or feed him small bites of the fruit from your lips, letting the juices run into his. . . . Delve into the heart of the matter, and you will have satiated him in all three ways.

As in life, there are a time and place for everything.

Nowhere are your manners more acutely on display than at the table. But you mustn't lose your appetite at the thought, for I will also impart to you the secret ingredients of etiquette.

One course after another, just as your food must be well seasoned, so must you yourself be in the rigors of the dinner table, lest you leave a bad taste in another's mouth by wearing on your person what rightly belongs on your plate.

Proper etiquette at even the most formal meal is merely a matter of observing the basic rules and, if you find yourself at a loss, watching to see what the hostess does. Once you have digested them, these rules will become second nature to you and will allow you to savor every meal and every occasion.

Sharing the memory of food with others is one of life's great pleasures. The experience will only be enhanced when you know what to expect and what is expected of you.

Enjoy these savory tales and the recipes that I have copied out for you. You will not be able to make them in exactly the same way I did, nor should you try. It is my greatest hope that you will instead find your own essence *and thereby fill your kitchen with the sweet aromas of love.*

Anyone who is willing to follow a recipe can cook, but only a woman's passion can sate her lover's hunger. When you feel moved to cook for someone, you will find, as I did, that the most precious ingredient in your kitchen is the one you mix with love.

Con amor,

Tu nana

uno: AT THE TABLE

When I was a child, my day began at six o'clock every morning. That was when Mayra, our kitchen maid, would begin preparing breakfast.

As soon as I smelled the aroma of freshly brewed coffee traveling lazily from the kitchen to my room, I knew that it was time for me to get up, and that Yamila would be along shortly to prod me into my morning rituals.

Then I would go downstairs to Mayra's delicious breakfast, elaborately served on a flawlessly set table and closely attended by her.

Back in those days, it was customary that a family's housemaid be sent to live in the house of the señorita who married first. The assumption was that the maid would have already mastered the kitchen routines and so could assist the young bride, who might well be overwhelmed by the task of setting up her new household. Prior to coming to work at our house, Mayra had been in the employ of Doña Victoria, my maternal grandmother.

Mayra was a gifted cook. I can still, just by thinking of them, almost taste her delectable *arepas,* made with fresh corn and served with *queso fresco,* and her perfect scrambled eggs.

One particular Saturday morning, I was tired and didn't feel like going through the elaborate routines of getting dressed, having my hair combed, and joining the family for breakfast, so when Yamila knocked on my bedroom door, I told her to go help my sisters instead. Then I went back to sleep. This was a mistake.

"*A desayunar,* Gabriela!"

When I heard my mother's voice booming down the hallway, I knew I was in trouble. The door burst open, and there she was.

"What's taking you so long? Look at that tangled mess you call your hair! And why aren't you dressed?"

"But Mami, it's Saturday. Why do I have to come down for breakfast if I don't feel like eating?"

"Because we're a family, that's why. Now please brush out those tangles and come downstairs, *now.* We're all waiting for you."

In our house, no meal could begin until every member of the family was seated at the table. My mother ran a scrupulous household in which manners mattered, in which food was to be enjoyed slowly and deliberately, and in which matters of taste must be fastidiously respected.

The conversation at our table was always pleasant and of a kind in which we could all take part. If one of us felt compelled to say something disagreeable, he or she had to wait until afterward, so that no one else's appetite would be spoiled. During meals, the talk had to flow like the pleasant breeze that blew through the kitchen window.

As I dragged myself down the three flights of stairs and wandered sheepishly into the dining room, I wondered what the point of it all could be. I wasn't even hungry. All of these rules felt like a heavy sack of flour falling on my head.

Once in the dining room, I felt everyone's eyes on me. The looks ranged from a kind of tolerant patience all the way to pity.

Although I was barely ten years old, Mayra greeted me as if I were an adult: "Good morning, Señorita Gabriela."

"*Buenos días,* Mayra."

"Would you like your *huevos revueltos,* señorita, or fried?"

I asked for the scrambled eggs, even though I didn't really like them. I just wanted to see her light the matches.

Before chopping the onions that would go into my eggs, Mayra would take a match out of the matchbox, light it, smell it for a few seconds, and blow out the flame. Then she would place the spent match between her teeth and hold it there to keep her eyes from watering. When she had a lot of onions to chop, she lit a lot of matches. That was what I liked about *huevos revueltos.*

A few minutes later, the smell of onions being sauteed in butter would fill the kitchen. When the onions sparkled, Mayra would add two beaten eggs and a trickle of cream, and begin scrambling with a wooden spoon. A few minutes before the eggs were done, she would remove the pan from the burner; that way they would finish cooking in the heat of the pan, and by the time she spooned them onto my plate, they'd be soft and moist.

When we had all been served and were ready to eat, Constanza, always mindful of manners and poise, winced at me and said, "*Hermana,* you're slouching off your chair."

My sister's charge was echoed by my mother: "Gabriela, why must you be so slovenly?"

Searching for some docility, I straightened up and smiled. But I'm sure I didn't fool my mother; she could always hear my loud thoughts.

Jacinta, eternally pleasant, only stared at her plate, a hint of pity on her face. Antonio, meanwhile, always my ally, winked at me. My brother's eyes were black like mine, and I could tell from his expression that in his wild heart, he was celebrating my small rebellion. With everyone at the table busy observing my every move, I thought to myself that not even the dining room was a safe haven from the prying eyes of decorum.

When we were finished eating, we all went back upstairs, except for my mother, who usually stayed on to give Mayra her next set of instructions for the day. Sometimes I loitered, trying to find out what we would be having for our next meal.

"Mayra, please make sure the plates are put away properly."

"*Sí,* Señora Grenales."

It was important to my mother that after every meal, the plates were stacked in order of size and put away, as if they had never been used.

"And Mayra, we'll be having lunch at Doña Victoria's today, so please don't bother cooking anything for us."

"*Está bien,* señora."

From all that went on in my mother's kitchen, I learned how great an impact rules can have on a person's character. They provide the discipline that develops our core—a discipline to which we might not otherwise wish to surrender.

Every single day, including Saturdays and Sundays, the routine remained the same: Yamila saw to it that I completed my compulsory beauty rituals; Mayra made breakfast and set the table, making sure each starched linen napkin was hugged tightly by a polished silver ring; and finally the entire family gathered, ready to eat.

With all this monotony of instruction came an odd sense of security and an almost innate craving for order. As a child, I found it burdensome, but when the time came for me to set up my own home, I followed my mother's example to the letter. Looking back, however, I'm not at all sure that was helpful for anyone. It wasn't until I was much older that I began to ask myself why we feel compelled to repeat what we are taught, even if we don't agree with it. By the time the answer came to me, I had already raised my daughter. This is why I want to pass on to you both things: the rules I was brought up to live by and the way I actually lived. This way, the choice will be yours.

My mother used to tell us that knowing what was the right thing to do was very different from being able to do it when the need arose, and that good manners came only through constant practice in the right way of doing things. That was why she posted the following guidelines for table manners on the kitchen door—so that whenever we entered the kitchen, we would be reminded of what was and was not permissible behavior at the table.

I can still hear her telling my sisters and me, "It is all about gentility, *niñas,* which goes beyond having money. Gentility is what is left over after the money is gone."

Throughout my life, I have tried to resist rules at every turn, but all the same, they have always stuck to me like glue.

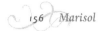

LOS BUENOS MODALES

Proper Posture

~Young people, when properly trained, should be easy and natural in their bearing at the table.

~Never slump in your chair, jiggle your legs, or play with your food.

~Sit up straight and keep your elbows off the table and close to your sides at all times.

~Each time you take a mouthful, lean over your plate. That way, if anything falls off your fork, it will end up on the plate and not on your clothes.

General Table Etiquette

~Always arrive promptly for meals.

~At the table, remain standing until everyone has arrived.

~It is customary for a man to help the lady on his left to be seated.

~Never read at the table unless you are alone.

~At a formal meal, food is always served from the diner's left.

~If you don't care for a dish that you are served, you may politely refuse it.

~Do not start eating until everyone has been served, unless the hostess invites you to do so. In that case, you must oblige her.

~Be sure to compliment the chef.

~If you must leave the table during the meal, politely excuse yourself.

~Do not push your plate away when you have finished eating; it is very rude to do so.

~Keep your mouth closed while chewing your food. Remember, you are not trying to load hay into a barn to beat the rain.

~Do not slurp or make any other unattractive noises when eating.

~Never talk with your mouth full.

~It is perfectly appropriate to use your fingers to remove olive pits or fish bones from your mouth.

Dining Protocol

~Silverware is generally arranged in the order of its use, from the outside in. If you realize you have made a mistake and instead picked up the utensil closest to the plate, do not try to exchange it; simply continue eating. Do not put a utensil back on the table after you have used it.

~In a simple table setting, the knife goes to the right of the plate, the fork to the left. The napkin is placed to the left of the fork. When soup is to be served, the soup spoon goes next to the knife.

~Utensils are not weapons. It is permissible to talk while holding a knife and fork, but not to gesture with them or wave them around.

~When using a fork, rest it on your middle finger and guide it with your index finger and thumb, keeping the thumb on top. Never use your fork as a shovel.

~Never raise your knife more than five centimeters above your plate.

~Always cut your food into bite-sized pieces, one piece at a time.

~Never rest your silverware to the sides of your plate. Instead, rest the knife across the plate, blade facing in, handle on the rim.

~If you have not yet finished eating but wish to rest your knife and fork, you must cross them on your plate, with the fork over the knife, prongs down.

~When not using your knife and fork, keep your hands in your lap.

~If you wish to take a drink, eat some bread, or dab your mouth, you must place your knife and fork in the rest position described above.

~When you have finished eating, you must always place your knife and fork side by side on your plate, with the prongs of the fork pointing up and the blade of the knife facing the fork.

Handling Cutlery

~There are two ways of handling cutlery properly: the American style and the European. While both are perfectly acceptable, the American style is less efficient and can appear awkward.

~In the American style, the knife is held only when cutting. It should be grasped with your right hand, and the fork with your left, prongs down, to hold in place the food you wish to cut. When you have finished cutting, you must rest the knife on the edge of your plate (blade facing in) and switch the fork to your right hand to lift the cut piece to your mouth.

~In the European style, the knife remains in your right hand and the fork in your left, its prongs facing downward, when you lift the cut food to your mouth. The fork is not shifted back and forth every time you cut a piece.

dos: LOS GOLFIADOS

As far back as I can remember, almost every Saturday after breakfast, my mother would take us to her mother's house for either lunch or *merienda,* the equivalent of an English tea.

The kitchen was always the center of activity at my grandmother's, but especially on those days when "all her girls," as Doña Victoria used to call us, gathered to make Venezuelan *golfiados* for the afternoon *merienda.*

"Good morning, Doña Victoria."

"Good morning, Jacinta."

"*Buenos días,* Doña Victoria. Does this day find you well?"

"Yes, thank you, Constanza. You are always so polite, my dear. But where is your sister Gabriela?"

Not far behind, I overheard Constanza's reply: "She'll be along in a minute, *Abuela.* You know how she hates to follow anyone."

I owe my love of cooking in large part to my grandmother, Doña Victoria. Her wonderful meals, carefully prepared and exquisitely served by her, always had an aura of bygone days. For me, the joy of living was wrapped up in the delight of rolling *golfiados* in her kitchen. When fresh out of the oven, these spongy cinnamon spirals melted sweetly on our tongues; had I not known better, I would have thought they were filled with air.

While the men went to the cockfights, all the women would crowd around the stove, where Doña Victoria presided as queen of the realm, ready to make pastries for every Saturday afternoon's *merienda.*

Much like the English afternoon tea, *la merienda* is an hour-long—sometimes longer—seated affair, at which the family enjoys homemade pastries and *café con leche.* Black coffee, or *café negro,* is and has always been preferred by the natives, for the coffee bean is indigenous to our country. But after the conquistadores arrived in Venezuela in 1498, they began to add milk to the potent local brew in an effort to soften its effects. Thus, sadly, our delicious *café con leche* is frothed with tasteless racist undertones.

For nearly fifty years, Doña Victoria managed to keep the burner going, as it were. It is to her that I owe the understanding that, whether or not we like it, life moves at its own pace.

Whenever we made *golfiados,* it seemed to take an eternity for the dough to rise. I can still hear Doña Victoria telling me, "*Paciencia,* Gabriela. Your watching it isn't going to make it rise any faster. Let it be."

In addition to patience, the secret of good *golfiados* lies in the *melado,* the sweet, sticky essence of sugarcane that, once melted, drips from these treats like *savia* from a tree. *Papelón,* the most important ingredient in these uniquely Venezuelan sweet rolls, is one of those local delicacies that cannot be bought at the market; it must instead be obtained through the networks of contacts maintained by those who harvest it from the land. That is, unless one is fortunate enough, like Doña Victoria, to own the land oneself.

LOS GOLFIADOS DE
DOÑA VICTORIA CONTRERAS

Ingredientes

½ tsp. yeast
¼ cup warm water
1 cup milk
1 tsp. salt
3 tbs. sugar
3½ cups flour
2 egg yolks
3 tbs. vegetable oil
½ cup butter, melted
1¼ cups grated *papelón* (if you can't find *papelón*, you may use brown sugar instead), plus ½ cup, melted, for topping
¾ cup grated *queso blanco duro*
Breadcrumbs
1 tbs. butter
½ cup water
½ cup grated *queso blanco duro* for topping

Preparación

1. Place yeast and warm water in a glass bowl for about 15 minutes, until yeast rises.

2. Bring milk, salt, and sugar to a boil, then remove from flame and set aside to cool. While mixture is still warm, add yeast, 3 cups of flour, egg yolks, and oil. Mix well. On a flat surface, knead dough over remaining ½ cup of flour until it no longer sticks. Place dough in a bowl, cover, and set aside for three hours until it has doubled in size.

3. Remove dough from bowl. With a rolling pin, make a rectangle about ½ inch thick. Brush with melted butter. Sprinkle with *papelón* and grated

queso and roll dough loosely away from your-self. Cut into 1-inch slices.

4. Butter a baking dish and cover with a thin layer of breadcrumbs. Place the slices flat on the dish, about ½ inch apart. Brush with leftover melted butter. Cover with a kitchen towel and set aside for 45 minutes.

5. Preheat oven to 425 degrees.

6. Bake for 15 minutes. Remove from oven and spread melted *papelón* and remainder of grated *queso* on top.

7. Let cool for 5 minutes before serving on a silver platter lined with wax paper. Enjoy with hot *café con leche* at the time of the *merienda*.

MAKES 25 GOLFIADOS.

tres: *PARRILLADAS LLANERAS*

When the time came to celebrate a birthday, wedding, or anniversary, the two sides of my family came together at my grandfather's hacienda in the Valles del Tuy for *parrilladas llaneras,* so called because they are traditionally cooked over an open fire, or *a la parrilla.*

On these special occasions, the men of the family would fire up the coals to re-create with sizzling pieces of grilled *churrasco,* chorizo, chicken, and corn the fabled flavors for which the *llaneros,* the rogue Venezuelan *rancheros,* are renowned.

The mandatory accompaniments to this feast were *cerveza fría,* much talk of soccer and politics, and, among the women, the sharing of recipes for *guasacaca,* the colorful blend of fresh avocados, garlic, and cilantro that was spread over the *carne asada* as soon as it came off the grill, to drip like liquid emeralds on the serving plates.

When I reflect on the most important moments of my life, I inevitably recall the smell of *churrasco* steaks roasted over an open fire. Seeing the men cut strips of meat with silver knives and place them directly on slabs of grilled bread, I felt a part of the almost mythical history of those who owned the land, my family included. Because our country has long been defined by its ability to produce enormous quantities of high-quality beef, *parrilladas* always inspired in me great pride that my family had played such a vital role in the development of the Venezuelan economy over the first half of the twentieth century. *Parrilladas* are as much a part of our culture as dance, unbridled politics, and pious Catholicism. And like those perfectly grilled *tiras de asado,* my family's *parrilladas* had all the sizzling heat that kept these memories alive like a constant open fire.

While the men drank beer and prepared the grill, the women

of the family would busy themselves in the kitchen making *contornos,* the side dishes that put the finishing touches on the grilled meats. The *contornos* always gave them an excuse to gather in the kitchen and gossip.

To be complete, a *parrillada* must include *caraotas negras* (the black beans that symbolize fertility and procreation), *guasacaca fresca,* and perfect white rice.

On the day we arrived at the hacienda, starting the beans was always our first priority because they had to soak overnight. Making black beans for a big *parrillada* was always an orderly procedure. First we scooped the beans into a big funnel made out of a rolled-up newspaper, which allowed us to spread them evenly over the kitchen table. Then we picked out all the blades of grass and little stones. As we picked and sorted, we chatted, gossiped, and talked above the radio.

We made black bean soup in honor of an ancient fertility ritual, so sacred that no menstruating woman was ever allowed to touch the beans, because during her time of the month, a woman is not able to conceive and would therefore spoil the others' chances at creating life.

Once the beans had been cleaned and every woman in the kitchen had administered a healthy dose of advice to every other, usually all of them talking at the same time, it was my job to place the beans in a pot, cover them with water, and add a tablespoon of bisodium carbonate to soften them. As soon as I had put the lid on the pot for the night, I began a mental countdown until the moment when Doña Victoria's *sofrito* would begin to fill the hacienda's kitchen with the rich smell of onion, garlic, and peppers frying in cumin oil.

When the *sofrito* was ready and the beans were simmering on the stove, we turned our attention to making the *guasacaca.* This green *mojo* may be found on every Venezuelan table, and almost every woman in the country has her own recipe for it, which leads to many interesting discussions about whose *guasacaca* is best. Like most everything in the kitchen, it's a matter of taste.

I was introduced to the making of *guasacaca* by watching my cousin Clara. She made it instinctively, with practiced ease, while we talked in the kitchen; she didn't even have to think about it.

Clara's secret ingredient was a few drops of orange juice. When I asked her why she used orange instead of lime juice, she just said, "It's my essence. You'll find your own one day, don't worry. Just keep trying different things." Then she added, "You'll find your essence when you cook for someone you love."

She was right: eventually, I did find my essence, that special touch that distinguishes one woman's cooking from every other's.

Whereas letting one's creative juices flow is the key to the perfect *guasacaca,* stirring the pot in which the rice is cooking is a sticky business.

"The secret to fluffy rice is to leave it alone, Gabriela. Just pour in the water and leave it alone": this was Doña Victoria's advice, and indeed, all who ate her rice marveled that they could almost count each individual grain on the plate.

"But I like stirring the pot, *Abuela,*" I said.

"That you do, Gabriela, that you do."

From plain white rice I learned more than I could ever have imagined I would. In rice I found the hidden beauty of simplicity and the overlooked importance of ceremony, because in our family, without rice, a celebration did not deserve any mention.

Whether served as sweet *arroz con leche* for a baptism, thrown at a new bride to celebrate her wedding, or cooked simply as *arroz blanco* for a big *parrillada,* rice would throughout my life continue to constitute the most basic and constant of ingredients.

"An accomplished cook does not need to measure the water to

produce loose, fluffy rice. But it is essential to leave it alone," Doña Victoria repeated, trying to stamp this lesson onto my brain. I guess my sweet grandmother must have known me well, for in my entire life, it would never occur to me to leave anything alone.

"How do you know how much water to add, *Abuela?*"

"Just enough to allow a wooden spoon to stand upright in the middle of the pan—like this. See?" She inserted a wooden spoon into the pot, and to my amazement, the spoon stood.

Because this was how I learned to do it, I always preferred this method to measuring out the water, but most women favor the latter, especially when using round-grain rice, which can get very sticky when the quantity exceeds two cups.

"I thought you said to leave it alone, *Abuela,*" I asked when I noticed that she was adding lime juice to the water.

"I did. This is the last thing I'll do before I let it be. The lime juice will break down the starch and prevent the rice from sticking. *Now* we can leave it alone."

"I see."

Once they were finished in the kitchen, the women took great pride in laying out festive linens and dishes and gathering fresh bougainvillea to arrange on the long tables that would accommodate the overflow of life.

The simplicity of *parrilladas* is perhaps what makes them so alluring. Besides bringing everyone in the family together, they call for only a few ingredients—good beef, chicken, chorizo, and corn—and a patient *asador,* a man ever ready to turn the meat over the coals. Of course, a *very hot* flame, as my father used to say, is also required.

Papi was right: the trick to perfectly grilled meat is indeed a very hot grill. To make the meat more aromatic, my father sometimes strewed orange and guava peels over the coals, but this was not the sort of thing with which any woman ever had to concern herself. It was always left to the men of the house.

PARRILLADA LLANERA

Ingredientes

2 cups oak chips
1 cup dry white wine
1 cup olive oil
½ cup fresh lime juice
3 tsp. dry oregano
1 tsp. crushed red
  pepper
2 tsp. coarse sea salt
⅛ tsp. black pepper

4 garlic cloves, minced
2 tsp. oil, to coat grill

CARNES
2–3 lbs. *churrasco* or
  other meat cut of
  your preference
2 medium chickens, cut
  into pieces

Preparación

1. Soak oak chips in water for 24 hours. Drain well.

2. Combine wine and other ingredients and whisk until well blended. Pour half of this mixture over meat and chicken and marinate for 6 hours or more.

3. Place oak chips atop charcoal and coat grill with oil.*

4. Grill each piece of chicken for 12 minutes on each side, turning frequently to prevent burning, and basting often with remainder of wine mixture. Chicken is ready when no pink liquid appears when pierced with a fork.

*This was how my father used to prepare the fire. The secret to getting stripes on the meat, he confided, was having a *very hot* grill.

5. Grill *churrasco* for about 10 minutes on each side, or to desired degree of doneness. Let stand for 5 minutes. Cut across grain into thin slices.

6. Slather *guasacaca fresca* over meats. Serve with black beans and fluffy white rice.

THIS IS A SMALL *parrillada*, FOR 4–6 PEOPLE, DEPENDING ON HOW HUNGRY THEY ARE!

CARAOTAS NEGRAS

Ingredientes

1 lb. dried black beans, soaked overnight in a large pot with 3 qts. water and 1 tbs. baking soda
10 cups chicken stock
½ cup olive oil
2 onions, finely chopped

2 large red bell peppers, seeded and chopped
4 cloves garlic, minced
2 tbs. ground cumin
2 tbs. salt
1 tbs. of sugar
1 cup fresh chopped cilantro, for garnish

Preparación

1. Discard soaking water and wash beans. Keep beans in pot and add enough of the chicken stock to cover.

2. Bring chicken stock and beans to a rapid boil for 1 minute. Reduce heat and simmer 2–3 hours.

3. Meanwhile, heat olive oil in a skillet. Sauté onions and bell peppers, stirring with a wooden spoon, for about 10 minutes.

4. Add garlic and cumin to skillet and cook for another 2 minutes. Let cool for a few minutes before adding to the beans.

5. When the beans are almost tender, add salt and sugar and cook for another 30 minutes, or until done. If necessary, correct seasoning with salt and pepper.

6. Garnish with chopped cilantro and serve.

SERVES 4–6 AT
A *PARRILLADA* CELEBRATION.

LUSCIOUS *GUASACACA*

Ingredientes

2 large avocados, peeled and cut into small cubes

1 yellow onion, finely chopped

2 cloves garlic, minced

½ green bell pepper, chopped

½ cup white vinegar

1 tsp. salt

½ tsp. pepper

Juice of 1 lime

¾ cup olive oil

½ cup cilantro, finely chopped

Preparación

1. In a large kitchen bowl, mix avocados with onion, garlic, green bell pepper, vinegar, salt, pepper, and lime juice.

2. Slowly add olive oil to mixture, whisking with a fork until all ingredients are mixed well.

3. Gently fold in cilantro with a wooden spoon until *guasacaca* begins to glisten like liquid emeralds.

4. Pour into a clear bowl and spread over grilled steaks, chicken, or corn.

MAKES ENOUGH FOR
A SMALL *PARRILLADA*.

ARROZ PERFECTO

Ingredientes

2 cups long-grain white
   rice
2 tbs. butter
4 cups unsalted chicken
   broth

2–4 drops lime juice
   (white vinegar may
   be substituted)
1 clove garlic
2 tsp. salt

Preparación

1. Wash rice under hot tap water. Drain.
2. In a small pan, melt butter.
3. Add rice and stir until slightly toasted but not brown.
4. Stir in remaining ingredients.
5. Bring to a boil. Cover, reduce heat, and, as Doña Victoria said, "leave it alone."
6. Cook for 15–20 minutes, until all liquid is absorbed. Fluff with a fork before serving.

SERVES 4–6 AT A *PARRILLADA*.

cuatro: CHIRIMOYA CREAM

Most years, we spent *semana de carnaval* at my parents' house in the town of Macuto.

Macuto's setting casts a magic spell on all its visitors. White-sand beaches fringe a sea stippled with periwinkle, while farther inland, blooming tropical trees wrap as if by chance around blue-green hills that descend majestically to flower-filled villages. Some of the trees are more than a thousand years old and twist out of the ground like Balinese dancers.

This heart-stopping jewel of the Caribbean, a paradise that no visitor has ever willingly left, is also home to the world's sweetest fruit, the chirimoya.

As children, my brother and sisters and I would clamber along the limestone terraces ribboning the nearby hills, where the air was scented by mango and passionfruit trees. From way up there, we could just barely see our house, a seventeenth-century Moorish structure that my father had restored to its original grandeur.

One year during carnival week, while our parents were entertaining guests, the four of us, along with Carmela and Jorge Armando, climbed to the top of the hill behind our house to play a game of *abacanto* among the tropical trees. Jorge Armando and his sister knew this challenging terrain well because their parents, too, had a place in Macuto, right next to ours. Back in those days, many families from Caracas owned second homes there.

That afternoon still lingers in my memory, for it was then that I learned the secret to eating a chirimoya.

Inspired by the asynchronous song of the native *tucánes* and *turpiales* and by the hovering scent of ripening fruit, Jorge

Armando plucked from a tree a plump chirimoya the size of his hand and invited us all to partake in the unforgettable sensation of sucking on the fruit's soft flesh.

There could have been no sight more seductive to a girl of fourteen than that of a flirtatious eighteen-year-old giving himself to a fruit with such obvious pleasure. Utterly entranced, I could not help but stare at him. I wanted to meet his eyes, which were as rich and dark as the soil beneath him but I was afraid that if I looked into them, I might suffer the same fate as the fruit. And then, as we ate, he began to regale us with a story unlike any I had ever heard, a story as ripe with suggestion as the flesh of the chirimoya itself.

At dusk, we made our way back down to our house, where I asked Jorge Armando to write down for me the tale of the chirimoya. Perfect gentleman that he was, even at that tender age, he complied.

Several days later, I received the following letter from him. Not yet aware that I had just had my first experience of pure, seeping lust, I nevertheless saved this missive, which would later be the only one of Jorge Armando's to survive my father's wrath. I have it still.

8 de Agosto de 1939
Querida piel de canela:

I am flattered that my chirimoya tale invited the color of pudor to your cheeks. Call me a devil, but it is always a pleasure to disarm a young woman, especially with something as harmless as a fruit.

I would not dream of refusing your request. Otherwise, who knows how you might preserve my innocent story in your mind? This thought alone was enough to make me put pen to paper as soon as I returned from Macuto.

Here it is, querida—*the story I told you, and a little more.*

Just promise me one thing: not a word of this to my sister or your brother. I will hold you to this promise, or else . . .

Legend has it that back in the sixteenth century, the village maidens of Macuto had to be closely guarded when the servants were outside gathering chirimoyas.

When ripe, this modest emerald-green fruit naturally releases a sweet, creamy essence, a nectar so alluring in its striking resemblance to a woman's gift that in chirimoya-gathering season, the air around Macuto is filled with lust.

I have it on good authority that only the tender persistence of a gentle hand, combined with the delicate touch of a fluttering tongue, can induce the bare fruit's tightly woven honeycomb to part with its innocence.

The stunning beauty that lies hidden at the chirimoya's core is not to be revealed to the squeamish. Only the lips of the right suitor will persevere to overcome the fruit's mild resistance, eventually to discover that the velvety white flesh pours out a honey-like cream with a sweet fragrance all its own, the just reward for a lover's efforts.

The secret is to be gentle but without hesitation, to dismiss any feelings of shame, and to embrace the pleasure with immodest determination.

This is one of those rare occasions when a luscious fruit tempts one's tongue, and one's tongue longs to return the favor.

Mil besos,
Jorge Armando

I did not know quite what to make of the curious mix of emotions that Jorge Armando's letter aroused in me. What schoolgirl of fourteen would? But had I been able to put words to my feelings, I expect they would have been as dithering and fickle as the tingle you feel when you first have a new experience: you wonder if it's all right that something so pleasurable is going on inside you, or if you should keep it a secret from everyone until you can figure out exactly what it is. In the end, reluctant to ask anyone else about it for fear of seeming naive, I decided to keep my feelings to myself, only to discover years later that my first intriguing encounter with raw desire had also been my first encounter with life.

cinco: DRINKING PARTIES

The ladies were not invited.

At these rollicking affairs where the freedom of male expression was sovereign, the women had to be content with doing most of the work while their brothers, fathers, uncles, and husbands went on and on about their secret dalliances, native erotica, the seduction of unwilling hearts, and the sexual urges of the fairer sex, with enough derring-do to fray the nerves of even the most faithful of wives.

A typical drinking party was held in a private home and organized for a man and his friends by his wife, with the assistance of her housemaids.

Ladies were welcome to be on hand in the early afternoon and to be occasionally visible thereafter as ornamental fixtures, but they were not to participate in either the drinking or the games that followed. This was just as well, for the men's society inevitably became odious after they had ingested a few drinks. Most women were grateful for the clement measure of their compulsory yet mercifully brief attendance, though it usually took them hours of beautification to get ready for it.

Thanks to my father's brothers, who had a great many friends, I was able to be present at a number of these parties. I remember eagerly helping to make some of the concoctions, and I credit to my participation both the refinement of my skills as a chef and my enviable knowledge of aphrodisiacs.

My brother, Antonio, remains to this day an enthusiastic frequenter of drinking parties, for he is an ace at dominoes and loves to win at absolutely everything. When the parties were hosted at our house, unable to sleep from a nagging curiosity, I waited until everyone had left and before drifting away to the sleepy world of dreams, I intercepted Antonio and made him share in vivid detail the unedited versions of the pleasures of his youth. During those nights of filial complicity, my brother would share tales so colorful that I was grateful it was night time so he could not see me blush. My dear brother, as prone to bragging as every *hombre* born in our country, considered the satisfaction of my curiosity both a duty and an honor: I was always his favorite sister, and as he saw it, the more I knew about the ways of men, the less susceptible I would be to their repertoire of seductions. But instead, his stories had the opposite effect, awakening in me an almost irrepressible fascination with the mysteries of the night and intensifing my curiosity about those times when men spent their nights forging the stories that would confirm their reputations as *puros machos Latinos.*

The native concoctions served at a drinking party often included *tisana Venezolana,* a punch inspired by sangría but made with fresh mango, pineapple, and passionfruit juices and spiced with dark Caribbean rum, and such aphrodisiac potions as the savory *pavita Trujillana,* an elixir that tastes like roasted vanilla and is reputed to increase a man's stamina and sexual prowess.

The star of one memorable evening of drinking was my uncle Raul. The father of my cousin Clara, Raul was the most ill-behaved of my father's seven brothers. As Antonio told it, at this particular party, Uncle Raul mixed a tangy blend of crushed ice, yerbabuena leaves, and raw sugarcane and instructed all the other men to take a big sip and hold it in their mouth. With this delectable drink, he said, a man could make a woman writhe with pleasure. The mint would cause her to tingle, and the unexpected chill of her lover's tongue would double her pleasure—if, that is, he managed to remember, along with everything else, to move his flitting tongue like the wings of a fluttering butterfly.

Later, as the evening was winding down, *Tío* Raul again bragged that he was the king of cunnilingus and, to prove his point, proceeded to stun every man in the room by sucking, before the crowd's disbelieving eyes, every bit of flesh from a fresh *mamón,* a nearly impossible task.

The *mamón* is about the size of a grape and grows tightly wrapped in a greenish shell that must be snapped open to release the fruit. With the texture of cornsilk, the shell's delicate pink center has a succulence that makes one's mouth water even before one tastes its tender flesh. For anyone wishing to suckle ripe juice, *mamón* is the only fruit.

Once shelled, the *mamón* splits evenly into two parts, its luscious garden now peeking eagerly from the top, yet remaining closed around the bottom. It is a strange, isolated, claustrophobic little fruit.

By the time my uncle Raul had finished separating the slippery pinkish silk from the stubborn seed without ever letting the fruit slip from his tongue—a nearly impossible feat—the wild uproar of earlier had hushed into apprentice awe.

At the conclusion of my brother's accounts, I used to wonder if I would ever be able to taste men's passion for life and all the things that made it sweeter. When, much later, I was able to appreciate the meaning of Uncle Raul's story, I was captivated because only then did I understand that when a dream of desire is rivaled by the riveting experience of it, the memory of both forever transcends surreal bliss.

seis: A SEASONED CHEF

"It was the paella, you know. . . ."

And with the memory of that incomparable dish still fresh in his mind, my uncle Raul closed his eyes and shared with me the story of how young Carlos Tavares had won my cousin Clara's hand.

My uncle was proud of the fact that his family had been prominent in Venezuelan society, and more specifically in Caracas, for generations. The city's picturesque cobblestoned streets and centuries-old red-roofed houses, many retaining their original doors and windows, spoke to him of deeply rooted traditions.

While the Spanish conquistadores discovered the lush coasts of Venezuela at the end of the fourteen hundreds, it was not until the next century that they ventured to colonize the interior. The indigenous tribes that occupied the territory tried to resist them, but to no avail. In the year 1567, Diego de Lozada led an expedition into Caracas and rechristened it Santiago de León de Caracas. Santiago was the name of a Spanish apostle and military saint; León was the name of the province's colonial governor at the time. The Ponce de León and the Caracas were the local native tribes, whose efforts to resist Spanish occupation have their legacy in the cocksure attitude of the city's people down to this very day.

Our country's natural resources and our people's uncommon ancestral mix have always inspired indulgence in the exotic worship of irresistible pleasures. In much the same way that the mingling of Indian and Spanish blood has produced women whose exquisite beauty men find it difficult to resist, so, too, does Venezuelan food offer a feast for the senses, by seasoning native ingredients with the flavor of the Spanish heritage.

Uncle Raul counted among his greatest treasures his three beautiful daughters, my cousins Clara, Corina, and Ercilia, whose beauty was as rare as that of the natural landscape into which they were born.

When Clara reached a marriageable age, her father issued a challenge to any man within the family's social circle who would be brave enough to ask for his favorite daughter's hand in matrimony. Young Carlos Tavares accepted this challenge.

Doña Marquesa Tavares, the mother of the prospective groom, was to prepare a meal that would prove that her son was the right man for my uncle's daughter. Whatever dish she chose was at once to underscore the natural bounty of our homeland and to sate the ravenous appetites of the *familia* Grenales.

The judges for this test would be, in addition to my uncle Raul, his wife, Mariela, and their three girls, Raul's seven rowdy brothers and their wives, for a total of nineteen guests.

As is customary in Venezuelan families, Clara's uncles were expected to play an active role in ensuring that she ended up with the right husband. If his mother's cooking failed either to indulge their senses or to honor tradition in every way, the engagement would be off.

Doña Marquesa, a legend in her own right, was no stranger to romance, and she was determined to help her son win my cousin's hand. Of all the cousins on both sides of my family, Clara would be the first to marry, so all eyes were upon her—and on her potential mother-in-law.

The menu that Doña Marquesa planned for the occasion was a tribute to Spain's major culinary contribution to the world:

vibrant flavors and colors derived from natural ingredients through the use of time-honored techniques.

Early on, Doña Marquesa decided that the main course would have to be her famous paella Valenciana, a traditional Spanish dish infused with saffron, the most delicate of spices. Her wonderfully old-fashioned recipe was famous for its ability to warm even the most reluctant heart and to satisfy the fussiest appetite.

The rich and colorful paella is one of the most difficult of dishes to master; indeed, many culinary careers have been ruined in the quest for the perfect paella. Without patience and correct technique, the rice will turn to curd and stick to the palate like glue. But with the proper touch, this dish becomes a rare indulgence for the senses. In the warmth of the oven, the varied array of *frutas del mar,* sensually spread over a bed of rice, releases its essence and bathes the golden grains in the rich flavors of the sea.

When the appointed evening finally arrived and all the guests were seated at Doña Marquesa's table, the air was charged with anticipation. After the paella was served, everyone ate in complete silence. This was most unusual, for no Grenales gathering was conceivable without boisterous remarks and constant roars of laughter.

When he had finished eating, my uncle Raul pushed his plate away and looked around the table. His eyes fixed on Doña Marquesa for a full half minute before shifting to his oldest daughter. A daring and rebellious soul just like her father, Clara held his gaze and said, "Well, then? What's the verdict, Papi?"

Everyone at the table waited for my uncle to say something, anything. But he didn't. Poor Carlos was nervous and fidgety, but Doña Marquesa just watched Raul placidly, her composure completely intact.

Seconds more passed in absolute silence. And then, finally: "May I please have some more?" my uncle asked. On hearing these words, everyone breathed again and began talking and laughing.

The Grenales challenge concluded with a *brindis* of sangría in honor of the now "officially" engaged couple.

The secret ingredient in Doña Marquesa's sangría was Jerez. This sweet liqueur takes its name from the famous town in southern Spain where some of that country's best *bodegas,* or wineries, have perfected the making of wines and brandies over generations.

While many consider this sweet cordial the brandy of Spain, the proud people of Jerez call it by its name of origin and reserve the name brandy for the similar liqueur made in France. Some sangrías are prepared without it, but the Jerez is what gives Doña Marquesa's its luster. When held up in a glass against the light, this lustrous liquid looks as if it were made out of polished cherries.

". . . and so it was that Carlos Tavares won my Clara's hand," Uncle Raul concluded with a sigh.

"*Tío,* did you at least get the recipe for the paella?" I asked.

"Why would I want the recipe?" he demanded in a gruff voice.

"For *Tía* Mariela."

I knew that any woman would count it as a victory to acquire another's secret recipes. But my uncle didn't seem to understand what I was getting at; he just sat there and stared at me in silence, shaking his head from side to side.

Not long after that, only a few weeks prior to my own wedding, I learned the truth about the paella recipe from Clara herself.

"*Of course* he tried to coax it out of Doña Marquesa that night, *querida prima.* But my father is far too proud to admit that he lost the challenge, his daughter, and his bid for the recipe all in one day. He was so sure that no suitor would agree to his conditions, and even surer that no mother could meet them." Clara smiled one of her sly smiles and then exclaimed, "How very little Papi knows about women!"

"Why do you say that?"

"Well, after Carlos and I were married, Papi again asked Doña Marquesa if she would write down the recipe for him. He said he wanted it for my mother."

"So what happened?"

"Well, believe it or not, Doña Marquesa turned him down a second time. She told him that sharing her recipe would bring bad luck."

"Bad luck?"

"Yes, she's very superstitious . . . or so she told Papi. She said it could destroy our marriage—it'd be a bad omen, that was how she put it. Can you believe it?" Clara started laughing her infectious laugh, just like her father's.

I laughed along with her. "Did he accept that?"

"He had no choice. But when he told me what she'd said, I just *knew.* Carlos's mother is every bit as proud as Papi. She had no intention of giving him her recipe! And probably she wanted to get back at him for thinking up that stupid challenge in the first place."

There was one more thing I'd been wondering about: "How did Doña Marquesa know that paella was *the* dish, Clara? And why was she so certain it would work?"

My cousin winked at me and said, "*Querida prima,* are you entirely without guile? *I* told her that paella was Papi's favorite!"

I was well acquainted with Clara's ways—she had always been my favorite cousin—so I wasn't terribly surprised by her admission. With her charm and her easy smile, she always managed to get what she wanted.

"Oh, and before I forget, *prima,* I got the recipes for you—the paella *and* the sangría. Here."

Out of her small purse, Clara pulled two pieces of paper that she handed to me.

I took them from her and asked, "How did you manage *this?*"

"I simply confided to Doña Marquesa that I needed her help in sealing another union. People love it when you ask them to help, you know. And besides, she's a romantic, just like you and me."

"What union are you talking about?"

"Why, *yours,* silly! I told her you wanted to warm the heart of an Englishman. Isn't that clever? I mean, I had to tell her *something,* and you never *did* say why you wanted the paella recipe."

"I guess I didn't, did I?"

"So?"

"So what?"

"*Prima* Gabriela, tell me the truth. Why did you want it?"

Without a trace of conviction, I said, "I guess . . . to warm the heart of an Englishman."

But we both knew I was lying.

DOÑA MARQUESA'S
PAELLA VALENCIANA

Ingredientes

1 whole chicken, cut in
  pieces
½ cup olive oil
1 lb. pork, cut into small
  cubes
½ lb. chorizo sausage,
  cut into small cubes
2 cups onion, chopped
4 cloves garlic, crushed
½ tsp. pepper
1 tsp. dried oregano
2 tsp. salt
1½ cups white or
  Arborio rice

½ tsp. saffron
3 tomatoes, peeled and
  chopped
1 bay leaf
3 cups chicken broth
1 lb. *langostinos frescos*
  (peeled, with tails left
  on)
½ lb. fresh black
  mussels
½ cup fresh green peas
½ cup red bell peppers,
  cut lengthwise

Preparación

1. Wipe chicken with a damp cloth. Heat oil in a
   large paella skillet, add chicken one piece at a
   time, and brown until golden. Remove from
   skillet and set aside.

2. Place pork cubes in skillet and brown well on all
   sides. Remove from skillet and set aside.

3. Place sausage in skillet and brown on all sides,
   about 10 minutes. Remove from skillet and set
   aside.

4. To drippings in skillet, add onion, garlic, pepper,
   and oregano. Sauté, stirring, for 5 minutes, or

until onion has turned golden. Add salt, rice, and saffron. Cook, stirring, for about 10 minutes.

5. Preheat oven to 375 degrees.

6. Add tomatoes, bay leaf, and chicken broth to rice mixture and bring to a boil, stirring gently. Reduce heat.

7. Add previously browned chicken, pork, and sausage, then arrange *langostinos* and mussels evenly on top. Bake in same skillet, tightly covered, for 1 hour.

8. After 1 hour, sprinkle peas on top. Do not stir. Bake, covered, for 20 more minutes.

9. To serve, remove cover and place paella skillet at center of dining table. Let cool for 5–10 minutes. Garnish with red bell peppers.

SERVES 9,
PLUS A FUTURE HUSBAND!

DOÑA MARQUESA'S SANGRIA

Ingredientes

1 bottle Spanish red
  wine, such as Rioja
1 tbs. sugar
1 lemon, sliced
½ orange, sliced
½ lime, sliced

½ red apple, cubed
1½ cups club soda
2 tbs. Spanish Jerez
2 tbs. Cointreau
20 ice cubes

Preparación

1. In a large terra-cotta or ceramic pitcher, combine wine, sugar, lemon, orange, lime, and apple. Stir until sugar is dissolved.
2. Stir in club soda, Jerez, and Cointreau.
3. Let marinate overnight in refrigerator.
4. Add ice cubes before serving.

MAKES 6 GLASSES.

siete: MACUTO PEARLS

What lay beyond my thirtieth birthday was an adventure of a different order from any I had known, though I had been contemplating a similar journey since I was a child: a kind of fantasy in which marvelous images followed one after another in rapid succession.

The outward sign of my inner stirrings was what Constanza described as my "frenzied look."

As I prepared to leave Caracas, on doctor's orders, for the solitude of Macuto, my mother and Constanza attended to the last-minute details. Strangely, I felt no remorse regarding what I was about to leave behind; somehow I had managed to convince myself that given my worsening depression, Cristina would be better off under the care of my mother and sister.

The journey toward personal growth was, I felt certain, a necessary one. With my family's approval, I abdicated all my responsibilities as a mother and wife in order to replay the lovely melodies of my early adolescence, a time of bountiful exuberance when the concept of duty had not yet made me deaf to the harmony of the tunes that made music in my heart.

My husband, Jonathan, was so concerned about my emotional health that he readily agreed to my sabbatical, comforted, no doubt, by the knowledge that in my absence, our beloved Cristina would be in the best possible hands.

I sensed that upon my return, whenever that might be, I would no longer inhabit the privileged world of my youth. I knew I had arrived at a point in my life where my sense of reason and my need for fantasy must battle between themselves, and that the hours-long trip to Macuto, one way or the other, would be a flight toward my destiny.

Immediately upon entering the courtyard of my parents' grand Moorish residence, I was greeted by the sharp scent of gardenias, a sweet fragrance that opened a clear path to my childhood. It was not a memory of the past but the past itself made real by that smell, and at that moment, I saw that the young girl of fifteen years before and the woman now standing in the courtyard were the same person. As I breathed in the scents of the past, I was able at the same time—for the *first* time—to look toward my unknown future without fear. I was suddenly regaled by the lifting of my spirits, thanks to the scent of a small white flower.

As soon as Yamila and I had settled in, I took off my shoes and went out for a stroll. As the breeze blew through my hair, I inhaled the unmistakable aromas of sun-baked sand and briny sea. All the other beachfront houses appeared to be empty; it was not the time of year when families abandoned the bustle and heat of the city to seek comfort in their seaside homes. Before the humbling majesty of the vast ocean, I felt a surge of reverence. The silence was broken only by the lulling sweep of the waves as they caressed the shore, my only company.

How astonished I was, then, to find, as though summoned by my dreams, the vision of my waking mind. Incredulous, I blinked, then blinked again, to focus on the figure sitting on its heels near the water's edge: a man, his back to me, his hand busy in the damp sand beside him. He must have noticed me before I ever noticed him.

Completely mesmerized and unaware of all else, it took me a moment to understand what the man was doing. He was writing on the sand. Turning, he motioned for me to come closer. And then I knew what I had known all along, and I felt a sharp and sudden pang of recognition that at long last, the world had righted itself.

Scribbled on the sand was his overture:

¿Estás sola?

I was not alone, for Yamila was back at the house, but I nodded just the same.

This encounter with Jorge Armando spoke to me like a divine revelation, like sunlight breaking. His unexpected presence justified all my romantic longings. He must have known in his heart that I would one day come to Macuto, for no one in my family would ever have betrayed my whereabouts to him.

After a dozen years of marriage and a life of circumscribed behavior etched in stone by the forces of tradition, I saw with sudden clarity that this moment had been inevitable from the first. Over all those years that had seemed like lifetimes, we must have been inching inexorably toward each other, each of us moving through the world carrying the other inside.

What I did not know at the time was that I was advancing my first pawn in a long game of chess that the two of us would play over the course of many months. Now would begin an intoxicating year of lust, longing, ecstasy, and regret.

I followed him back up the beach as if it were the only possible thing to do, perhaps because since the moment I first saw him again, my heart had felt like a mountain of dry leaves onto which he had thrown a lit match.

As he walked, I noticed the wet sand clinging to his bare feet, and the few gray hairs just starting to be visible among the black, and the curve of his forearms below his rolled-up sleeves.

He stopped abruptly and turned to look at me. When I met his cocoa-seed eyes, something jumped inside me. Not a word passed between us. But we both heard the sound of a mating call. It was the echo of unfulfilled desire.

When we at last reached his family's house, he asked if I was thirsty. I was.

"Would you like some sangría *fresca?*"

"Sangría? Please don't go to any trouble."

"No trouble at all. There's plenty of fruit."

I followed him into the kitchen, where we stood staring at each other, not moving, not speaking. The silence made me nervous, and the way he looked at me reminded me of our long-ago kisses in the shade of the mango tree. That made me even more nervous.

"What are you doing here?" I blurted out, addressing the question as much to myself as to him. At least I had broken the silence.

"What do you mean, what am I doing here? It's my house."

"You know what I mean, Jorge Armando. What are you doing in Macuto?"

"I told you that the last time we saw each other . . . but I guess you must have forgotten," he said.

And then I did recall hearing him say, through the spinning blur that was my thirtieth-birthday party, that he stayed in Macuto between trips to the Canary Islands, where he now spent much of his time working in his father's import business.

Had my subconscious mind brought me here—to this place, this moment—without my even being aware of it? I wondered. No: I preferred to regard our encounter as a coincidence, perhaps because it is always difficult to admit to ourselves that we would knowingly pursue something that we know is wrong.

"I remember now," was all I said.

I looked at the fruit he had spread out on the kitchen counter: bright-red apples, sunlit oranges that looked like small balls of fire, and ripe mangoes packed with the sweet juices of youth. My mouth was so dry; I was so thirsty. And seeing the fruit made me even more so.

Jorge Armando must have read my thoughts, for at that moment, he picked up an orange, split it in two halves with his thumbs, and offered me one of them. He peeled the other half and started cutting slices to put in the sangría.

I ate the fruit in a fever, letting its juice trickle down my arms to my elbows.

When I was finished, I handed him the peel. He took it from my sticky hands and said, "Lucky orange."

"Do you know the secret to making a good sangría?" I asked, trying to make conversation while hypnotically watching his hands cut fruit.

"I know a lot of secrets, Gabriela. Wait here."

He left the kitchen, only to return a minute later carrying a bottle of Jerez. "My father imports it," he explained. "Best brandy in the world."

I smiled at him. "I know."

"*How* do you know?"

"Well, because years and years ago, right before I got married . . . it's a long story. Are you sure you want to hear it?"

"Absolutely."

"One day, I was talking to my uncle Raul about my cousin Clara's wedding, and he told me this story about a paella, and . . . I remembered that paella was your favorite dish in the whole world . . . and I just had this feeling . . . this feeling that I wanted to learn how to make it, even though I knew I'd never be able to make it because . . . because, well, you know . . . but all the same, I asked my cousin for the recipe. Somehow I felt I had to have it—just in case, you know?"

By now my voice was quavering, and tears had started running down my cheeks like drops of juice from a blood orange, thick and sweet but bitter, too, at the memory of all those years, all those lost years of love.

"After Clara gave me the recipe, I studied it carefully, thinking I might make a paella for my husband after we were married . . . but every time I pulled it out of my recipe book, I had to put it back again . . . because I couldn't imagine doing all that work for someone . . . someone . . ."

He nodded and looked at me tenderly, waiting for me to go on. I could see that his eyes, too, were moist with tears.

". . . so along with the paella recipe . . . my cousin Clara gave me a recipe for sangría, even though I hadn't asked her for it. I only wanted the paella recipe because I remembered your telling me about your mother . . . in her kitchen . . . frying the chicken, browning each piece so patiently . . . and your saying you could tell how much she loved you because . . . because she went to so much trouble for you. I wanted to learn to make it, too, but I never did. So that's how I came to know about Jerez . . . it's one of those things I didn't mean to learn but ended up learning anyway."

"One of those things . . . ," was all he said.

The entire time I was talking, he'd been watching me closely, barely glancing away from time to time to attend to the sangría—adding thinly sliced apples, oranges, and mangoes, squeezing an orange over the pitcher, and stirring, stirring. Stirring his love into it.

We were both silent for several minutes after I finished my story. Then he poured a glass of sangría for each of us and exclaimed brightly, "I didn't even think to ask if you were hungry!" And with his characteristic courting of temptation, he added, "Have you ever tasted a Macuto pearl, Gabriela?"

"A Macuto pearl? I've never heard of such a thing."

"It's what I call the oysters around here. I got some fresh ones from a fisherman this morning. Shall I open them?"

I shook my head. "I don't like oysters. I used to watch my father swallow them whole when I was little, and they looked so, so . . . disgusting. I could never eat an oyster." I winced as I said this and took another sip of my drink, which was starting to make me feel a little dizzy.

"They taste better than they look, you know. And they're different when you're grown up."

"Different how? Is this another one of your famous stories?"

"Let me show you. Do you trust me?"

"I trust you."

I watched as he shucked an oyster, squeezed a fresh lime over it, and sprinkled it with coarse sea salt that made it shine.

"See? Doesn't it look like a pearl?"

To encourage me, he held the shell to my lower lip. I tried to suck in the oyster, but it danced tentatively between my lips, so I ended up swallowing the liquid instead. Seeing this, Jorge Armando tried to rescue me and recover the periling pearl by placing his lips on mine.

It was a deep kiss, deep as the waters of yearning.

After we stopped kissing, Jorge Armando saw that I was flustered, and in an effort to put me at ease, he teased that one day soon, he would have to teach me the game of tongues.

"The game of tongues?"

"You're not supposed to swallow the liquid," he explained with a smile.

"What *am* I supposed to do, then?"

"Put your tongue in the way. Like this."

He took another oyster and, with his tongue, showed me how to gently slide out the pearl while leaving the liquid in the shell.

"See?"

"Maybe next time," I said.

AS TIME WENT ON, WE FELL INTO A DELIRIUM OF passion. We spent whole days contemplating each other in the drowsy peace you feel when you are lulled by the satiety of love. I felt as if we were in Paradise, and in many ways, we were. I was reminded often of the Original Sin. We spoke of faith and doubt, of how lonely one could feel in the midst of such conviction. We spoke of my shame and of what might constitute redemption.

For months, I existed solely for the bliss of our communion. In his presence, my being was half light, half love, flesh only under his spell. With him, I found the sympathy of the cosmic communication that is possible only between two people who are perfectly and closely attuned.

In the months that followed that first day, I would make for him the most delicious paellas, eat ripe fruit he picked for me under the sweltering Macuto sun, and drink water from the lips of the man who would forever dominate my inner life.

Every time we were together, I experienced a peaceful wave of oneness in which I entered pure communion with him. I remember wanting to lock myself in that place, safe, completely understood.

I existed only in his essence. I knew bliss.

By the time Pilar's plane landed in Chicago, it was late Sunday evening.

Although she was physically spent, she longed to feed her hunger for life. Her grandmother's stories had made her feel as if she could get drunk on milk. She wanted, now, to sit at the table of life's banquet and satisfy her every craving.

Nana's rapturous unburdening of her secret journey toward the consummation of her true love had made Pilar realize that spending her life with someone she didn't love was the biggest mistake she could ever make.

How unforeseen and unforeseeable this revelation had been, she thought. She had gone home to attend her grandmother's funeral and returned with an unexpected bequest: the insight that would give new meaning to her life, the wisdom that would put an end to every one of her doubts and settle, once and for all, the question of where she belonged, and to whom.

Thanks to Nana, she was ready to commit herself to living her own life and not the life that others, however well meaning, wanted for her. At long last, she felt free of insecurity and of the fear of making a mistake. No one on earth could have persuaded her that she was not taking a step in the right direction.

The first thing she did after turning her apartment key in the lock and dropping her bags inside the door was check her voice mail. She skipped through most of the messages: her landlord; her friend Stacy, asking her over for drinks later in the week; her mother, hoping she'd gotten home all right. Then came Patrick's voice: "Hey, Dimples, give me a shout when you get back." The last message was from Rafael: "*Hola, muñeca, es Rafael.* Just wanted to make sure you arrived safely. I can't wait to see you at the end of the month. *Mil besos.*"

She settled herself on the couch and stayed there with her knees drawn up to her chest and stared at the phone, daydreaming about new beginnings and marveling at how simple it all seemed now that she'd made up her mind.

III

The *Courtesan*

And then God bestowed upon her a love that would desert her forever upon her first sigh of earthly satisfaction, and a sweetness that would vanish with her first awareness of flattery.

—KAHLIL GIBRAN,
THE CREATION

Secrets *of*
the Bedroom

Mi querida nieta:

The time has come for you to receive the key that will unlock the bedroom door.

As you have already learned, my full physical, erotic, and sensual awakening did not coincide with the knowledge I had gleaned as a wife. Instead, I gained access to the hidden treasures of the bedroom through a different door.

By forsaking the pledge and bonds of matrimony, like a courtesan, I put an indelible stain on the fabric of my life.

Through a twist of fate, I came to realize that pain and pleasure are irresolvably intertwined; that while sex without love has its place, it is the marriage of the two, the sweetness of romance complementing the decadence of desire, that brings all other aspects of sensuality to the fore; and finally, that only in the hands of the right man, can a woman's true self begin to emerge.

Before all else, however, you must be aware of the cardinal rule governing the world behind closed doors: the pursuit of sensual pleasure need never extend beyond your own predilection.

Most people are surprised to learn that like the living room and the kitchen, the bedroom has its own protocol. The sole difference is that sexual manners concern only that which is tasteful to a couple. It is within the close quarters of similar inclinations that favorable liaisons tend to flourish.

As you seek refuge from your passions, you will be pleased to know that the bedroom is a place where decorum may not matter—but only if it matters not to the two lovers so engaged.

The stories that follow concern themselves not with erotic curiosa but rather with the satisfaction of bodice-ripping sexual appetite, a key element of intimacy. Only a liar could deny that love affairs are as necessary to us as the air we breathe, for we all fall prey to the yearnings of the flesh, those intense manifestations of desire that feel like hunger pangs.

You will find, as I did, that under the best of circumstances, there is nothing more seductive than having an affair with a man you have always known. If that man should happen to be your husband, what might otherwise be considered impropriety becomes, instead, domestic harmony.

Most of the secrets of the bedroom apply in the living room and the kitchen as well, for each is but a different venue in which to express love for and devotion to another.

In the arms of my lover, I learned about ravishing lust and the designs of desire and discovered that seduction and submission are seamlessly interwoven; that a slow, tender touch can spin the silk of the most fervent desire; that the lavish worship of a woman's every curve and sinew can feel like soft lace on her skin, but only when the right hands do the caressing. And, too, that the threads of existence can embroider themselves into the wrong pattern, even if one starts with the most precious of fabrics.

To seduce, to conquer, to surrender, and to love: you will stand in good stead in the other areas of your home if only you can forge a happy alliance in the bedroom, for a woman's primary relationship must be with her husband, between the sheets.

Unlike a mere seductress, a real woman must, if she wishes

to lure a man into her bedchamber, reveal more than her flesh. She must learn to bare her mind so as to intrigue his, and only after this should she beckon desire.

I never deliberately sought to probe the mysteries between the sheets; rather, they revealed themselves to me through the unfolding of my life's experience.

As a child, I spent a great deal of time in the company of my father's brothers. In their company, I was inadvertently admitted to the contours of a world where men pressed to get entry but I was still close enough to be able to observe how our men learn to master their bedchamber gait. Later, by unfolding the delicate bed linens myself, I discovered the enigmas that coiled around the fabric of a bedroom's bay.

Through my brother's rite of passage I learned that like a priest donning the collar, a man must undergo a sacred initiation rite if he is to rip the seam between boyhood and manhood.

Eventually, I realized that every man wants to be thought of as a Don Juan. And while no woman wants to think that her husband, after their marriage, would frequent prostitutes, we all desire to be with dexterous caballeros whose style, manners, and appearance sow in us the seeds of lust.

Through the painful loss of my own virtue, I recognized that when a husband is unfit for his wife's bed, the door is left wide open for marital discord.

To become "a lady, a chef, and a courtesan," you must apply yourself diligently to the acquisition of knowledge and observe the rules of etiquette; learn how to work with the right ingredients in the kitchen; and acquire the discipline to keep your lust in check until the right moment. In time, I came to understand that the true meaning of this dicho is that a woman must behave like a lady no matter what company or surroundings she finds herself in; must desire to stir her lover's sexual appetite by *including a measure of love in every dish she prepares for him; and must practice amorous restraint until she can be with the man she loves. This last is of the essence.*

At twilight, just as the sun is caressing the last curve of the horizon, ask the man you love, "What is your pleasure tonight?" and listen to his answer, but not with your ears. Listen with your heart. Aim to please him, not like a servant but as a lover. And always hold allegiance to the quintessential secret of seduction: that which men can't have makes them want it all the more.

The cuentos *that follow will, I hope, shed some light on the cultures of wooing, cooing, and courting. But, please don't be surprised when you don't find any map to help you navigate love's uncharted waters of the heart. On the matter of whom to love, I must leave you on your own, for no one else can possibly tell you how to give what must flow freely, like the sweet juice of chirimoya, from every lover's brimming heart.*

The mysteries of the bedroom will reveal themselves to you through untold tales, in their own time and through your own experience of love.

Con todo mi amor,
Tu nana

uno: HOUSE RULES

If our men know how to make their women come completely undone behind closed doors, it is because they have learned it at the brothels.

My brother's first encounter with the ways of our men began one night in his seventeenth year, when, accompanied by Papi and his seven brothers, he paid his first visit to El Palacio, the finest brothel in Caracas. Later he would describe to me in great detail the polished black marble bar, the red velvet curtains, the soft satin cushions, the fluffy, snow-white carpet—and the women whose lavish beauty justified every extravagant fixture in the magnificent mirrored gallery.

After entering the main lobby, patrons were whisked in a hidden elevator to the mezzanine, where they were greeted by the spectacle of twenty-one stunning beauties of all shapes and sizes, standing on each side of a spiral staircase that led to the private rooms upstairs. All were in various degrees of undress, and all were smiling invitingly at their prospective customers. My uncle Raul was disappointed, however, to find that the naughtiest girl in the house was not there that night. Without her in the lineup, he said, it felt as if something were missing.

"*Bienvenidos al Palacio,*" announced the mistress of the house in her butterscotch voice. "These are the ladies available to you this evening. Señoritas, please welcome our guests and introduce yourselves."

El Palacio was what was known as a bar house, meaning that visitors could opt just to have drinks at the bar and not select a girl. This was a more elegant house than many others, at least in that regard. The bar was where my father and his brothers would wait for Antonio as he crossed the threshold from boyhood to manhood.

"Now what?" Antonio asked with feigned nonchalance after the girls had recited their names.

My uncle Raul replied, "You choose."

After scrutinizing the array for ten more seconds, during which time he lost all memory of which name went with which girl, Antonio finally offered, "I'll take the one with the pretty smile and the feathers."

Her name, as it turned out, was Zuleima, and my brother would later claim that he was so ready to meet his fate that even had he been blind, he would still have been able to follow the feathers that caressed her back as she swayed her hips seductively before him all the way up the staircase. In recounting the episode, he said that the sight of white lace against her mocha-colored skin had made him want to grab her at once from behind, but he had been warned in advance by Uncle Raul that if he seemed too eager, he would give himself away as an amateur.

The presence on the mezzanine of eight older *machos* emboldened Antonio, and much as he cherished the notion of being insolent with his first woman, he wasn't going to let her beauty turn him around.

My seventeen-year-old brother apparently received quite a warm reception from Zuleima, for he remained in her company longer than was customary for *primerizos*.

The morning after Antonio's rite of passage, I woke up to an unusual burst of Papi's raucous laughter and heard him brag to my mother about how there were now "two *machos* in the house" and how proud he was of their son for "taking that woman like a man" the night before. It wasn't until years later that I fully grasped the implication of such rites of passage, those prescribed rituals that, when observed, transmute.

As Antonio came to the table to join us for breakfast, I remember noticing that he had a curious gait and a self-confident grin that he had not had the day before.

"When is it going to be my turn to have fun with you and my uncles?" I innocently asked my father.

"Not anytime soon, Gabriela. Now please eat your breakfast."

When, as a grown woman, I at last heard the whole story from my brother's lips, it confirmed my suspicion that my own love of the clandestine had begun to grow in the ripe and fertile soil of the forbidden.

dos: UNFIT FOR MY BED

The morning after my wedding night, I remember looking out the window at the scene that greeted me. Tabay, a small pueblo *indígena* located in the Venezuelan Andes, near Mérida, was the setting for Jonathan's and my honeymoon.

Dating back to the 1550s, the town now comprises a series of small huts that honor the hallmark architecture of its original settlers, the Tabayones or Tabayes Indians. The Tabayones spoke Mucubache and worked the land, growing cotton and yucca root crops. Fried yucca is still served at most Andean *posadas* as an accompaniment to the main course.

Located in the Mesa del Salado, between Mucuy Baja and Mucunután, in the coldest part of the country, Tabay is home to white *frailejones* and more bird varieties than any other part of Venezuela.

When I finally opened the window, hoping to get some fresh air, I heard a pair of agitated *paujíes* in what sounded like a lively argument. I was grateful for the distraction and for the breeze, which at least stirred the deadening decay of the prior night's leavings. The ever-present Andean fog now began to clutch at my heart.

How could he seem so unruffled after what had transpired between us? I wondered. In time, I was to learn that my husband was most dispassionate about precisely those things that in others tended to provoke extreme reactions.

I let my mind drift with the motion of the *forasteros para-meños,* a local species of tree capable of thriving amid the inhospitable temperatures of the Andean climate.

Feeling overwhelmingly defeated as a woman, I tried to assess the new order of things. The realization that this was but the first leg on the rigorous journey of matrimony sent me into despair. Despite my efforts to forget, my mind kept mercilessly replaying scenes from the night before, when my husband had, without warning, entered me like a weapon.

With the entire weight of his body on mine, I had felt that at any moment, I must break in two at the waist. I did not know whether to submit or to struggle. I wanted to push him away, but I knew that would merely postpone the agony. The locks of my black hair, pasted to my face, allowed me to conceal the hostility I had already begun to harbor toward this man, for whom I now felt not the slightest affection. At that instant, I waged war against him, secretly, in my heart. He continued to hurt me with the intrusion of his flesh until I realized that I might suffer less if I forced myself to ride his frightening rhythm. The merciful resulting numbness was the only thing that allowed me to endure the agonizing pain.

Only moments into the act, he seemed to choke on his own breath and then began thrusting deeper and faster into me. Suddenly I heard a loud grunt, followed by a groan of relief. I shrieked and called my mother's name. As he lay collapsed on top of me, I wondered if he had died. Hot tears ran down my neck.

I think I must have fainted then, for I remember coming to. My tense muscles reminded me of the assault. Rather than a painted red *cayena* flower on the sheets, dried blood, caked and crusty between my legs, was the painful reminder that I had been taken without regard.

Hopelessness descended over me as I found myself face-to-face with the fact that the romantic dreams of an eighteen-year-old virgin had been so viciously sacrificed.

By dusk, as the sun began to hide behind the Andes, the trees were bathed in a diffused, lingering red light. As I watched its slow descent, I wished with all my heart that I could be buried with the last glimmer of the day.

That night, my heart began what would become a familiar throbbing in my chest, a beating that took over my entire body and consumed most of my energy during the many unhappy years of marriage to follow. But at that moment, I was not yet ready to submit to my fear, and in an effort to calm my nerves and to suppress my desperate desire to flee, I rested my head on the pillow and prayed for the strength to stay.

In the first year of our marriage, I committed the newlywed's cardinal sin by trying to "fix" my spouse. It seemed to me, then, the only way to add some color to an otherwise black-and-white existence, but over time, I found it increasingly difficult to share my bed with a man whose public role had been laid out for him at birth and for whom love was nothing more than a necessary service.

After a while, I resolved to make my marriage work by becoming the perfect wife. I hid my unhappiness, as so many women do, behind a flurry of activities that took up most of my time and served the questionable purpose of keeping me from coming to terms with my immediate reality.

I justified my predictable script of lovelessness by reminding myself what I had always been taught: we must show gentleness when we love, and affect it when we do not; I began teaching piano lessons and planning charity events to keep myself occupied. And whenever I began to feel suffocated, I sought refuge in Constanza's company, accompanying my sister on the numberless errands that gave meaning to her life.

Ironically, over all those years, no one who knew us would ever have suspected that Jonathan and I had anything other than a successful marriage. That was perhaps my greatest victory: like a magician, I managed to induce others to look in precisely the wrong direction, so they could never see the hand that was putting the rabbit *into* the hat.

In due course, I allowed myself to accept the fact that I did not love my husband, and that our life together was hardly a paradise. It was this realization, I suspect, that enabled me at last to make peace with myself, to rethink my own aims in life, and to plant new seeds where once there had been flowers. My altered disposition in turn afforded me enough maturity and compassion to try to understand the icy world in which your grandfather lived. Bookish and intense since his father's premature death, he was a recluse even from his own family. As a result of a deeper understanding of his core and because I came to bear his child, I learned to find peace in our union and began even to enjoy our quiet times together. I eased into accepting that the fire of passion would never burn in our matrimonial chambers, and abandoned the notion that in order to be complete, a woman must have a man attending to her every whim.

In the end, our marriage would be best served by the cordiality that often develops between two people who have much invested in their life together.

My ultimate decision to be celibate within my marriage had less to do with my husband's lack of skill as a lover and more to do with my own realization that Jonathan was not the man who would evoke the woman in me.

Finally, I also came to revise my position regarding womanly virtue. This is what I now believe: the courtesan is not the woman who, as I was always taught, in being solicitous to the man she loves, seeks to earn due regard for her skill as a lover; nor is it the woman at the brothel who is paid to sleep with men, for the honest exchange of money for sexual favors, repulsive though it may be, is far from disingenuous. Instead, I reached the harsh conclusion that of the three, it is the woman who shares her bed with a man she does not love, while pretending that she does, who rightly deserves to be called a courtesan.

tres: REFLECTIONS

In sharp contrast to my wedding night, on one of the most special evenings of my life that year of complete and unrestrained abandon in Macuto, *mi amor* regarded me before the mirror.

That afternoon, I had found a surprise from him on my bed: an elaborately wrapped gift box.

After carefully untying each binding ribbon, my anticipation growing by the moment, I at long last reached the prize. On seeing it, I wept with joy that a man had finally come to regard me as my mother had taught me a man should. The exquisite item inside the box made me unexpectedly travel back to that special day in the years of my youth when my mother had unwrapped before my sisters and me the secrets hidden inside her delicate *piezas.*

Nearly hidden beneath this wonderful present was a second surprise: the same red velvet jeweler's box that I had asked Yamila to deliver to Jorge Armando on my wedding day. I didn't need to open it to know that the golden milagro was still inside.

When evening came, I donned the gift he had left on the bed for me and contemplated my reflection in the mirror. At that moment, Jorge Armando walked in. Before that mirror, he would perform the most delicate of acts, requiring tact, grace, trust, agility, and exceptional courage.

Under the spell of his fascinated gaze, all the imperfections of which I, as a woman, was so keenly aware seemed magically to disappear into the glass. I felt like a statue coming to life one limb at a time, breaking out of a centuries-old marble pose.

Fully aware of his presence and hoping to put myself at ease, I started to make conversation about the two nudes that hung on each side of the mirror. One was a reproduction of *Venus at Her Mirror,* by Velázquez. The other was a copy of *La Maja Desnuda,* by Goya.

Before the nineteenth century, paintings of nudes, even if based on living models, ostensibly depicted nymphs or goddesses. In the Velázquez, for example, which was commissioned from the Spanish painter in 1647 by a patron said to be fond of both women and the arts, Cupid studies the reflection of a reclining Venus—his mother!—in a mirror.

Inspiration for such works could be readily found in any of the numerous episodes of the *Metamorphoses,* by the Latin poet Ovid, most of which had a sexual theme. In Ovid's imagined world, divinities lesser and greater pursued one another with wild abandon.

Almost a hundred years after Velázquez, Goya overlaid a similar sensuality and eroticism with the unmistakable influence of the Gothic. His *Maja* is nonetheless a symphony of soft lines and sloping curves.

Between the two, toward the late eighteenth century, a shift had occurred, with the female form beginning to acquire the more active quality found, prior to that time, almost exclusively in representations of the male figure. Because art inevitably reflects prevailing social norms with regard to gender and sexuality, Spanish painters' approach to the depiction of the female nude slowly moved from modest to playful.

With trembling fingers, I reached out and touched one of the paintings.

"Had you been alive then, which one would you have chosen?" I asked nervously.

At that moment, I wanted to trade my awkward ignorance and self-consciousness for all the experience of all the courtesans of the world.

"Have you ever seen, have you ever contemplated—no, have you ever *admired* the grace of your own curves before a mirror, Gabriela?"

My memory took me back fifteen years, to the image of Yamila during my daily beauty routines. But as I looked back on it, that reflection seemed to have separated my physical being from a spectacular other self.

Who was this woman in the mirror pretending to be me? Lost in thought, I began to imagine that there had always been two of us, one whom I could see, and another, now reflected in this mirror, who could see me.

As familiar with my moods as a locksmith must be with every kind of lock, Jorge Armando knew the only answer to my question. Looking as deep into my eyes as anyone had ever done, he said without hesitation, "I would choose *you, encanto.*"

Removing a merry widow—the most precious undergarment ever created—from a woman's body, is, by all accounts, one of the most delicate and sensitive of tasks. Just as my mother had said, lingerie is a mystery to be revealed proudly by a woman, but only to the man she loves.

Starting with my garter belt, with expert hands, Jorge Armando made slow but steady progress toward uncovering my allurements. He clearly understood that when a woman dons such a garment, her natural apprehension and anticipation may be enough to cause her to shiver.

After giving my lips a soft, tender kiss, he began to caress my waist, gradually making his way toward the curves of my hips, over the garter belt. He moved on to touch the stockings, while continuing to get closer to each object of his affection. He ran his right index finger slowly up and down one garter strap, gently stroking my leg as he did so. My knees went weak and nearly buckled under me, but his arms held me firmly upright.

His bold exploration did not go unrewarded. At last he discovered the first snap, hidden under the garter's silky end. With admirable dexterity, he slipped his index finger under the strap while tautly placing his thumb atop of it, as if the two were stuck together with glue. With unnerving precision, he then slid the snap backward, toward the loop of the hook, which at once obediently disengaged. With patience as his virtue, he soon received his recompense. When the four grippers had been freed, one at a time, my stockings gave up and fluttered helplessly down my legs.

Unleashing all his rogue charm, he then began to loosen from my bosom the embroidered corset containing all my desires.

Deftly he moved behind me and with one hand began to unfasten each hook in turn from its corresponding eye. As he lightly caressed my breasts with his free hand, the corset, too, gave up its fight and joined the stockings on the floor.

I was now down to a single piece, the garment that goes on first and comes off last, the final obstacle that a man must overcome if he is to claim his coveted prize.

As desire besieged me, I seemed to awaken from a trance, and observed, as if for the first time in my life, my nearly naked reflection in the mirror. Through his eyes, I was able finally to see that hidden self that had always been able to peek at me while itself eluding my gaze.

When at length he caressed the last silken piece from my trembling legs, I had proof that his persuasion was capable of stealing the heart of even the most virtuous of women.

After swiftly removing his own clothes, he took me by the waist and legs and lifted me into his arms. Looking lovingly into my eyes, he held me tight as I sank into the warmth of his chest.

He carried me to the bed and placed me on it as one might the most delicate of flowers. And with a tenderness that I had never known, he restored to me the virginity that I had so longed to hold in my possession.

On this night, there would be no bewildering emotions or savage passions. He merely sat beside me and regarded my body ever so sweetly. I allowed his fingers to meander over every part of it, his soft caresses making me feel like a child being put to bed rather than a grown woman being made love to. With gentle kisses, he covered every part of my body and loved me so, the night long.

After he had lured me to that lazy lulling place between the last few seconds of a waking moment and the inviting world of sleep and dreams, my heart was luminous with the clarity of the discovery of the riches hidden inside a woman's treasure chest: the almost undistinguishable brilliance of two almost identical gems, having sex and making love.

Such adoration suffused my face with a virginal radiance—that exquisite bloom that can never be obtained through artifice and only at the hand of the right lover. Mother Francisca had been right: there *was* a special glow that graced the face of a happily married woman. How I longed for my lover and my husband to be one and the same.

Not infrequently over the years, I have thought back to that night, but I have never gotten any closer to an answer. All I know is that sometimes, during one of those brief daily pockets of silence, between rings of the telephone or in the pause between the turning of the dial and the sound of the first voices on the radio, I catch myself asking the same question: How can the love of another so completely alter one's image of oneself?

cuatro: AGUA FRÍA

On the night that I became forever his, the Macuto air was so hot and dense that it almost hurt to breathe. I can still remember my feverish thirst. Despite the fact that the house had been built next to Playa Azul so that the ocean breezes would cool the house, as the night closed sharply in, it only grew hotter and hotter.

The linens on the bed were soaked, my mouth dry as beach sand at noon. I finally rose from bed to get some water, trying not to awaken Jorge Armando, who lay peacefully on the bed, seemingly unaware of the asphyxiating heat.

I walked toward the kitchen, barefoot on the cool tile, the only surface that would not be entirely suffocated by the unrelenting heat.

A beautiful moon streamed through the window. As I contemplated its almost full shape, the motion of the beach waves lulled my senses. I decided to lie momentarily atop the soft oak table where baskets of fresh mangoes and a pitcher of well water rested for the night. I could hear the sea waves washing against the rocks, smashing and reshaping them with every move.

I closed my eyes and immersed myself in thoughts of water. Shored against the table, I felt life's essential liquid caressing the tip of my fingers, streaming gently up my arms, its ebb and flow building higher, sliding slightly downward at the points of my breasts, which seemed to emerge then submerge into the water until rippling cascades released forcefully and shot straight down to the world between my legs. For a moment, I experienced a wave of peace, the ripples now a distant murmur.

Lying there, I thought about what I was going through and

about the person I was becoming—no less a stranger to myself than I would have seemed to all who thought they knew me. Fleetingly, I wondered if I could reclaim the world I had inhabited before my time in Macuto.

Moments later, I heard footsteps coming toward the kitchen.

He was always capable of reading my mind, and, as if it were the most natural of things to find me lying there, Jorge Armando's gentle fingers began to seek my curves. They caressed me slowly, as if my body were a precious harp whose beautiful music they wanted to extract.

He then moved to the far end of the table and began to lick me. I could feel my feeble flesh begin to swell with pleasure. After a moment, he stopped, as he often did, leaving me to wonder if he would do it again. He always waited long seconds between one caress and the next. I marveled at how a few seconds could really seem like hours. He knew this tiny pocket of time left me desperate, moaning for more. Since the first time he had put his mouth to my lips I knew I had been ensnared forever.

Gently, he parted my legs, as one would a flowering bud, and slid his fingers inside me, lifting me up and down, then coming to shore softly. This came as a benevolent release that felt like raindrops caressing me inside. He kissed me lovingly and lingered, making me only more aware of the small space that beckoned to be filled.

I was lost, my resistance waning with every caress.

"Again," I begged weakly, my skin suddenly invaded by the color of flame.

The word came from a different source, a spring deep within me that had been hidden since I was born and would remain so after he was gone.

"Please be patient," he whispered.

He began once more to massage my eager cleft, a feeling I

was afraid I would never know again. *Hilos dorados* I learned to call this gentle threading because he seemed always to be weaving my pleasure with delicate threads of gold.

What had I done to deserve this pleasure? Blessed, delicate, drenching love, the kind that comes only once in one's life, the kind of love that must be offered up at a place of worship to which sacred oblations are brought. The kind of love that defies rational explanation and can only be appreciated by experiencing its sublime meaning, its profound power, its spiritual potency, in another.

The two of us always came to our communion with open hearts and souls. From the depths of our need, our soulful cries of anguish and joy were the result of the deep desire each of us felt to touch and be touched by the other. This pure love gave me the answer to the inherent human longing for the sacred, for the spiritual, for the eternal. Through our worship, I satisfied my longing to connect, to communicate with the mysterious force that had given me my very existence. Through our union, I learned to respect love as one of the awesome wonders of the universe and completely understand the human yearning to be assured of the protection of our heart, for in his arms, I finally knew peace.

I waited, but it never came again, that feeling of gentle waves swirling between my legs, taking me both to the depths and the heights of my emotions, a voyage that transcended time and space and transformed the very essence of my being. I missed it desperately, even then, even in its vivid presence.

He paused, silently, and I felt the flood of my warm arousal meander indecorously down my legs, onto my knees.

I could still hear the sound of the sea, now amplified, as though someone had put a seashell to my ear. Cooled by my own sweat, I experienced, for a moment, relief from the heat.

Aware of the tiniest sensations, I looked up to find him still threading my pleasure with his tongue. He was completely engaged, fully participating, and wholly affected by the encounter. His touch had a balanced, rhythmic cadence, a poetic modulation, up, down, up . . . down again, until I had no choice but to collapse in ecstatic exhaustion. Another gasp.

He kissed my softness one more time, the smooth motion calming me but for a second. Soaked yet again, the cove between my legs surged wetter than the ocean, giving way in anticipation of what was to come. He slid his finger inside my mouth. I began to suckle it and continued to moan, impatiently, desperately, rolling in billows, begging for more. I could not stop moaning, every sigh a lost whisper. Every time he stopped, a terrifying disappointment rippled through my entire being. During those few seconds, I grew afraid that my body would never hear the sounds of this rare harmony again.

With his face and fingers buried deep inside me, I began to thrust against the table, a euphoric yet buoying movement that no amount of self-possession could restrain. I lost myself again. I learned to trust.

"Please don't stop," I moaned. "Don't ever stop." My body and brain intertwined, forever attached to the hot spring between my legs.

His adoration felt as though my ears had been clogged for years and suddenly, without a warning, I could hear more acutely than any other time in my life.

And then, all was quiet.

Still bewildered by the burning thirst, I reached for the pitcher on the table, but he grasped it first and filled his mouth with water. He then placed his mouth on top of mine and tenderly poured the water into mine. I swallowed the water feverishly, gratefully. Though the water was no cooler than lukewarm, I never understood the meaning of quenched thirst until that moment. Fresh water trickled slowly down my throat, almost sweet, made sweeter by its having been given to me by my lover. I felt drunk with pleasure. He asked if I wanted more, and I nodded fervidly, no sounds coming from my dry mouth. He fed me more water from his lips, making each mouthful smaller and smaller, each feeding longer and longer.

A strange passion engulfed us both. At last, he dipped his finger into the pitcher and began to trace the silhouette of my body, making a line from my throat to my stomach, stopping at my navel. He left my side then and crossed the kitchen in search of something. I heard a drawer being opened and then he was beside me once again. In his hand was a small knife with which he began to caress my flesh.

He whispered in my ear. *"No tengas miedo.* This is not a feeling you seek, it's one you discover."

I should have been afraid, but strangely, I wasn't. Rather, I felt a blessing, a familiar awareness, the ultimate recognition that I had known him in another life. This realization came to me with all the clarity and luster of a gem newly polished.

He barely approached my entrance with the knife's tip, but I screamed, a primal scream of possession, a ritualistic shriek of pain and pleasure that reminded me of a sacrificial offering intended to bring the worshiper into a closer intimate relationship with the adored.

I drank the moment in slowly with the sobering realization of one who gets to a place from which there is no way back.

The surges of pleasure now seemed to grow stronger, more passionate, the motions reminiscent of a gathering storm.

He put the knife down and parted my legs. As ever, he was reading my mind: I wanted desperately to feel the rush of him inside me. He moved to the foot of the table, and still standing, pulled me toward him, his rhythm a perfect ebb and flow ascending toward my welcoming relief until he could remain standing no longer. With mounting pleasure, he filled me until we were no longer two separate bodies but one swelling wave of passion breaking onto itself. Between us only a series of concomitant, exquisite, intoxicating bursts.

I felt like shouting for joy and crying in anguish, both intimate whispers from my core. I knew the satiated longing of returning to one's source, the elusive perfection of the soul.

After a time, he picked up the knife again. My heart thumped in anticipation, but I lay perfectly still on the table, my arms draped on each side. He smiled tenderly at my innocent whimpers.

His constant desire to court physical sensations was a mesmerizing and addictive trait. Every night, at lust's fervid conclusion, I hoped there would be more and prayed that this exhilaration would be a constant in my life.

I knew that no one and nothing else would ever provide me with such a titillating sense of both possibility and risk. Years later I would recognize that it is only by taking risks that we can dominate our spirit; without risk, we are bound to lose our balance as we deny ourselves one of the most extraordinary sensations imaginable, that of getting lost in an experience while braving it.

I squeezed my eyes shut for an instant. When I opened them again, he was still standing there, drenched in moonlight, holding the knife in his right hand. Slowly, deliberately, he made a small incision on his left thumb. I stared at him, stunned, searching on his face for evidence of the pain I knew he must be feeling. But I could see none. And then he handed me the knife. I felt the anticipation of a thousand tiny pins slowly pricking my veins and drawing my life's blood. I sucked in my breath.

"Go ahead, *nena,*" he said softly.

Despite the sheen of the sharp blade glistening against the moonlight, I trusted him.

Obediently, I pressed the knife against the soft flesh of my right thumb and slid it downward. It made a short, sharp cut that yielded just a few beads of blood. He took my hand and pressed his thumb to mine, joining the cuts, blending our blood. He kissed me then, a lingering kiss that mingled pain with pleasure and that gradually stopped my head from spinning. I hoped the cut would form a scar that would live forever as a memory of the marriage of our blended souls. That night, I swore in my heart that I would never love again, for I was his. All the same, I ached to think of my betrayal.

We had loved each other until we were only nerves, with no senses left. Having stripped down to my bare soul, I had become a woman to the bone. I knew then, for the first time, that I was in love, for it is impossible not to love when you are loved so perfectly, so completely.

He fed me water one more time, then carried me back to bed.

After my body drank in the last burst of the essential liquid of life I was certain that in the depths of my quenched thirst there would be no rest.

cinco: TAPIZ

I had waited patiently.

In the raw of the morning, Yamila led into my room the woman who would help me bring into this world proof positive that I had loved and had been loved in return.

On June 1, 1955, I should have achieved the sum total of my earthly desires. Our love had finally borne fruit. But this day would be bittersweet, and my ecstasy short-lived.

As life was about to burst from my womb, Jorge Armando asked me if I was ready. He, too, had waited. A few months earlier, he had offered me a life with him and away from the sacrament of matrimony. If at the end of this time I had not the courage to risk my marriage over our destiny of true love, he said, he would return permanently to the Canary Islands, and we would cease to be.

The moment I'd dreaded had now arrived: I had to decide before our child came into the world. I remember how I struggled with those words. When at last I managed to speak, they trailed slowly, synoptically, out of my mouth: "I . . . I can't . . . I can't choose my passions over the destiny of my birth."

My labor was intense. Life and death were intertwined in a battle in which I knew there would be no victor. As if I were drinking simultaneously from a cup of pleasure and one of pain, life and love lost struggled within me. Then life pushed aside all my fears and transformed me, if only for a moment. This pulsating life inside me belonged to him. My beating heart felt twice as heavy as my body—so heavy, indeed, that long afterward, I would still carry its heft with me.

After hours of labor, I let out a primal scream, and Tapiz's head crowned. Heedless of all else but the feverish desire to breathe, she emerged and almost immediately began to wail, her soft, purplish face a tiny relief of life.

I was too scared to close my eyes and too scared to open them.

He was still in the hallway when the midwife left my room, but a sudden tightening in my chest, like a premonition, told me that he would not remain long. Unable to face the certainty of grief, after making certain that our baby and I were both well, Jorge Armando stole away from Macuto that very night.

Yamila later found, pinned to Tapiz's crib, the most beautiful love letter I have ever read. The gems of his words, in a setting of shared sorrow, still glint in my heart like rare jewels.

1 de Junio de 1955
Querida piel de canela:

All of us are blessed with one great love, one object of longing so extraordinary that it remains in memory, forever untouched. No, in fact, this one passion, this true desire that comes in the form of a stabbing blow to the soul, improves beyond all reason with the passage of time.

Our daughter's birth has made me recognize just how long I have carried you inside. In loving you, I have learned the difference between love and love for one woman. But our union also brought an end to your precious innocence, and for that I will be eternally sorry.

My soul yearns, even more so now, to be one with its other half. It is this permanent ache that assures me that our lives, so randomly united, will remain so to win over the passing of time, for the milagro of love owes no debt to death.

I am certain that you will think of me as the afternoon begins to lose the splendor of its light, in the same way that I will think of you as I embrace the darkness of each night.

I vow I will stay away so you may live in peace and in accordance with the prescriptions of your birth. But please know that in that sacred place that hid the burning fires of our passion, you will always sigh in my arms as if it were our first embrace.

Con todo mi amor,
Jorge Armando

Never before had I felt the force of loss and love as I did then, and never have I since. I belonged to my lover. The blood-drenched sheets seemed the physical evidence of my ruptured heart.

My journey through life and death was filled with raw, agonizing terror as I awakened to the belief that darkness was not the only thing that would stalk me. The almost preternatural, spine-tingling silence that followed would haunt me for years to come. Life had chosen me, but with Jorge Armando's absence, death had determined to continue lurking within my soul.

Over the months that followed, I readied myself to reenter my old life with all the solemnity of a nun about to take the holy orders. In preparation for my pilgrimage, I wrote out in my journal my plans and wishes for the future, chief among these being receiving God's blessing; ensuring Cristina's well-being, even as I raised Tapiz in secret; and renewing my vows to the holy sacrament of matrimony.

In rejecting my life as a mistress, I aimed to seek, through faith, the answers to the central question of my universe, the substance of my existence—a question that could be answered only upon the completion of a personal spiritual journey. In seeking God, I hoped to remain eternally connected to this life-sustaining love.

I knew I had a few months to recover before my return. In coming home with an unexpected newborn, and with the screams of pain still echoing, I wrote triumphantly, if not altogether frankly, to my mother:

After my yearlong retreat, I am happy to report that my stay here, made possible by your much-needed assistance, has at last brought the hoped-for results. I must thank you in advance, as I find myself in perfect health of both mind and spirit. A most pleasant surprise from Yamila awaits the family. We expect to be ready to be fetched on September 9. The very thought, my dear mother, fills me with such joy as I have not known since I was a child. I count the days until our reunion and can think of nothing but the delights of home and motherhood with no onerous distractions. How I have longed for this complete happiness! Please give my love to Cristina; while Jonathan tells me that she is well, only you can know how much I have missed my darling daughter. Give my best to Constanza and tell her that I hope by the time I see her next, my spiritual journey will have been completed without any great jolts.

Yamila and I had agreed that Tapiz would live in my home, but as *her* daughter, not mine. This resolution gave me the courage to brave the immolation of my soul. I would raise our daughter in close proximity of body and spirit. For this ignominious task, I discovered a mountain of reserve that I never knew I possessed.

Thus compelled by the unrelenting forces of duty and propriety, I tore myself away from the love of my life. His absence suffocated me—so much so that at times, I would have thought myself dead were it not for the constant reminder of my hemorrhaging breath.

On the morning of our last day in Macuto, shortly before my sister and her husband, Mauricio, were to come for us, I saw with utter certainty that I would soon be closing the door of my parents' Moorish home for the last time. I would be nailing shut the coffin that held all my impossible dreams, my sudden explosions of desire, and everything else I had discovered through my encounter with true love. At that moment, my life flashed before me as I clung to the lintel of the door, sobbing and kissing it.

From now on, tears would be my only traveling companions through the arid desert of my life. With his leaving, a part of me had begun immediately to die: the part of me that he had awakened. But now, despite my overwhelming grief, I willed the rest of my heart to strike a balance in favor of my existence.

Suppressing all signs of sorrow, I donned an elegant black lace cloak in preparation for my sister's arrival. In its right-hand pocket, I placed what I had written to myself, *"La Guía de la Esposa Ideal."* These were the exacting new standards I had set for my roles as wife, mother, traveling companion, and confidante. I would be a mistress only once.

Overwhelmed *by what she had just read, Pilar wiped tears* from her eyes and wondered how her mother would feel if she ever found out about all of this. Probably refuse to believe it, she thought.

A love child, two broken hearts, and a woman caught in a loveless marriage: for a moment, Pilar considered how many lives had been shattered when just one person failed to follow her heart. She realized that she must not make the same mistake. What would her grandmother's tears be worth if she couldn't learn from them?

Pilar now felt sure that her grandmother's stumbling block would have to become the cornerstone of her life.

She felt an urgent need to speak to her mother.

While she knew that what she was planning to say would cause a panic in the family, she no longer feared how her mother might react. Nana's wisdom had given her the courage to assert her will calmly, without the disquieting anxiety that had tainted all past conversations on this subject.

She should do it before going to the supermarket, she thought. Patrick had called her back the night before and agreed to come over for dinner tonight so they could talk: she'd have to start cooking as soon as she got home with the groceries. Better to get this over with first: early afternoon on an ordinary Monday was as good a time as any to make the phone call she had long been dreading. After reading her grandmother's diaries, she knew it had to be done.

As she dialed, she wondered if every woman had to have, at some point in her life, at least one such unpleasant conversation with her mother.

"*Hola,* Mamá," she said as soon as she heard her mother's voice.

"*Hija,* did you get home all right? I was starting to worry, since I hadn't heard from you."

"I'm sorry, Mamá, but it was late when I got home, and I didn't want to wake you. Plus, I had a lot on my mind."

"How was your drive to the airport with Rafael?"

Pilar smiled. She had to give her mother credit for trying.

"It was fine. But actually, that's why I'm calling. I have something to tell you."

"You do?" Cristina's voice was filled with sudden expectation.

"Yes, I'm calling to tell you that I've decided."

She must have heard the conviction in Pilar's voice, because for the first time, she seemed to be truly listening to her daughter, rather than waiting for her to finish talking so she could give her another round of unwelcome advice.

"*Sí, hija?*"

Pilar felt a pang of guilt in the pit of her stomach, but she kept repeating Nana's words to herself: *When you find your orchard of truth, you must find a way to enter it . . .*

"You've decided what, Pilar?" Cristina prompted.

"That I'm not coming home. At least not for a while."

"I see . . . and just when did you decide that? When you left here yesterday, you said you were still undecided."

"I know, Mamá, but now I'm sure."

"I see."

Pilar knew that her mother must be devastated, but there was no turning back. She could hear it in her own voice: an unwavering determination that had never been there before. Nothing Cristina could say would change her mind.

With an air of resignation, her mother asked if she was at least planning to come home for Christmas.

"Yes, Mamá, I'll be home for Christmas. And Mamá . . . tell Ana Carla that I'll call her this weekend, *por favor.*"

"*Muy bien, hija.* I will." Then, "Pilar? I just want what's best for you . . . you know?"

"I know, Mamá. I know."

For a moment, Pilar regretted the distance between them, and the disappointment she was causing her mother, but she knew now that choosing happiness always had a price. She had imagined this moment for so long, and in her mind, it had always been a victory. The reality was proving less satisfying than she'd expected, however, because for one person to be happy, someone else had to suffer. Even Patrick had said as much: "If you wanna eat an omelet, you gotta break a few eggs."

Cristina had one last question: "What am I going to tell Rafael?"

"Don't worry, Mamá. I'll take care of it."

And so she did.

As soon as she had hung up with her mother, she called Rafael on his cell phone.

"*Muñeca,* what a pleasant surprise!"

To Rafael, Pilar said, firmly, that she would not see him during his upcoming visit to Chicago. This time, unlike in the past, she did not waver, for she no longer wanted to give him the impression that he could try again some other time. Pilar knew that most Latin men subscribed to the belief that when a woman said no, she was really just waiting for additional encouragement to say yes. So she made sure that Rafael understood that this was her last word on the previously always-open-for-discussion subject of their getting back together.

True to character, Rafael accepted defeat gracefully. "You leave me no options, *querida.* Obviously, I'm disappointed for myself, but I must say, I am glad for you. Your voice sounds different, Pilar. You sound . . . happy."

"I am, Rafael. I am."

Afterward, Pilar marveled at how smoothly everything had gone, as things usually do when one has made up one's mind. Like all riddles, it seemed crystal clear when one knew the answer.

She had only a few more pages to go in the last volume of Nana's diary. First, though, she had to run out to the store. When she got back, she would finish reading, kiss the diary shut, and move on to what she knew her grandmother would've wanted her to do next: see Patrick.

seis: SANGRE CALIENTE

This is the first and last time that I will give voice to the full story.

All our days are numbered and we must not waste any of them by leaving anything unsaid. Every sunrise is a gift from God.

At sixty-two, I still feel the need to nestle in the sheltering space between the light caresses of his hands and the constant beating of his heart. I would have done anything for him, except destroy my family, or its good name. Instead, I have chosen reverence for the ordinary pleasures that have become the bedrock of my life.

The peace of walking outside with my husband and the satisfaction of watching our daughter as she observes her parents' quiet respect for each other; the simple pleasure of preparing countless meals for my family; the joy of receiving a thousand sweet kisses from my granddaughters and the enduring friendship of a woman who has borne in silence the fact that she cannot have a child of her own for carrying the burden of mine. These are my blessings.

During the last thirty-two years, I have gradually made peace with my past. This is, finally, what enables me to share with you this story of transcendant love, a feeling that most people find difficult, perhaps impossible, to understand. The story of a woman whose deepest passions were tenderly awakened by a lover to whom she gave the world; a woman who would never belong to her husband and who would one day find herself arguing helplessly against the unbridled passion that depleted her confidence as a wife and mother as she acquiesced completely to desires that were not entirely hers to own.

The day Tapiz was born, her father begged me, one last time, to be his. I could not, I would not, say yes.

Thinking strictly of myself for a moment, I am certain that I made the wrong decision in choosing a life away from the love of mine. Thinking strictly of my family, I have the certainty that I did not. I gave my family my life. And I gave Jorge Armando Caballero my soul; a place he would come to forever inhabit because he was the only one, in an entire lifetime, who ever touched me there.

Every time we made love, we traveled to a previously unknown, sacred place that always beckoned us back. Such was the feeling that bound us; that binds us. I have peace in my heart only because he never really left it. In my bones, I know we are both breathing the same air, even if we are constrained by a different physical reality. Does that sound like sorcery? It is.

Although we never spoke with each other again, we became bound by the milagro of love, as tightly bound as two people whose one soul has been arbitrarily split into two separate bodies. The best way to describe it is that as soon as we loved each other for the first time, we both realized that were we to get physically separated, our one soul would be left to wander in the vastness of the universe. Each one of us created, completely, the other. While I experienced the intensity of this feeling every time he loved me, I only grasped its significance to a human life, gradually and over time. Had I fully understood it at the time, I would have probably left with him.

From time to time, I find myself replaying every second of our time together. Each time, I run the images meticulously through my mind, imprinting all of them again, not unlike the ritual of repeating a story over and over to ensure it will survive for generations. But generations live on earth, and our love does not.

I remember everything about him. I remember *su gracia y su gentileza*. I remember how he smelled of the sea breeze and the sultry Macuto air. I remember how his *café con leche* skin felt against mine. And I will never forget the intermittent whispers of pure pleasure that escaped from the depths of my soul as he prepared to move me temporarily away from my permanent home.

I miss his cocoa-seed eyes that always managed to find my beauty. His eyes would plunge into mine and a few minutes later would bring out the treasured beauty that surfaces from the depths of every woman when she is desperately in love with a man. If bliss were a color, it would have to be that unmistakable rosy glow of love that even Mother Francisca had been eager to point out.

Sometimes, as I am moving through my day, I reach for the silver milagro that still hangs around my neck and try, as he once asked, to *Find Music in the Silence* of his absence. Whenever I do this, I wonder where he is and I try to imagine what he is doing at that moment. At sunrise, I imagine waking him with a kiss; at twilight, I imagine him in my embrace. I often wonder if he has ever been able to drink in the juice of a ripe mango again. I have not.

Jorge Armando discovered my essence and taught me what it was like to be a woman, in a way that few others, perhaps none, will ever experience. Throughout the years, his love has caressed me like a pleasant, constant breeze. Sometimes I trail my fingers along my body and pretend they are his, adoring my every curve as they did a thousand times.

Oftentimes, I also ponder what would have otherwise been a beautiful friendship; my friendship with Yamila. Except that *la ama de la casa* can never truly befriend a servant. But in the sanctum of my heart, Yamila has been my closest and dearest friend. Why did she quietly bear the burden and responsibility for what is essentially sanctioned as an immoral act? It is true that she had no choice. When you have been brought up to live the life of a servant, you don't think of yourself as having choices. But what of her devotion? She did have a choice about her devotion; which was hers and hers alone to offer.

"Señora Gabriela, por favor no sufra," she would tell me when I cried in desperation in the months that followed our return from Macuto. *"Usted sabe que"* he will always love you, don't you?" In the midst of my suffering, I would be comforted by one of Yamila's greatest gifts, the simplicity of her thinking. "We have a saying in Canaima, *señora,* when a man's seed burns inside of you, you belong to him forever," she would say. I marvel at the wisdom with which her simple truths are impregnated.

On my return from Macuto, Jonathan seemed puzzled by my desire to take some of my meals in the kitchen with Yamila and her daughter. One more breach of custom by Gabriela, he must have thought: the mistress of the house should never sit at the same table with her servants. Only a mother could comprehend that a woman always feels at home in the presence of her child. I could not do otherwise.

Tapiz has grown up happy. She has never suspected that your mother Cristina is her sister; nor she hers. Neither one would understand it, nor desire it, for we all get accustomed to the life we know.

Every time I hear Tapiz call me *señora* instead of *mami,* my heart breaks again. But the music of her voice keeps her father's song alive in the chambers of my heart. The distinctive timbre of his voice will always echo in my heart like a bolero. And whenever I smile at her, she returns a different smile; a complicit bond that only a mother and a daughter are able to recognize. The other thing she does not know is that in our silent recognition of each other lives the love that gave her life.

I am a grandmother now. As Yamila likes to say, "You are supposed to be the voice of wisdom, Señora Gabriela."

Yes, I am to be the wise woman to those around me.

Cristina learned what I had to teach her. She learned how to attend to a household, how to be married, and how to cope with the inexplicable loneliness that overtakes a woman after childbirth. Through my respect for her father, she also learned how to regard a husband and a gentleman, which is quite different from how to regard a lover. I never taught her how to love a man by preparing a meal for him.

In the years that followed the breaking of my heart, I often asked myself, How does one learn to live with an impossible love? I eventually came to accept this condition as one would any other kind of pain: by enduring one day at a time. Unlike other wounds, however, a broken heart never truly heals.

A few years ago, when your grandfather died, I felt an old heaviness return to my heart, and I recognized the weight I had been carrying for so long. But the burden of my heart was made of sorrow, not of regret.

I am not ashamed of having loved; on the contrary, I am proud to have experienced life's incandescence, even if, at times, the light was blinding. I have come to believe that through the force and the intensity of our love, I was given the gift of an extra life, or perhaps, in the end, the gift of the one life I had.

One day, when I was sitting on the back patio reading "Absence by Moonlight," that beautiful poem Jorge Armando had written for me long before, one of Cristina's girls came to sit on my lap and asked me to tell her about my family.

"Nana, is it true that you had seven uncles? Is it true that they broke girls' hearts? Can you tell me the story?"

I nodded and patted her on the hand. "Some day, little Pilar, I will tell you the *whole* story."

I am finished now. You are the vessel into which I have poured this story of love, loss, and strength; it is to you, my dear granddaughter, that I entrust my treasures, the riches of my heart.

Now that I have poured the salty waters that my life has cost me, I hope that the currents of yours flow in a less turbulent stream, in a more fluid ebb and flow of smiles and tears, of the dreams and sighs that inevitably course through the unknowable depths of a human life.

Jorge Armando Caballero came to me on October 10th, 1955. It was late afternoon in Macuto. I was thirty years old. I was hot. I was thirsty. Even though he quenched my thirst with agua fría, *his* sangre caliente, *like my name, runs through my blood, hot and never still . . .*

This is how it all began.

As she closed the last volume of her grandmother's precious gift, an image of the man beside Nana's grave appeared in her mind. She could see his face now, sharply in focus, and that clarity strengthened her resolve.

In giving up the love of her life, her grandmother had given Pilar the courage to claim the love of her own.

She expected him in a couple of hours.

The longing she had felt for him the whole time she was gone now acquired a new significance.

Feeling that the very air she was breathing had changed, Pilar went into the kitchen, unpacked her groceries, and, before starting to cook, looked up at the ceiling and said in a barely audible voice, "Nana, I'm going to follow your recipe. Wish me luck."

While she was chopping the onions, her eyes started to water, so she reached into a drawer, took out a matchbook, lit a match, put it between her teeth, and continued chopping. Would it really work? Yes! She hoped the rest of the evening would be as simple as lighting that match. She thought about what she was going to tell Patrick. She had not seen him in over a week and was anxious to talk to him—so anxious, in fact, that she wasn't at all sure she'd be able to find the right words.

After putting the dish in the oven, Pilar took a long shower, and then, when it was time for her to get dressed, instead of wearing jeans, she put on a fitted black dress. When she was ready, she looked at her reflection in the mirror and was able to smile at the woman who looked back. Before going out to the other room to set the table, she said aloud, "Nana, I hope you approve."

When the doorbell rang, she greeted Patrick with a welcoming, "I missed you."

Patrick, being his usual self, looked her up and down and then exclaimed, "Dimples, you look good enough to eat!" Smiling, he twisted his right index finger into one of the divots in her cheek.

Realizing how much she had truly, truly missed him, she embraced him, so tightly that it seemed as if letting go would never be an option.

"How was your trip?" he asked, pulling away just a little to look at her face.

"Well, it's a long story, Patrick. I want to tell you all about it. But first, would you like something to drink?"

"Sure."

Letting go of him reluctantly, Pilar went into the kitchen and returned to the living room with a cold beer in her hand.

"Here, your favorite."

"It smells good in here, Dimples. What are you cooking?"

"Oh, that's a surprise. It's part of the story," she said, smiling at him.

"OK, what's the story?"

"Let's see, where should I start? . . . Well, my grandmother left me her diaries."

"She left you her diaries? What's in 'em? Did you read them yet?"

"Oh, yes . . . yes, I did. In a way, they were more than I expected . . . and in a way, I guess they were less."

"Less?"

"It's so sad, Patrick. It turns out she didn't really love my grandfather the way we all thought she did. That's what I mean by 'less'—it really hurt to read that. But she was in love with someone else."

"Someone else? Do you know who he was?"

"No, I don't. Well, I guess I do, actually—he was at the funeral, but I didn't talk to him . . . none of us had ever seen him before. Still, even without reading Nana's diaries, I could tell he had been someone special in her life by the way he . . . well, that doesn't matter now."

Patrick looked puzzled but nodded for Pilar to continue. As always, he encouraged her in whatever she did, no matter how trivial it might be.

"The thing is, Patrick, the more I read, the more I began to see my own life in hers. This love she had . . . it *owned* her. I mean, she didn't intend for that to happen, but it did. She said they lived inside each other, they became the same person. I don't think their love was of this earth. But in a strange way, it was that love that kept her going all those years."

"So how come she never left her husband for him?"

"She couldn't, Patrick, not in those days. You don't know what it's like because you're not *from* there—there are traditions . . . a different sense of responsibility. But in the end, it was as if they'd never parted: he stayed inside of her for the rest of her life."

"She wrote all that?" Patrick looked at Pilar's somber expression. He moved toward her and put his hand on the back of her neck. "Dimples, it's all right."

"She wrote her story down for me so *I* wouldn't . . . that's what I wanted to talk to you about . . . she wrote it all down with such love, to make sure I wouldn't waste my life. And that made me realize that this kind of love is given to us only once in a lifetime, and it's not our gift to throw away."

"You mean . . . ?"

"I mean that clarity, the certainty that there is one and only one person with whom we can share our love and our soul . . . which is different from just sharing a life with someone. Nana called it the 'orchard of truth.'"

"I see."

"This may sound corny, but I've found my orchard of truth, and I wanted to tell you as soon as I knew because . . . because I don't want to lose you, Patrick."

She hugged him and looked into his eyes. And then she began to cry. She cried for her grandmother, grateful tears of love and loss, and she cried for herself, because she had finally found the courage to admit what *she* wanted, after twenty-six years of agreeing to what everyone else wanted *for* her.

Patrick pulled her onto his lap, and brushed the hair out of her face, and kissed her tear-stained cheek. She hugged him back, taking in his tenderness, feeling the pull of him, and thinking that in a world full of uncertainty, she had never felt more certain of anything in her life.

He carried her into her room and gently laid her on the bed and began undressing her. She closed her eyes and allowed his touch to transport her. His slow caresses seemed to go on for days. With the soft brush of his fingers, light as the tickle of a feather, Patrick began to draw shapes on her body. As his hands wandered up and around her belly in lingering lines and sweeping curves, Pilar felt her future move closer and closer toward her.

In concert with her undulating hair, their bodies now moved in a mesmerizing cadence of willowy movements. Pilar arched herself slightly up and down. She clutched the sheets with clenched fists. Eyes tightly shut and lips slightly parted, she felt her whole body quiver, again and again, until she had no choice but to let go of both the fabric she held in her hands and all sense of control. And with that, she allowed life to overtake her.

She was inside a dream, and all she could see was bright light. She saw the shadow of her soul lifting, luminescent. Peaceful. At last.

While she did not know what lay ahead, more than ever before, Pilar felt the warmth of Patrick's love. As she watched him sleep, she hoped he was dreaming of her. And in her heart, she thanked the grandmother she now knew better than anyone else. She thanked Gabriela for her love and for sharing the secrets that now allowed her to begin shaping her own destiny.

Lying there in Patrick's arms, Pilar could smell the simmering paella, still in the oven, moist with her love, still warm, nestled in the dish like a child in its mother; that saffron-kissed bed of rice that Nana had said would win even the most indifferent of hearts, and the beautiful midnight mussels with their promise of life, remained there, split open atop the warm bed of rice.